WILDE MAGIC

IMMORTAL VEGAS, BOOK 1

JENN STARK

Off the grid and on the run since she was a teen, Sara Wilde has made a name for herself as an artifact hunter with an edge—finding the most magical treasures on the planet with the flip of a Tarot card.

But when she's hired to steal a powerful fertility idol on the last night of Carnival, Sara discovers her rough-and-tumble skills are no match for the new, mysterious buyer she's attracted. Rich, demanding, and sexy as sin, this Magician promises to be nothing but trouble. Yet, for what he's willing to shell out for her services, Sara can afford the risk.

Or so she thinks.

As the danger—and the payoffs—mount, the power of Tarot leads Sara from the rollicking party of Rio de Janeiro to the grand historical cemeteries of Savannah, then on to the ostentatious museum halls of New York City. Meanwhile, the relentless Magician weaves an ever more seductive spell, hinting at a world she's barely glimpsed.

To keep from getting burned by passion, power, or betrayal, Sara's going to need some *Wilde Magic*.

--

Wilde Magic is the new series starter for the Immortal Vegas Series, which continues next with Getting Wilde. The opening adventure of Wilde Magic was previously published as the novella One Wilde Night. That story has been changed and expanded here, and leads Sara to all-new adventures to introduce the world of Immortal Vegas.

For Sabra
You have been a gift since the moment I met you.

THE FOOL .

1

No one could say I didn't have enough skin in the game. Not for this job.

I inched forward, barely squeezing between two breathtakingly naked women. They writhed in vigorous counterpoint to the pounding music, D cups smacking me full in the face. Thanks mostly to the heavy oil I'd slathered on myself from neck to toe, I wriggled my own naked body free of their Twister competition to claim exactly one square foot of open space in the subbasement rumpus room.

Finally. Oxygen.

The throng of nude humanity spun out around me in all directions, a mosh pit of groaning decadence. All of them were dancing. Some of them were fornicating. And one of them was damned well thinking she should have asked for more money for this assignment.

"Mmm, Deusa." The thickly accented Portuguese word purred past my ear. Heavy hands latched onto my shoulders. With a quick jerk, I was pulled ass to groin against a particularly enthusiastic admirer. Again with the help of my oil, I turned in the guy's embrace and smiled as wide as I could, my gaze raking over his face.

Nope, not my target.

Nope, not anyone I recognized from the trade.

I pursed my lips into a kiss, then shot my fist forward and gut punched him a little lower than his gut. He fell back with a high-pitched squeak of pain, releasing me. Turning back around, I plunged deeper into the crowd, desperate to get to the center of Crazy Town before I got trapped again.

The music blasted with the interminable samba strains that had pretty much been encoded into my DNA over the past four days. It was Carnival week in Rio de Janeiro. Ordinarily, that would find me with my fingers wrapped around a beer at a local block party, dancing in the street, then eventually passed out on some beach south of the city.

Not this year.

Not when there was fifty grand at stake for a chunk of jadestone now only twenty feet away from me.

I slithered between two heavily oiled male backs, one boasting some really impressive ink. Etched in vibrant greens, blacks, oranges, blues, and golds, a rugged sun god looked right at home between a pair of the most amazing shoulders I'd seen in recent memory. The god presided over the flowing waters of the Amazon, which in turn cascaded down to an exceptionally fine ass. An ass currently twitching against my—

"Is that truly your target, Miss Wilde?"

I popped into another pocket of air, turning quickly to defend myself. But there was no one leaning into me, whispering in my ear. There was no one paying attention to me at all.

The voice had been in my head.

Again.

"You're getting annoying." It took a pretty amped-up psychic to play phone-a-friend with my mental receptors, but there were a select few high-level Connecteds who could do it when I was distracted. Like right now, for example.

I'd picked up the anonymous psychic passenger the first night after I'd landed in Rio, and hadn't been amused that he'd known my name, especially since I had yet to figure out his. After his initial contact, however, he'd gone silent long enough that I thought he'd slunk off to haunt someone else's brain. Him showing up tonight was crappy timing, but I couldn't spare the mental energy to repair the shields at the moment. The dilithium crystals would have to hold.

I turned toward the center of the room. For good luck, I patted the thick frog-shaped pendant I'd had made to order for tonight's assignment, which hung on a leather cord around my neck. Almost all the women in the room wore a similar amulet and nothing else. In my case, a second leather cord held my ponytail. A tug confirmed it remained in place.

I pushed forward again.

The lights of the enormous subterranean chamber shifted, pointing the way to my target. On a small stage at the center of the room, an exquisite woman stood amid three highly dedicated attendants, all of them male, all of them built like Mack trucks.

I'd been following Fernanda Magdalena Santos for the past three days since I'd locked on to her at the Copacabana's Magic Ball. To the adoring public, she was simply one of this year's most beautiful and vivacious Carnival princesses. According to my client, she was also a priestess in the Cult of Icamiabas.

Based on what I was seeing, my client was right on the money.

Standing on her dais, Fernanda looked every inch the dominant Amazonian high priestess. And tonight was her night to shine.

Her and her necklace of supreme power. Or whatever it was.

A carved jadestone frog dangled from a thin leather cord from Fernanda's neck. That frog was currently having the time of its life bouncing around on the woman's impressive assets as she was alternately kneaded, stroked, kissed, licked, and a few other things I needed to remember for later.

Granted, there were approximately seventeen million similar frog charms being sold in the streets of Rio this very night. But this one, my client had insisted, was different. This one contained powers far beyond the norm. Powers of fertility, yes—hence the sexapalooza going on around me—as well as transcendent powers of luck, health, abundance, and long life. Maybe even a set of steak knives.

Ordinarily, I wouldn't waltz into a religious cult's crib and take their prize, at least not while they were still worshiping it. Most of the relics I secured for interested buyers were from long-dead tribes or forgotten family vaults. However, this particular strain of devotees rubbed me the wrong way. According to my client and verified through my Connected buddies south of the equator, these guys weren't just a Brazilian sex club rocking it old school. They demanded sacrifices too. Generally big brawny male ones.

Being a fan of big brawny males, that didn't sit right with me. The world didn't have enough of those as it was.

Adding to my motivation, my client had already transferred two-thirds of my fee into my bank account, not twenty-four hours before the start of Carnival. I needed that money badly. It was heading overseas to help fund a ragtag rescue network for psychic kids who never asked to be special, never understood why they were being targeted by the foulest players in the arcane black market.

Once they were identified as possessing psychic abilities, these kids would get attacked at their schools, taken from the streets, ripped right out of their beds by agents of the arcane black market. What happened to them after that went beyond obscene. The only thing that would stop the trafficking of these psychic children? Money to fund those who stood in the breach to protect them, and money to help heal those we hadn't protected in time.

I was going to nail this payday.

I pressed forward through the crowd, trying to keep my chin up, my focus on the prize and not on the naked rave around me.

At least Fernanda had been criminally easy to track. Her samba "school," a loose group of neighborhood residents who competed in the Samba Parade at Carnival, had been putting their lovely princesa on display across the city in ever-more flamboyant costumes. Each appearance had been tailor-made to build buzz for their triumphant parade through the Sambadrome later tonight, when Fernanda would be dancing her ass off in an elaborate headdress and very little else. She'd rolled out her particular version of the samba at every promotional stop throughout the city, like a mama showing off a jiggly baby. It made me exhausted to watch her, but I'd stuck to her like white on snow.

And when she wasn't on some stage shimmying her tan off, I'd been able to peg her location with a few well-chosen Tarot cards.

Tonight in particular, my cards had been straightforward and clear: the Tarot trump Justice had led me to a coffee shop next to the old capital district. The Fool had taken me to the Municipal Theatre, which was playing *Parsifal*. Then the Devil card had led me to this hellhole, O Diabo, where I'd hit...pay dirt.

The one card that hadn't been played out in an obvious way was the Magician. Since the "finding stuff" part of this little adventure was all but over, however, I really hoped that card meant I was performing at the top of my game.

The music jumped again.

Here we go.

I'd make the switch in the next few minutes, hole up for the night, then meet my client as planned tomorrow morning. Simple. Clean. Easy.

A new sound brought my head up with a snap. Either Fernanda was miked up or the acoustics in the room were unreal because her multisyllabic moans were the stuff of legend. Bracing herself on the shoulders of one pair of men while another grabbed her hips, the princesa gave a five-star shudder, then cried out with pure, undiluted, triple-X-rated pleasure. Loudly. And at length.

The crowd around me answered back with a roar of its own.

Clearly, it was party time.

2

Everyone surged toward the center dais, which was impressive given the multitasking going on. The dancing gave way to a full-on orgy, in multiples of two, three, and...five, it looked like. Based on an unofficial survey, I seemed to be the only one in the chamber with all my orifices unclaimed.

In the center of the room, Fernanda held the stone frog aloft and wailed with authoritative gusto. I was mideyeroll when a wave of energy blasted me back a full three feet, and all I wanted to do was...

Uh-oh.

I struggled to retain my focus, but it was like holding on to a dandelion in a tornado. An overwhelming need to dive onto every able-bodied man in the room consumed me, head to toe. I needed someone's—anyone's—hands on me, his body surrounding me, his mouth—

"Resist it."

Not him again. "I'm busy here," I practically moaned, swaying toward the closest pair of groping hands.

The voice in my head persisted. *"It's a spell. Only a spell. You can resist it."*

But the voice was wrong. Super wrong. Everything was spinning around me, whirling faster and faster. I couldn't stem the rushing tide of desire. I couldn't even breathe right anymore. A wave of lust so strong it seemed almost a living thing coursed through me, demanding to be satisfied. Immediately. Like now, already.

"Resist—"

"Well, help me, dammit!" I bit out. "I can't do it alone!"

A groan of what sounded like real pain shuddered through my mind, but this time, it was accompanied by a sensation of hands cupping my breasts, pulling me back against a broad chest. I gaped down, trying to understand what was happening, but nothing was there except the scent of cinnamon, jasmine, and—

I sucked in a breath as the massage turned insistent, and heat radiated through me. How long had it been since I'd been touched so intimately? Besides when I'd gotten stuck in that elevator with those guys from Cirque du Soleil?

"What—what are you doing?" I gasped.

"Keeping you safe until you break through the spell. Break through it now, if you would."

I didn't want to break through the spell, though. Not for this hot second, when my whole world vibrated with need, with want. My eyes drifted shut as I inhaled the heady spices, and I imagined the guy who I was pretty sure belonged to that voice, those hands. Rich bronze skin, sleek dark hair, golden eyes. It was always the same picture, and the picture was *good.*

My imaginary friend had shown up in my dreams only once, but it had been the perfect tease—leaving me wanting more, craving the touch, the whisper, the kiss that wasn't real because it was in my head and not my bed. The deliciously perfect lover, minus all the pillow talk.

But this wasn't a dream. This was really happening.

Though my eyes reported no one in my peripheral vision, a man's teeth bit down on my shoulder, like a wolf pinning its prey. I tried to maintain my dignity, but there was no denying the surge of need that originated somewhere near my core and gained intensity as it moved up my body. My head spun and my senses lit on fire as the very large, very male hands abandoned my breasts to skim down my torso, locking on my hips for a tantalizing second until the pressure continued, sliding down, down—

"Princesa! Princesa!"

The carnal tsunami ceased as suddenly as it had started, and the sensual cocoon I'd been wrapped in unraveled just as fast. I shuddered and gasped like a dog bursting out of cold water. The psychic touch that had so enthralled me eased back, replaced by words that were far too crisp and certain.

"The spell has been interrupted. You'll be safe now." He paused. *"However, Miss Wilde, should you need me again, for anything, you have only to ask."*

"But who—?"

A sudden rise in the volume of chanting broke through my daze the rest of the way, and I twisted sideways as the crowd lurched again toward the dais. My brain came back online barely in time to avoid me face-planting amid a forest of stomping feet.

As it was, I was caught up in a tide of humanity, their desire a living thing. Thankfully, my focus was stronger now, sharper, which probably had something to do with the elbow in my left kidney and the meat hook that had clamped down on my upper arm.

"Cadela," growled an insistent voice—my admirer from several rows back. I decided I liked "Deusa" a lot better. I turned to tell him so, bending my fingers into a tight double-knuckled battering ram and punching him in the throat.

Down he went, a half dozen eager, sex-starved women piling on.

That should keep him busy for a while.

The damage had been done, though. There were now too many people between me and Fernanda. The pulsing crowd carried me past stage right, where two massive guards blocked the way with crossed spears. Still, this remained the only path Fernanda could take, so all was not lost. She'd have to head this way with her sacrificial boy toys to reach the ceremonial bed. Tonight, through Fernanda's carnal and not to mention fatal offering while she wore the Trinket of Awesome Power, a whole new set of amulets would be consecrated, and the cycle would start all over again.

Unless I got to her first.

I scanned the room again, then halted abruptly, my eyes narrowing. Apparently, I wasn't the only wallflower at the dance after all.

Nigel Friedman stood naked and leaner than I remembered him, lingering on the outskirts of the crowd, ever so slightly poleaxed at the sheer immensity of skin on display. He wasn't a tall man, nor was he particularly short. He wasn't muscle-bound, but neither was he soft. He was the kind of man you might miss in a crowd, mainly because that's what he wanted you to do. His blond hair was buzz cut, and his jaw was looking extra chiselly this evening, but his blue eyes were the most arresting thing about him— constantly shifting, on alert.

Now that sharp gaze was fixed on something deeper in the crowd, and I followed Nigel's sight line until I saw what held his attention. A grim-faced woman was on the move, not appearing at all interested in the carnal delights she was being offered left and right. She was small bodied but fit, and completely focused on Fernanda.

I vaguely knew of her, a Russian with coal-black, blunt-cut hair, dark eyes, and a round, pale face dominated by heavy lips. *Great.* Russians were always a pain in the ass.

And this was my orgy, dammit. I'd gotten here first.

Fernanda chose that moment to issue another ululating howl that sounded completely unlike the pretty, vivacious Carnival princess she'd been for the past week. Instead, she was transforming more and more into an Icamiabas high priestess, her body flexed and proudly on display, her adoring men falling back to stare at her like slack-jawed yokels.

She shoved her fist toward the ceiling and spoke a stream of fluent Portuguese, to which I joyfully responded along with the rest of the crowd, something like "Keyara-mus!" Which didn't sound at all like "Yes," but who was I to judge? Beyond three or four emergency words like "Mojito," I sucked at languages.

This time, the word appeared to be some sort of signal, because the crowd reacted differently, reaching up with eager hands. Fernanda and her male entourage threw themselves into the throng. The Queen of the Naked Mosh Pit was handed over one admirer at a time, heading for the door the guards were barring.

I could work with that.

Taking up my position, I shoved one slender woman out of my way, then struck out with my heel at a hard angle, connecting with the man directly in front of me. He buckled with a satisfying scream.

"Keyaramus!" I shouted again as I took out the guy to my left. He was no more than eighteen and certainly *not* old enough to be invited to an orgy, even in Brazil. I almost felt bad when he went down amid a squeal of excited feminine voices, but I figured he'd rally. Then there was one more...

With five sets of arms down to two, the knot of mosh pitters in front of me faltered. Then Fernanda was there, toppling into my arms. Our mutually oiled-up bodies created a tableau out of Dante's inferno, with everyone grabbing at her face, her arms, her hair, her breasts.

Including me. But I had a slightly different endgame in mind.

Fernanda's cry of ecstasy became one of alarm as she hit the floor. The two giant guards bolted forward and thrust their spears high, roaring as if they'd been waiting to do it their whole lives. People shrieked, but refused to fall back as Fernanda thrashed around. Her long hair tangled around her, blinding and binding her.

I yanked my amulet from my neck and slid the catch, baring the sharp blade at the base of the frog. A slice, a swipe, and a sheathing of my blade later, I seized hold of Fernanda's arm and pulled her to her feet. She swept aside her hair and patted her chest, panting. I placed my own jade amulet into her hand. Glassy-eyed, she clutched the stone, and her lips curved for just a few precious seconds.

Time to go.

The crowd converged on Fernanda again, their hands stretched out greedily like supplicants at the altar. Plunging back through them was like swimming against a tidal wave, but I kept my head low and my hands working fast. I pulled the leather cord out of my hair, hastily restrung the amulet, then tied it around my neck.

The freaking frog was hot—way too hot, actually. Hot enough to burn.

Nothing I could do about that now.

I was halfway to the door when Fernanda screamed.

3

Truth to tell, when I'd taken this job, I hadn't been entirely sure about the jade amulet's legitimacy, no matter what my client had been willing to pay. But the moment I touched the thing as Fernanda tumbled into the Sea of Grabby Hands, I'd revised my opinion.

Now the blasted frog was practically frying my chest, but I couldn't reach for it or act like it was anything other than another pretty, fake bauble in a room full of them.

Given my naturally cynical nature, I'd also questioned Fernanda's legitimacy as a Connected. I hadn't been sure how sensitive she was, or even if she was truly a member of the psychic community. She certainly wouldn't have been the first "priestess" chosen simply because she had a nice ass.

Yeah, no. Fernanda was the real deal. The moment I'd broken the fall of her muscled, curvaceous body, I realized the princesa had zinged with power. If she hadn't been so locked into her high priestess zone, I'm sure she would have figured out that I was a Connected as well. I wasn't about to give her time to consider the finer implications of that realization.

Another stream of Portuguese wailed out over the crowd, louder this time, and everyone finally panicked. From what I could tell, they were being ordered to stop, to hold, and this group knew better than to think that good things were going to come from that.

They ran for the door, hurtling me forward, all of us pushing and shoving as we burst out of the room and up the wide stairway. We erupted in a naked geyser straight onto the dance floor of O Diabo, the nightclub that had already been raving when I'd first shown up here in broad daylight, three hours before.

Now the place was manic. Night had fallen. The city's energy had jumped a few more notches, hitting fever pitch as the evening wore closer to the final night of parades at the Sambadrome.

O Diabo was a stone's throw from the enormous venue where Fernanda was due to march in a parade in a little under an hour. She was on a tight schedule.

In fact, for one sweet shining moment, I hoped the sight of the Sambadrome looming over us would be to my advantage. Fernanda might hit the open air and realize that, ritual shmitual, she had a booty to shake.

Dare to dream.

Raucous cheering filled the club at our arrival. I snuck a glance at my watch—then realized I wasn't wearing one. My clothes were stashed behind O Diabo's bar, courtesy of a very agreeable bartender who'd expressed significant doubt that there was actually a full-tilt orgy going on in the club's subbasement, but who'd been more than willing to help me strip. A good man, but there was no way I could stop for my clothes at this point. Not with at least two other artifact hunters after me.

"Sara!" As if on cue, a hand snaked out of the crowd and latched on to my bicep, wheeling me around. Of course, the dashing British operative had managed to recover his clothes. Nigel was nothing if not a strategic thinker. Which was why his chest was covered in black tech material, his legs encased in running tights. The bastard had on shoes too. Actual shoes.

And, more to the point, there was a knife in his other hand.

He slashed at my neck. My instinctual reaction to jerk away actually helped Nigel as he yanked the amulet free— taking what felt like a good chunk of my skin with it. He dangled his prize for just a moment to gloat. I grabbed for it, but he was already dancing back.

"That's mine!"

Nigel, apparently unimpressed with my jurisdiction over the amulet, turned and dashed out of the bar, his laughter floating back to me. I hadn't taken three steps after him when a powerful feminine hand snagged my left arm, whipping me around the other way.

Fernanda's eyes were bright, almost manic. Before she could eat my face off, I pointed ahead. "Vamos! I don't have it, *he* does. Get him!"

She apparently understood enough of what I said, because she took off again, her burly bodyguards pounding after her. She'd also somehow managed to find a microdress and platform heels, but I didn't have that kind of time...or concern for modesty. I raced into the street after them, ignoring the cheers and catcalls as I focused on my quarry dead ahead.

They weren't hard to spot. Nigel might have been ex-

Special Forces, but he wasn't Batman. I could see him racing ahead of the lumbering guards. As for Fernanda, the girl could move. She charged after Nigel with her arms bent and her legs cranking. Never mind the platform heels, she was gaining ground.

I followed about fifty paces behind, mainly because I had no shoes and was running through the streets of a city in full Carnival mode. Granted, losing that amulet would hurt a lot worse than sliced heels. Trying not to wheeze, I picked up the pace.

As we rounded the corner, Nigel braked sharply. A fifty-person-strong samba school shimmied in place, waiting while three-story stadium doors swung open in front of them. I blinked as every sense was assaulted by light, color, and an unbelievably raucous wall of noise.

We'd reached the Sambadrome.

Enormous screens lit up the world like a revolution. Music blared over loudspeakers, intense enough to vibrate my bones. An explosion of brightly hued revelers erupted from impossible-to-believe, larger-than-life parade floats that lumbered forward like elephants among ants. And everyone—everywhere—was dancing.

This was Fernanda's home away from home. Showing that her lungs were nowhere near as crapped out as mine, she shouted loudly, her voice carrying over the music like a call to arms.

A high priestess of Icamiabas was not to be denied. The men and women prepping an enormous Day of the Dead float reacted instantly, abandoning their positions and throwing themselves at Nigel. The cagey Brit changed direction on a dime, skimming around that parade float and racing toward the next one in line. Fernanda's laugh was exultant, as if she'd somehow chased Nigel into a cage.

Gritting my teeth as my bare feet encountered sticks, chicken wire, gravel, and a swath of shattered glass, I matched strides with the guards. We tore around the skeleton-festooned float with its hundred white-robed, white-faced dancers...and smack into a forest of spinning, five-foot-tall chocolate cakes with little red cherries on top. Those were followed by three-foot-high white cupcakes with feet.

I shook my head hard, but the hallucination held firm.

With another scream from Fernanda, the cakes burst apart into multiple slices. The cherries popped up and swiveled around to reveal faces painted crimson beneath bulbous red hats, while the chocolate cake pieces hurtled toward Nigel, a sight that threatened to put me off sugar for good.

Not to be taken down by a carbohydrate, Nigel leapt onto the fourteen-tier wedding cake float. Fernanda launched herself at him. She cried out in pain as she slipped and banged against the base of the float, but she still managed to snag his foot. As the float lurched forward, the princesa collapsed against its side with another bone-jarring thump that earned a gasp of horror from more than a few cupcakes.

Nigel tried to kick Fernanda off him as fondant red roses swung into action all around the wedding cake. Hard seed-encrusted balls rained from the second layer so furiously that the Brit hunched over and covered his head with his arms.

I scrambled past Fernanda and onto the lowest tier, where Nigel continued to fend off the dessert assault. Taking advantage of his distraction, I reached into his pants and yanked out the amulet.

Thankfully, he wore his trousers tight, or I would've had to guess at what to grab.

Nigel jerked away, only to find himself directly in front of a pristine white rose, who smacked him topside with a man-sized wooden spoon. His next kick went wild, connecting with Fernanda's chin at the exact moment she started to rise.

Once again, the Carnival princesa went down. Once again, her guards came to the rescue. One scooped her up in his massive arms. The other lunged at Nigel and bashed the side of his thick British head with a ham-hock fist. A brigade of pink bows shoved Nigel off the float. He landed in a heap on the Sambadrome floor, immediately set upon by cupcakes.

Not something I'd ordinarily wish on any man, but he should have kept his sticky fingers to himself.

Jumping from the float, the jade amulet in a death grip, I grimaced with satisfaction. *Got you.* I struggled to retie the amulet around my neck, but my hands were shaking too much. If only I could get—

"Ochacontesooka Princesa!" Or at least that's what it sounded like to me. I jerked back as one of the chocolate cake pieces raced up to me, shoving my arm. "Princesa!"

I was sorry I hadn't learned the local language, but really. Could they not at least *try* to speak English?

"Ochacontesookam elah?" The cake slice shouted again.

"Um... No?" My understanding of Brazilian Portuguese was nonexistent, especially under pressure. "No" seemed safest. I whirled around, taking in the fallen princesa, the battered Nigel, and about three dozen dessert forks and saucers bearing down fast. I sensed the cutlery was about to turn on me, so I backed away, feeling naked.

Probably because I still was.

"Sim!" An exceptionally overlarge man positioned himself squarely in my path.

I stiffened my spine, ready to rumble even if he did top me by a good foot. My hand closed tight around the amulet, the frog face now positioned between my fingers. Not quite brass knuckles, but it would have to do.

"Vocha Devay!" he roared.

Immediately, two young girls ran up, their white tights and shoes betraying them as part of the cupcake brigade, sans the actual cakes. Instead, in their arms they held what looked almost like clothing, but with way too many feathers. "Vocha Devay!"

"Vocha what?" I reached for the clothes with my left hand out of a knee-jerk reaction to put something on my body, but stopped myself in time. When another half-dressed baked good dashed toward me with a sopping-wet towel, however, I abandoned good sense completely and lunged for it. Putting the now blessedly cool frog amulet between my teeth, I wiped most of the oil from my skin, so disgusted by the amount of DNA I had sticking to me that I didn't at first notice the white bra the youngest girl was dangling in front of my face. When I realized what it was, I seized it.

"Thnkmmphf!" I shouted around a mouthful of amphibian. I shoved my arms into the overconstructed straps, white and glittering with little tufts of tulle. The bra was definitely enthusiastic about my proportions, but at least I could stash the amulet inside it. And about six of my closest friends, but still.

As I struggled with the back fastening, the girl in front of me dropped to one knee. She tapped my right foot, then my left, making me hop. By the time I had the bra on reasonably tight, she was pulling something up my legs that looked like fluffy floss.

Realization began to dawn on me.

"Mmph—" I tried again.

"Perfeito!" An old man with a few teeth left in his wide grin wheeled around the corner, dressed like a wedding-cake topper, all black hat, bow tie, and tails—only his hat was the size of a golf cart. He leered at me as he bowed. "Princesa!"

Sweet Christmas, no.

4

I spit out the frog and stowed it in my bra, belatedly realizing that the getup was some sort of effed-up idea of a wedding gown. Without the actual gown.

"Guys, guys. I'm not your princesa." A quick glance confirmed that Fernanda wasn't either, not anymore. She remained out cold, currently draped over the shoulder of one of her guards as the confections hastily resumed their positions. I swiveled back to the cake committee. "I don't even know how to dance."

"Perfeito." The old man grinned again, turning me around toward the school. Something heavy settled on my head and floated around me—a veil. A freaking wedding veil, festooned with feathers. As I struggled to redefine my center of gravity, my feet were tapped again, and suddenly, I was being strapped into white high-heeled gladiator boots.

"Seriously this a bad, bad—"

I stopped. Entering the crowd behind the glitter-dusted origami napkins was an all-too-familiar resting bitch face. *Crap.*

The Russian woman from O Diabo's subbasement had

followed us here, no doubt on Nigel's ass. Which meant she was now also on my decidedly less covered one. Worse, she had her own collection of goons with her. They were scanning the school directly behind us even as the Russian grabbed a man in a death-mask outfit.

Resolutely, I wheeled around, staggering a little as I considered the option of faking my way through the parade. The towering boots almost fit, and I went up on my tiptoes, spreading my arms to steady myself.

"So what all do I—" I flapped my hands and tried a wiggle. Watching Fernanda shake her moneymaker for the past four days wasn't helping me figure out how to get the loose change out of mine. "Do I just samba?"

"Samba!" That word connected, not surprisingly, and the cake topper smiled broadly. "You are English."

"Oh thank Go—"

"You are English!" He announced again, and I realized he'd exhausted his entire repertoire of the language. But he started dancing anyway, a stutter step, move, and shake that I could barely follow, let alone emulate. This was not going to be good.

Still, I couldn't exit the Sambadrome the way I'd come. Not with From Russia with Love back there sharpening her shoe spikes.

"Come, come." My bridegroom grabbed my hand and pulled me out in front of the enormous wedding cake float as the music started. He squeezed my hand. "*Perfeito.*"

That wasn't going to help me samba either, but I appreciated the enthusiasm.

The lights swept over us, and sweat pooled between my shoulder blades as a flood of cupcakes trotted out around us, followed by their grown-up chocolatey counterparts. With that kind of frosted camouflage, maybe this would work. I just needed to get far enough along the parade route to find an exit, right? Piece of...never mind.

I struck a flourish. I could do this—seriously, I could.

The music started.

I froze.

Right there on the Sambadrome runway.

5

Even as my panicking bridegroom threw a desperate smile my way, a different set of hands settled on my hips, warm and sensual, anchoring me.

"You can do this." My psychic passenger's voice breathed into my ear as his invisible hands moved, pushing my body the way it was supposed to move. *"Dancing is as natural as breathing, as swimming in the open sea."*

I gritted my teeth. "Haven't done a lot of that last one, just saying."

"I have. Relax." The hands firmed on my hips, biting into my skin, forcing me to roll my step forward, then back, to twist and turn this way and that. I didn't know how he was managing the extrasensory dance lesson, but I was more than grateful. As my muscles warmed to the task and the crowd responded to my attempt at a samba, my blood began to stir. The burst of energy started slowly at first, then picked up the pace until it was racing through my veins, jacking up my heart rate, and flowing out in a wild flutter of my hands

as I strutted my way back and forth across the Sambadrome floor.

I wasn't samba-ing, but I was doing this! I was pulling it off. Sort of. "How are you *doing* this?" I demanded of the voice in my head. "Is this some kind of remote control tech?" The members of the arcane black market were constantly upping their game, but this...was seriously throwing me.

An amused chuckle sounded in my ears. *"Just enjoy it, Miss Wilde."*

The shock of hearing my name again in that lilting, foreign accent jolted me back to awareness. The man opposite me, Samba king to my princesa, grinned as his gaze dropped to my hips. "Sim, sim!"

I swung my hips like I was rotating off my axis as I scanned the parade route. Throwing kisses to the crowd, I sashayed to the right, then the left. There was no clear exit on the left, but the right appeared more promising. A dark stretch that might be a tunnel loomed ahead, guarded by official-looking attendants.

Maybe...

The music changed and the cakes exploded around us into several individual pieces, swirling and twirling to their own dance moves. My shimmying became less about form and more about function, trying to stay out of the way. Following the lead of my bridegroom, I threw back my head and laughed at odd intervals, flinging my arms out like a wounded albatross. Eventually, I realized that the unseen guiding hands had left as well. You just couldn't keep good help these days.

I continued to work it hard, and by the time we were a third of the way through the Sambadrome parade route, I was almost getting the hang of it. In fact, I had to admit...I was hot.

No really, I was *hot*.

With the fifty-pound wedding veil forcing me to keep my gaze straight ahead, I couldn't afford to glance down, but the frog amulet currently nestled against my cleavage had suddenly decided to cleave me in two. Electricity sparked around the piece and arced out along my skin, igniting my nerve endings and making my feet move even faster out of sheer desperation.

What was going on? The amulet was South American, yes. But not even I was willing to believe it was somehow activated by bad samba dancing. Worse, if I'd somehow tapped in to a Connected-synching amulet...then every *other* Connected in the Sambadrome would feel it too. I had to imagine someone in the crowd of eighty thousand was noticing this.

Especially since I suspected my hair was on fire.

"*Princesa*. She glows!" cried my bridegroom, as if this was a good thing. I grinned back at him, squinting through the sparks my headdress was now spitting, the electrical current also somehow igniting my bloodstream and making my skin stretch way too tight over my bones.

I shot another glance at the dark tunnel leading out of the Sambadrome, up and on the right. That was my ticket out. That was my exit strategy. That was my...

A woman I was already beginning to despise rushed out of that same tunnel, coming fast. Before any of the attendants could stop her, the Russian vaulted the barricade and was on the runway, gunning for me.

There was nowhere to run—not forward, not back. And not out the tunnel, not anymore. Russia's goons had to be there, waiting for me to make that move. Instead, I swung myself and my towering headdress to the side just as the woman caught up with me.

Oblivious to the fact that she was in the middle of one of the most-watched televised events in the world, the Russian tackled me like a linebacker and sent me sprawling. At least she had the grace to wrench my oversized feathered bridal veil from my head while she was at it.

With a scream, she tumbled to the ground engulfed in electrified feathers as I skidded painfully across the asphalt. The moment I stopped moving, the amulet began shooting flames—as in real, actual *fire*. They hadn't covered that in Wardrobe Malfunctions 101, so I improvised. I rolled into a tight ball to beat down the blaze, then somersaulted off to the side to avoid glazing any cupcakes.

The crowd roared its approval. At first I thought it was for my impressive acrobatics, then I realized that behind me, the Russian was struggling to her feet.

Oh, for the love of Kansas. I turned to flee, only to be pulled back around in the woman's surprisingly strong grasp.

"Back off!" I growled, using her momentum to drive my fist into her jaw. She feinted, more agile than I would've expected, and I barely got my arm down in time to block her next punch, aimed at my kidneys. I would have been peeing blood for a week if that'd connected, and my eyes narrowed. "Who hired you?"

"Someone smarter than your client. Give me the amulet," Russia snapped back. "You shouldn't be handling it. You don't know what it is."

"I do so!" Never had I been accused of arguing like an adult. Barely restraining myself from pulling the woman's hair, I launched myself at her torso, and we both hit the deck.

After that, it was pretty much a mud-wrestling competition, minus the mud. My cake-topper bridegroom gamely rolled us along with a giant cake server, as if this fight was all part of the show, and the crowd howled its approval as the woman got her nails hooked into my bra and almost yanked it loose. God love the costume designers of Rio, though: it held and to spare. I think she ripped a nail.

As she wrenched her hand free, however, I pressed my advantage. Rolling over on top of her, I pinned her shoulders to the ground with my knees and cracked her once, twice across the face. A satisfying stream of blood spurted from her nose, which I shouldn't have felt good about, but I did. Unfortunately, the pain seemed to ground her.

I always forgot that part.

With a strength that once again belied her tiny frame, Russia got her foot up against my inner thigh and kicked out hard enough to bruise bone. I collapsed to the side, grunting in pain. She got off her own roundhouse punch, sending me over onto my back. Instantly, she scrambled over me, her hands going again for my bra, but I shook off my daze and grabbed her wrists.

I pulled her face toward mine and head-butted her.

The soccer-crazed crowd did not miss that move. "*GOL!*" they howled.

As the cheer intensified, I shoved the concussed operative to the ground, then staggered to my feet. Striking another flourish, I grinned mightily. There was blood on my hands, blood in my mouth. Definitely in need of a new escape route, I turned to throw another kiss to the crowd—and heard a sharp whistle.

A man stood near the end of the parade route, at the edge of the runway. Nigel? How had he...

No. Not Nigel. I squinted harder, my heart doing its own shimmy, my palms going all sweaty. *No way.* What was Will Donovan doing here?

Tall and distinguished, with deep black skin, jet black hair and whiskey-colored eyes, Will Donovan was the quintessential academic with a dash of archeologist flair. I hadn't seen the guy in two years, but it wasn't like we'd parted enemies. Hell, he'd been one of my first mentors when I'd started searching for artifacts four years ago.

Nevertheless, what were the odds that he'd be here, exactly when I needed him? I mean, sure, Rio was an open party. But an antiquities prof from Philadelphia randomly hanging out in the Sambadrome?

Watching me?

I had a bad feeling about this—but I wasn't about to look a gift Trojan Horse in the mouth.

I bolted for him.

6

Once Will realized he had my attention, he bounded forward through the crowd, his arms held out as if to greet a long-lost lover. Which wasn't too far off the mark.

What *was* he doing here?

Will wasn't a Connected, but as an esteemed professor of very old things and a linguistics expert, he and I had worked together on a number of jobs. He'd been one of my earliest contacts when I'd come back on the grid, new to a bonkers black market that wheeled and dealed anything and everything arcane. Realizing all too quickly that I had an uncanny knack for finding things that didn't want to be found, Will offered to show me the ropes and make a few connections. We'd had an on-again, off-again relationship for a few years, and as it had become more off-again, we'd gradually lost contact with each other.

Still, now he was here, and I needed to get out.

Turning with an exaggerated hip swing, I waved goodbye to the cakes, my bridegroom, and the cheering crowd, then dashed off to the side, gaining speed. I gripped the top bar of the parade runway railing and vaulted over, landing in Will's long arms. He swung me around and kissed me full on the lips, and only then did I realize we were being tracked by the Sambadrome cam, lighting up the giant video screens.

Oh well. It wasn't like I was keeping a low profile on this job.

Under the cover of the crowd's roaring response, we ducked and ran, threading our way through the stands and down to the first level, then eventually out to the street.

"You have clothes?" Will gasped. I always did forget he was more professor than tomb raider, but when he grinned at me, it was almost like old times.

"Back at my hotel." I wasn't going to risk going to O Diabo again. "I probably shouldn't be seen at the hotel quite yet, though. I'm on a job."

His expression turned wry. "Since when are you not on a job? Anything you can deliver now, or do you have to wait for the moon to be full on a cloudless night?"

"What time is it?"

He checked his watch. "Slightly after ten. Your client is close?"

"He might be." I frowned down at my barely there bra and even-less-there thong. "Walk with me for a few minutes. I have another go bag tucked away at—"

"Never let it be said I wasn't a gentleman." Will waved his credit card and turned to hail a taxi. "I'll give you the full concierge treatment. I'll go in and get your clothes, together we'll go visit your client, and then we'll have dinner afterward down at Copacabana. Sound good?"

It sounded more than good. Fernanda had been one exceptionally mobile target. I couldn't remember the last time I'd eaten while actually sitting down. Smote by a wave of gratitude, I piled into the taxi with Will. For a few glorious minutes, I planned to let myself wallow in the relief of something going right on this job.

Will interrupted my ruminations just as they were getting to the good part. "How dangerous is it going to be, me walking into your hotel room?"

"For you? Shouldn't be bad. You see anyone lurking around my room, though, keep on going. But I doubt anyone will be inside."

"How strong is your doubt about that?"

I considered. "Not strong."

He swore softly under his breath. "Ever since I met you, I can't turn around without running into trouble. I'm just glad I found you in time."

"Found me?" I pulled myself a little more upright in the cab. With the flush of adrenaline out of my system, everything was starting to hurt. "What do you mean?"

"Why do you think I'm in Rio?" He looked at me, surprised. "You contacted me."

Now it was my turn to stare, all my half-formed suspicions flying out the window along with a few feathers. "What are you talking about? I never contacted you."

"Well—someone did. Said you would be in Rio, in danger. Maybe with a stolen artifact that I'd want to see. I've been running around the city for the last three days following up on dead bodies and hoping they weren't yours. I happened to be in the Sambadrome tonight because I'd given up and it's the last night of Carnival." He offered me that lopsided smile again. "Leave it to you to make an impression."

"You came all the way down here, based on a call you didn't confirm was me?" I didn't know whether to be touched or infuriated. "Will, you have to be more careful."

He shrugged, appearing a little embarrassed. "It seemed like a good idea at the time."

"You're an idiot."

"I've been accused of worse."

With Will as a tagalong, though, I didn't need to go to the hotel—my bag was still at O Diabo, which provided me with both clothes and a burner phone. Granted, I didn't have my gun with me, but that wasn't too much of a problem. I generally preferred not to shoot the hand that fed me, and Will had always been squeamish around guns.

Raising my client proved more difficult. I texted him to meet me as we'd originally planned, down in Nuva Sol at 6:00 a.m., but got no response. Then I spent the next two hours eating everything put in front of me at a pizzeria off the tourist quarter, up to and including dessert. Will and I caught up on his work and his promotions, and I fought off my continued desire for sleep as I sank more deeply into a food coma. When Will offered to host me in his hotel for the night, I was too tired and strung out to argue.

We walked the short distance to where he was staying. The city streets were filled with dancing and singing, and the cachaça we'd shared over dinner had gone down far too easy. It was only when we stopped in an alcove in front of his hotel and Will leaned down to give me a long, searching kiss that my sense of unease finally got the better of me. I'd been kissed by this man before. Will was too tense, too alert. Especially for a professor away from the university on holiday.

My brain kicked into gear, about four hours after it should have. Better late than never, I always say.

Still, I wasn't about to give up on a good smooch midway through simply because the guy I was kissing was about to double-cross me. I leaned into Will, sliding my hands up and around his shoulders, pulling him closer. My lips left his and trailed up to his ear, where I blew a soft breath against his earlobe.

God love him, the man actually shuddered against me. Then I ruined the moment with the million-dollar question. "Why, Will?"

He tensed a little more, but my grip held him in place. After a long moment, he sighed against my neck. "Made a promise to an old friend that I couldn't live up to. I had to make amends."

"But to follow me all the way here? How? There's no way you could have known about this job ahead of time. I didn't even know about it until a few days ago."

Will shrugged, not resisting as I angled him slightly to get a better view of the street beyond the alcove. This wasn't good. I didn't have my gun, and Will undoubtedly had a tracker on him. Stupid.

"The Connected community is tight, Sara." His voice was soft and almost sad. "You've made a name for yourself as an artifact hunter, and you should. You're good. For a while, you know, I was hoping you'd find us."

"That's beautiful. Be sure to include the part where you betrayed me."

"Not a betrayal." Will pulled back and eyed me, his gaze so earnest that it almost made me not want to knee him in the groin. Almost. "I'll make it up to you, Sara. I just—I needed to get out of a jam, and this was my best shot. Please." His gaze grew more earnest. "I—I have a family now."

"A *family*." Shock radiated through me as I fairly barked the word, the barb digging deeper than it should have. "Can you explain why you just freaking *stuck your tongue down my throat* when you have a *family*?"

"I didn't know how else to keep you in place!" He almost wailed the words in his horrible sotto voce whisper, but he leaned back from me, rightly guessing that I was about to go full-on Hannibal. "Why do you think I agreed to feed you? We were too early."

"Not at all, Professor Donovan. You're exactly on time."

The laser-pointer light indicating a sniper was aiming for Will's temple didn't faze me all that much, but the second one flashing in my eyes did.

"Oh, shut that stupid thing off." Showing bravado instead of the flash of fear that bolted through me, I pulled out the amulet and waved it toward the man now exiting one of the cars parked along the street. Bright lights flared behind him, rendering his features invisible. "It's here, I've got it. Which means you've got it."

I poked Donovan in the stomach hard. What had I ever seen in him? "And that means you owe me big-time, weasel. Why couldn't you just have asked me for help?"

The voice boomed again. "Mr. Donovan, you can leave."

Will's face was ashen and his eyes filled with misery, but I was in no mood to make this easier on him. No sooner had he stepped away, though, than a second man came up to me, this one wearing a cloth face mask and tech-knit clothing not unlike Nigel's, flashing the universal "Gimme" sign. I tossed him the amulet, the wrench of its loss like a physical ache.

For a second, Mr. Gimme held the amulet up to the light, then he secreted it away...in his pants. *Sweet hell.* It *was* Nigel. Nobody else could have that big a penis fixation.

The man in front of the bright lights didn't move. Instead, Mr. Silhouette watched me as I shoved my hands into my hoodie pockets and resolutely ignored the sniper light flickering over me. "You're taking this rather well, Sara Wilde," he said.

I shrugged. "Karma's a bitch."

"Mm." He paused a long moment. "Don't try to recover the amulet. Your role in this is complete."

"Oh yeah?" I frowned as a car turned onto the street half a block down from Will's hotel, if this actually *was* his hotel. Something about the car bothered me, made me take a half step back into the bower of trees that had served as the romantic setting for Will's and my thirty-second tryst.

"Yes. Your client has been notified. As has yours, Mr. Donovan," Mr. Silhouette continued, pressing his point home. "Tell him if he wants to negotiate with David Galanis, he is free to do so. He'll know how to reach him."

David Galanis? The name sounded vaguely familiar, in the way that all the money flowing into the arcane black market tagged itself with pretentious-sounding monikers. Although the artifact-stealing asshat had a Greek surname, I was picking up a decidedly American vibe. The name triggered thoughts of shadowy museum hallways and glinting gold, but nothing more. Either way, the arrival of Mr. Galanis's operatives on the scene most likely explained my own client's lack of response to my texts—he probably suspected our frog had been gigged. Kind of presumptuous, really, counting me out so quickly.

The car heading toward us picked up speed, leaping forward with an aggression that had only one end, and not a good one.

"And it goes without saying, don't bother to—"

Unfortunately, Galanis's bagman didn't get a chance to finish his statement. Not with the flying bullets and all.

7

I checked into my second hotel in Rio, which I'd booked under one of my half dozen fake IDs, and slogged my way to my room. I'd stopped off at the bus station to pick up my primary duffel bag, so I had my computer and a spare set of clothes. I deeply regretted not being able to grab the gun I'd hidden in my original hotel room, but I could go back for it later. There was a chance the bad guys hadn't found it. They clearly needed help with their spy skills.

Then again, so did I.

Stupid. I shouldered my way into the room, performing all the usual checks as I deep breathed my way through wave upon wave of delayed fear—all the hysteria I should have felt during the orgy heist, the race through the streets of Rio, the dance in the Sambadrome, and finally the shootout at the Not Okay corral. Sweat snaked down my back and made my hands clammy, and I grabbed a towel from the bathroom to swipe at my face.

I was good at my job—very good. But that didn't mean I

was bulletproof. Tonight the bad guys had gotten way too close, and as usual, I had zero margin for error.

Once I finished my room recon and sweet-talked my heart rate into taking it down a notch, I took in my surroundings with a more appreciative eye. This hotel wasn't as swank as the Copacabana, but it was pretty high grade. Which meant the only criminals I really had to worry about were the organized ones. Given the givens, I needed those guys to feel comfortable I was locked down for the night in a hotel surrounded by really bright lights and lots of people.

I slung my computer bag on the table, my side throbbing with pain.

"Suck it up, buttercup." I checked the impromptu bandage I'd made out of one of my cleaner shirts. The bullet from the street ambush had grazed my waist, taking out a chunk of skin that I probably wouldn't miss, eventually. Blood still oozed from the wound, though, and stitches would probably be a good idea. With any luck, my bathroom would have a complimentary mending kit.

But first things first. I pulled out the laptop and an energy bar I'd stashed in my go bag for good measure, then collapsed into a chair while my machine booted. At least Will had fed me dinner before running his little scam on me. I had to give him props for that.

But what in God's name had he meant about a family? We hadn't exactly been Facebook friends, but didn't he think that little detail merited an "Oh, by the way"? Ideally before he'd kissed me?

The computer beeped, and I clicked the screen open, hitting one of three icons that appeared on my taskbar. A schematic of Rio came up, and sure enough, a bright blue dot appeared dead center on the map. *Excellent.*

I peeled the wrapper off the bar and squinted at the screen, triangulating the amulet first in relation to Galeão International Airport. It was nowhere near there, and I breathed a sigh of relief. Wherever the jadestone frog was heading, it wasn't out of the country yet. According to the system, the dot had continued moving slowly for over an hour, so slowly that the runner must have been on foot. Was that runner still Nigel? Or had he been taken out in the crossfire?

I fixated on the flickering pixel, mesmerized by its little flare. "Where are they taking you, buddy?"

I wouldn't know anytime soon, I suspected, but I didn't mind that so much. The security program for which I'd traded a very select set of services would do its job and record the amulet's location unless and until the tiny, almost transparent wafer seal I'd managed to transfer from my leather thong to the stone was detected and removed. Given the number of hands the thing was probably passing through, not to mention its probable position in Nigel's briefs, I didn't think anyone would pay too much attention to it for the next few hours.

Nigel. I scowled as I munched. Was he working with Mr. Silhouette and this Galanis guy, or simply dipping in to double-cross them? It was one of the Brit's favorite moves. And either way, who was behind the shoot-'em-up at Will's hotel? The Russian woman? Fernanda and Company? I hadn't stuck around to play count the bodies. After fleeing up the street and hiding out in the nearest bar I could find, I'd kept my head down until I heard the sirens start to wail. By then, the shooters were long gone, and I'd split for points south.

It had been a long night, and it wasn't over yet. I needed to catch a few hours of shut-eye.

But first...

I pulled out the new burner phone from my duffel. I'd brought three of them with me on this trip and was already down to two. I didn't have high hopes for how long this one would last. Might as well get my minutes in when I could.

Swiping the phone on, I dialed the digits from memory. Thanks to another serendipitous relationship with some enthusiastic gearheads in Duluth, my calling plan was configured to bounce off several different satellites, ensuring my calls wouldn't be tracked.

Because nothing said "Call me sometime" like an untraceable number.

The phone connected on the third ring. "Bonjour, Saint-Germain-des-"

"Father Jerome." I spoke louder than I needed to, somehow convinced that the thousands of miles of ocean separating us required enhanced vocalizing skills. "How are you? How is Michel?"

"*Sara.* It's so good to hear your voice. Your trip is going well?"

Instantly, I was on my guard. He didn't answer the question, and Father Jerome, like most Parisians, was a master at the nuances of communication. "Tell me he's not dead."

The priest's long sigh made my gut twist. "He's not dead, Sara. He is a strong little boy. But he is in significant pain." He paused. "He misses you. I don't know why you are where you are, but you should come back. Perhaps sooner rather than later."

I forced myself to keep my voice steady. "The morphine isn't helping?"

"It is when he allows us to use it. But he doesn't want to lose his sight, he says. He's afraid if he goes to sleep, he will wake up blind."

My heart shriveled a little in my chest. Michel was a Parisian boy I'd met years ago during my first visit to Father Jerome. I'd gone to the priest because he was an acknowledged expert in antiquities and familiar with the object I'd been asked to "reclaim" at the time. The good father hadn't been alone that day. He'd been shepherding young Connected children to a social outing at the zoo, and he'd commandeered me to help as chaperone. Over the course of that fateful day, Father Jerome had told me each of their stories—horrific stories I'd never imagined possible. Stories I certainly couldn't forget.

Back then, young Michel hadn't truly understood his abilities. Nor had he learned to use them. Back then, he hadn't yet experienced what arcane trophy hunters would do to the Connected—especially to kids. The fact that he'd *ever* experienced such an atrocity... Michel had been taken himself three years later for several harrowing hours before we'd run his captors to ground. The child's abduction was something Father Jerome would never forgive himself for.

Now, however, Michel should be recovering from his trauma, but his nightmares and the pain racking his young body stymied the most gifted of normal doctors and frightened those docs who were Connected. No one wanted to draw the attention of the dark practitioners who'd done such terrible things to a child.

Which meant that all we could do was wait to see if the little boy would come back on his own.

Either way, it had become clear that Father Jerome couldn't watch the children every day. There were too many, and he was only one man. Another facility, this one outside Paris, was being identified. But facilities took money to run. So did morphine drips.

"I'll be there soon," I said firmly. "With enough seed money to start the home in Bencançon. You'll see."

"It is more important that you come back safely, Sara. Promise me that you will."

I smiled into the phone. The old man had become the father I never had, a fact I suspected he knew, since he was so skillful at manipulating guilt. "I will, Father. Give Michel my love. Tell him I will teach him how to samba when I see him next, but he must be well enough to stand."

"I will do that."

We talked for a few minutes more, going over the plans for the halfway house and the latest gossip he'd heard about the arcane black market. I told him in the briefest terms about the jade amulet that had brought me to Rio. He listened without speaking, and when I was finished, he startled me with his response.

"This amulet you have found, have you touched it? Worn it?"

I frowned into the phone. "Well, yes. But it's not like it was under glass. It was being, um, worn by someone else when I first saw it."

"And how long did you wear it?"

I blew out a long breath. "For about ten minutes the first time, sadly. Then maybe four hours the second? Something like that. Why?"

Father Jerome's voice grew agitated. "How did you feel when wearing it? Did it become unusually cold or hot, or create any sort of physical reaction?"

I thought about the sparking flames shooting from my headdress. "Ummm... Why are you asking?"

"Because of a journal article I read, several years ago now. Given its relation to the Icamiabas, there's a superstition about the frog amulet's reaction to strong women. They're a female warrior tribe, you know that, right?"

"Hence the name 'Amazon,' yeah." Fatigue was beginning to scratch at my eyelids, and I fought back a yawn. "Is this reaction anything like hives? Because I don't have time for hives."

He chuckled. "Not exactly. It merely leaves its mark, it's said. For use in time of need."

I glanced down at the frog-shaped welt on my chest, one of easily a dozen injuries I needed to address. I was a strong woman, sure, but I didn't have much need for an amped-up sex toy, not on this job. My frog tattoo needed to take a breather.

"I'll let you know if something like that turns up." My yawn practically cracked my jaw. "Okay, I'm crashing for the night. Tomorrow I'll get the amulet again and finish my transaction with the client. I'll be back in Paris before either you or Michel knows it."

"Good night, Sara. And be careful. The Icamiabas are also known for taking the hands and feet of those who cross them."

I blinked, the energy bar suddenly feeling too heavy in my stomach. "Ahhh...good to know."

I waited while the priest said a benediction in Latin and felt better for it. I might not agree with all aspects of Father Jerome's faith, but I had faith in *him*. That was everything I needed.

Well, almost everything, anyway.

8

A fter I hung up the phone, I sagged back in my chair. I needed to do some personal recon before I passed out, but passing out sounded like the far better option. Gritting my teeth, I hauled myself up and trudged to the bathroom, then flipped on a light so bright, it made my eyes water. What did they plan to do in here, surgery?

Wincing with effort, I pulled my shirt over my head, then stripped off my jeans in one long movement. That done, I stared at what was left of my once healthy, unmarked body.

I was a mass of bruises and burns.

The bruises, now starting to swell, were the easiest to write off. They chronicled the long day's worth of abuse I'd suffered, first squeezing my way through the orgy enthusiasts, then at the hands of Fernanda's flailing. After that, I'd done pretty well until Nigel had nicked my neck with his blade, and things had gone downhill from there. My feet were a disgusting, scraped mess from my impromptu run through the streets of Rio. My side still seeped blood.

The deepest damage had come at the hands of the Russian, though. She'd made the most of her small frame and had beaten the crap out of me with swift kicks, grabs, and punches that ended up making my skin look like a patchwork quilt of jagged, uneven welts. I checked my teeth for good measure, relieved they remained in my head.

"Shower," I muttered to myself, knowing that when I woke up, I wouldn't be in any mood to deal with it. Still, it took another five minutes of me staring at my reflection with hollow-eyed confusion before I could move again. The water in the hotel proved to be blistering hot, and I hugged the tiled wall and whimpered as it pounded my muscles into jelly. By the time I stumbled out of the shower, I was lousy with fatigue.

Wrapped in a towel, I made it across the room to recover my clothes. I swiped for my go bag, too groggy to focus, and merely managed to push the bag off its perch. Its contents spilled onto the carpet, and I frowned down, trying to make sense of what I was seeing.

Cards. Several of my Tarot cards had tumbled out of the bag, landing faceup on the carpet like abandoned toys. *Great.*

That sprawl of cards might not matter to most people, but I wasn't most people.

For the past several years, I'd made my living as a finder of lost things. My compass of preference was a Tarot deck—seventy-eight cards, each with their own unique images, which arranged themselves into spreads I could decipher with remarkable success. Whether the cards aligned properly out of luck, coincidence, or because secret fairies made it so, I never much cared. I just knew they worked.

My skill in using Tarot cards to find what was hidden wasn't unique, but my mastery of it was, and word had gradually gotten out that I could unearth some of the most interesting treasures the world held secret, particularly those treasures with a psychic or magical energy. Those kinds of trinkets went for big money on the arcane black market, and finding them had been just the ticket I'd needed to stage an arcane community comeback four years ago. Everyone who'd chased me off the grid was dead, after all, no thanks to me. Being a Connected was not for the faint of heart.

Now I knew I should pick up the cards, but that would involve getting down on the floor. If I did that, I'd likely stay there.

Nevertheless, habit and a sense of self-preservation forced me to at least review them where they lay, to note their image, position, and placement...

I blinked.

They were all the same card. The Magician.

Six Magicians littered the floor, like soldiers marching off to battle. "What the...?"

In most Tarot decks, there was one Magician card. That's it. One. Even the Thoth deck only had two, for reasons I'd never quite figured out. But six? Six wasn't possible.

Bracing myself on the chair, I leaned down for a closer look—

The cards changed.

They *weren't* all Magicians after all. One of them was, certainly, the card farthest out of the bag. But the others were a mash-up of majors and minors, exactly what you'd expect to see. Read all together, I knew they meant something. Probably something important. They could literally point the way, in fact, for those with eyes to see.

"Tomorrow," I muttered. Now that they were behaving, the cards weren't going anywhere, and neither was I for a few hours. Instead, I swiveled toward the suite's separate sleeping chamber, the enormous bed almost embarrassingly plush to my exhausted eyes. As I staggered to it, dropping my towel to the floor, I thought about what Father Jerome had said about the amulet and its potential to have a strange effect on its bearers.

Other than Fernanda, I'd arguably had it next to my skin the longest. Was it a good thing or a bad thing that the amulet had reacted to me? Had it found me weak or strong?

And how had it reacted when it'd come into contact with Nigel's unmentionables?

The sound of my own grudging laughter echoed through the room as I crawled beneath the covers. Even my eyelids ached. Still, sleep wouldn't come. I lay there for several long minutes, eyes closed, willing myself to sleep.

No dice.

I tried meditation. Deep breathing. Even planned a grocery list for an imaginary future when I'd learn how to cook... Nada.

"Please, God, make me stop hurting," I finally moaned.

A long, slow chuckle seemed to shimmer through the air. *"Close enough."*

My eyes snapped open. The room had gone completely dark. Had I turned the lights off? I tried to recall, but my mind remained in a fog, my muscles as heavy as concrete. Every punch and jab from the Russian shot-putter was making itself known on my body, and not in a good way.

A soft breeze riffled through my hair—though there sure as hell weren't any windows open in my room. Alarm jolted through me, though I still couldn't move. It took all my energy to stifle a whimper. I did *not* have the stamina for hand-to-hand combat right now. I barely had the stamina to shiver. Which would be a problem if I had to fight.

Was that someone *breathing*? No—no. There was definitely no one breathing except for me, and I was an exceptionally quiet breather. But if no one else was breathing... that meant no one else was here. Nothing but my overactive imagination, anyway.

"You did ask for help, Miss Wilde."

"I—what?" My nerves prickled as a long-fingered hand drifted over my shoulder, my reaction reminding me all too much of the amulet sending sparks along my skin.

"Am I dreaming?" I didn't think this was a dream, though. If it were a dream, there'd be sunshine and unicorns. And ideally, drinks with little umbrellas in them.

The hand pressed, and a soothing wash of warmth flowed through me. *"Do you want me to stop?"*

"I...I don't think so," I mumbled. The wall of blessed heat spooning up against my backside blew something against my ears, and I felt myself sucked beneath conscious awareness. Ready or not, I was going down.

"You're ready," the voice assured me.

Words to live by, I always say.

9

There was no sound, no breeze. I floated on a soothing ocean, somehow not at all concerned with drowning, though my usual water wings were conspicuously not in evidence. Instead, I was buoyed up by waves that eased my battered body into unclenching its muscles and unkinking its knots.

It took me a moment to realize I wasn't alone, but the touch of lips against my neck seemed an almost disembodied experience, not something I needed to react to or necessarily understand. I groaned as the trail of kisses drew a line of fire down my back, curving in a graceful arc along my waist, until somehow, I managed to flip over onto my back, and those lips burned a brand against my hip bone. Energy sparked somewhere deep inside me, healing me with equal parts fire and brimstone.

"I do not understand you," the murmured voice came again. *"I can only reach so far into your mind. Why?"*

"Hummm?" I turned again into the water, reveling in the sensation of hands kneading my legs, my hips, my lower back. Everything that had been abused in the past twenty-four hours was devolving into blissed-out euphoria. When the touch moved around my belly and up to my breasts, however, I hissed with pain.

The fingers froze, retreated. *"There is no pain in this place."*

"Well, there damned well is in *that* place." I attempted to shift away, but the Magician held me fast, and...my eyes popped open. "Hey!"

I scrambled off the bed, taking half the sheets with me, shaking my head like a stoner flushed out from beneath the stadium bleachers. I frantically scanned the bed, the floor... then the walls and ceiling for good measure. No one was there. Had I just been spooning with the *Magician*? As in the *Magician* Magician, the Divine Trickster, Trump One of the Tarot? *That* was who my psychic passenger had been since I'd started this job in Rio?

No. No, it wasn't possible. The Magician was a character on a card, not an actual human. My psychic passenger was definitely at the top of the arcane community food chain, but he wasn't some sort of god. Even if he no doubt thought he was.

I hobbled into the living room, flailing for the light, but the sudden flood of illumination made me sag against the wall. "Make it stop," I whimpered.

The room went dark. Well, not completely dark. The same lamps flared, but at about a quarter of what I suspected their usual brightness was. "Do you also do windows?"

The voice was back, whispering against my skull. *"You need to trust more."*

"Yeah, and you need to get out of my head." I made it to the table and took a seat, putting said head in my hands for a long minute. I wasn't sure what was happening to me here, but this was *not* the time for me to have a psychic meltdown. And more to the point...

I scowled down at my body, swaddled in the hotel sheets. Leaning back, I peeled away the top layer to expose my chest. I'd surveyed this area when I'd hit the shower, but I hadn't registered more than "Ouch." Now, based on my body's reaction when the Magician or whoever he was had hit the area with his magic fingers, something was seriously wrong with my...

I frowned. The skin of my chest was unmarked. There was the hint of pink, as if an old burn was fading, but unless you peered closely, there was no scar at all. Barely a shadowy outline of a frog remained on my left breast, like I'd ghosted it in with makeup. I touched the skin, tensing up for the shot of agony...and nothing. I pushed a bit more firmly, right on top of the burn mark, and—nothing.

"Well, that's weird." I dragged my fingertip over what was left of the frog's head, and—

Pain ricocheted through me so hard, I shot out of the chair, stumbling back several feet until I connected with the couch. My entire body hissed with electricity, the burst of energy complete and absolute and gone just that fast, leaving me lying in a heap on brightly colored cushions, breathing shallowly. My hands gripped the couch's edge as if that hold was all that kept me tethered to this plane.

"Um... Any idea what that was?" I asked the air around me.

Silence.

Apparently, the Magician had stepped out for a smoke break.

I noticed something else as I lay naked and panting on the hotel room couch. Besides the fact that the ceilings were exceptionally clean in this establishment.

I didn't hurt.

I stretched out my toes to double-check, as it seemed a safe place to start. They wriggled enthusiastically. I flexed my battered legs. Not a problem. Other than my chest area, I remained covered with bruises, scrapes, welts, and swelling, but the actual pain was gone. It was as if my nerves had been fried, no longer allowing any sensation to pass through their receptors.

Well, that wasn't quite true. I drew my fingers along my arms, hugging them to me. I could feel that. I pinched the skin ever so gently and could definitely tell the moment my nails dug into my skin. So, pain wasn't off the table, at least not new pain. But all the pain of battles past...

Slowly, gingerly, I sat up, trying to reconcile how I looked with how I felt. My eyes refused to ignore the fact that I was a Neosporin "Before" ad waiting to happen, and the bruises snaking along my skin did not inspire confidence. But as I lifted my arms and extended them to their full length, nothing made me twinge.

Even when my shoulder made an interesting crunchy noise, and then a wet pop, I could feel the blood drain out of my face, but not the pain that was surely causing that reaction. Bracing myself on the edge of the couch, I pulled myself upright, then took an exploratory step. My swollen feet complied. I drew in a deep breath—my lungs obligingly expanded. I was moving normally. I was breathing normally. This was definite progress.

My gaze swept the room, taking in the TV and its bright digital display. The clock read 4:16 a.m. By my reckoning, though I hadn't realized it, I must've slept for more than three hours. That was plenty. And apparently, whether thanks to the Magician or my commemorative Kermit the Frog amulet, most of my pain receptors had shorted out, which I didn't even know was a thing. Still, I wasn't complaining. Give me a quart of coffee and a doughnut, and I'd be ready to go.

Warmth fizzed along my nerve endings as I crossed to the table, picking up my discarded sheet along the way and wrapping it around me, more for the sensation of something on my skin than modesty. Plus, the AC had dropped to subarctic, and my gooseflesh was starting to hatch goslings.

I stopped at the edge of my impromptu card reading, staring down. The six cards still lay on the carpet, topped by the Magician, whose meaning I'd already figured out. The rest of them presaged a raft of crazy heading my way. The Page and Seven of Swords indicated that electronic communication and stealth would be the order of the day. The Chariot generally meant an overland journey, which made sense since I didn't think the amulet was lurking somewhere in my hotel.

Unfortunately, after that, the cards took a turn. Lying side by side were the Five of Pents and the Tower. The Five of Pents could mean poverty, but its literal imagery depicted a church. So maybe a holy place of some sort? Either way, the Tower was generally no fun at all. It indicated that yet another surprise lay in store for me...or possibly a bomb. Toss-up.

Settling in at my desk, I swiped the keyboard of my computer, and the machine whirred to life. Before I could start thinking about whether or not my suite came equipped with a coffeemaker, a line of text appeared on the screen.

I CANNOT REENTER YOUR MIND WITHOUT PERMISSION.

"Seriously?" The line winked out, and I glanced to the floor. The cards were still there, the Magician at the top of the makeshift spread.

Was it my imagination, or did ol' Trump One suddenly look a little peeved?

I couldn't help it—a broad grin stretched across my face, and I bounced on my toes. My psychic passenger had somehow managed to short-circuit my brain on multiple occasions—first as a very appreciated distraction in the Icamiabas mosh pit, then as a dance instructor at the Sambadrome, and then as Dr. Feelgood. I didn't know how he'd accomplished any of that, but it was a definite relief to discover there were limits to his psychic repertoire. "Well, okay then, Mr. High and Mighty Wannabe Magician. I guess you're in time-out. I hope you brought snacks, because it might be a while before I get around to chatting with you again."

My computer beeped, and I refocused on the screen. The geotracker program had come up and, along with it, my cheerfully glowing tracking pixel. "I love you, little blue dot," I murmured. It wasn't moving, which meant Frogger had been tucked in for the night. Even better.

I expanded the map and leaned close. They hadn't traveled that far, which made me happy, but they were definitely outside the city, which made me less happy. They appeared to have holed up to the south, a little inland, apparently right in the middle of a national park. Which meant I wouldn't be able to sneak up on them.

Then again, it also meant they wouldn't be hard to find. I eyed my cards appreciatively, smiling at the Five of Pentacles and Chariot.

"Holy place and overland drive, check and check," I murmured.

Tijuca Forest National Park boasted arguably one of the most recognizable tourist attractions in all the lower Americas, if not the world: the one-hundred-and-twenty-five-foot-tall gleaming-white statue of Christ the Redeemer, perched atop Corcovado Mountain.

"Interesting location."

The Catholic Church wasn't exactly unused to the idea of co-opting pagan places of worship to celebrate its own faith, so it was entirely possible that once upon a time, Fernanda's deadly fertility ritual had played out in the open sky on that hunchbacked mountain overlooking the sea. Maybe some pious Portuguese had come along, appreciated the view as much as the next person, and settled in for the long haul.

Either way, I had a feeling my little amulet wasn't going to be found out in the open, at the feet of the enormous statue. Given the location, I also suspected that the current possessor of the amulet was Fernanda and not the Russian woman or Nigel...because either of them would've already fled the country, whisking the amulet off to their client for a big fat payday. That also meant Will's creditor, whoever he was, and one Mr. David Galanis had gotten screwed too. Did he know? Had Galanis's bagman, Mr. Silhouette, even survived the drive-by shooting? If so, I should definitely keep an eye out for him, because he would be pissed.

Speaking of eyefuls...

I tilted my head, considering the mountain from a different perspective. The Icamiabas high priestess and her cult had a decided preference for sky-clad soirees. That wouldn't fly in front of a Christian icon, not even during Carnival. So where would they be?

I eyed the park at the bottom of Corcovado, Parque Lage. A few clicks brought up a photo and description, listing an old estate given over to tourism, a steep trail up to the Christ, several manicured gardens...and a cave.

Bingo.

I checked my side wound, by far the worst affront, only to find it handily healed from Mr. Wannabe Magician's triage. The guy might not be the Great and Powerful Oz, but he did have some skills, I had to admit.

I dressed hurriedly in a cleanish tank top, pleather hoodie, and leggings, then pulled together my meager belongings with care. The park would normally be closed at this hour, but it was the morning after the last night of Carnival. There was no telling what that could mean. The trail to the statue would probably be blocked off, but perhaps the gardens were accessible.

Either way, since I'd gotten a temporary reprieve from my exhaustion and pain—either courtesy of my erstwhile psychic passenger's magic fingers or my own personal frog prince—I needed to hit it. I had a feeling that the blue dot would be moving again come dawn.

I shoved my laptop into my bag, my phone into my jacket. Then I turned to my go bag of tricks for additional supplies.

Before leaving for Rio, I'd packed for the standard Amazon adventure—jungles, caves, cities, water. I didn't need most of what I'd brought, though. A gun would've been handy, but ricocheting bullets in a cave probably wasn't a good idea anyway. Instead, I pulled a few knives out of my kit and stashed them on my body. A lighter and some sticks of live dynamite sounded like a poor escape plan, but I picked them up locally for good luck anytime I went underground, and tonight was not the night to ignore superstition. I slid them into a pocket in the lining of my jacket that I'd prepared for exactly this purpose, and my mood immediately improved. Then I tucked a line of thin rope into my jacket as well, and a spare Tarot deck, just because.

Burdened of body but no longer of soul, I slung my bag

over my shoulder and left the hotel. Even at this hour, a cab was easy to come by, and I directed the driver to a café about six blocks away from the mountain. During the drive, I stared up at the magnificent statue of Christ the Redeemer, which was bathed in bright white lights as it presided over the reveling city. It seemed an oddly serene counterpoint to the chaos in the streets—the dancing and singing, the drinking and laughter. As if it knew secrets that none of the rest of us did.

Since my driver was focusing on the road, I edged open my laptop. Sure enough, the blue dot was holding steady. I snapped the machine shut, satisfied. I'd have to ditch the laptop somewhere close to the mouth of the cave, then pray I got out of the cave with my hands still intact so I could recover it. Losing my hands would be bad. I'd become very attached to them.

We pulled over next to a café, which was, as I'd hoped, popping despite the early hour. After handing over my fare and a tip so sizable, the driver met my gaze with instant understanding, I exited the vehicle and watched him drive back toward the brighter lights of the main city. Around me, revelers showed no sign of taking a break for Lent, and I shouldered my pack again.

I hadn't gotten two steps when my phone rang. Which was a problem, because no one had the number. Not even Father Jerome, since my feed was scrambled.

"Wrong number," I muttered to myself, willing it to be true.

It wasn't.

10

I fished inside my jacket pocket, then pulled out the device and swiped it on. The caller ID read a name, not a number, so that made it easy.

Even if the name was sort of obnoxious.

I put the phone to my ear. "How did you get my phone to recognize you as 'The Magician'? Is that a new feature I need to shut off?"

"As I mentioned, I can no longer enter your mind without your invitation. You need to allow me access."

"I'll think about it."

"You really should." The guy's voice sounded like chocolate dipped in butter toffee. Suddenly, I realized: man, I was hungry.

I kept the phone up, because most women out at this hour would want someone to know where they were. I eyed the restaurants on either side of me. Chances were, the dining options at 5:00 a.m. weren't going to be stellar, so maybe I should hold off until after my little amphibian rescue campaign. The last thing I needed was to be barfing up bad shrimp when I was running for my life.

I turned onto the Rue Jardim Botânico and started hoofing it for the park. As soon as I got out of eyeshot of anyone who would be impressed with my mad acting skills, I inserted my wireless earbuds and stowed my phone. I needed to keep my hands free. High above me, Christ the Redeemer stared out benevolently over his flock. I really hoped I didn't have to climb all the way up there. My boots were sturdy, but the trail looked like it'd been designed by mountain goats.

"I can help you, Miss Wilde." The toffee-chocolate voice was in my ear again, and my ear was happier for it. "If you're trying to determine how far you'll need to climb the mountain, you'll be pleased with this answer. The amulet you seek is three levels below the entrance to the cave you found on your laptop. You'll find it near the converted mansion used as a welcome center for the park."

"Uh-huh. And how do you know that?"

"If it's a matter of Connected interest, then I'm interested as well. I know some of the players in this game, but not all of them."

"Yeah?" I returned, peering into the shadows. "So, are you and David Galanis besties? Because he's definitely in the mix here, and I've never worked with him before. Or against him, at least as far as I know."

"I'm aware of his interest." Was it my imagination, or did Mr. Magician sound annoyed? Unfortunately, he didn't give me the satisfaction of dishing dirt on the guy. Instead, he went on the offensive. "Why did your client choose this amulet in particular? He appears to be playing his hand quite close to the vest."

"Stop right there, Magic Man. I don't kiss and tell." Instantly, I was assaulted by the memory of Mr. Magician's mouth on me, burning into my hip bone. My voice was a little strained when I spoke again. "You got anything else I can use?"

Silence floated across the airwaves.

"What, now you're playing hard to get?"

Still nothing. I crossed another street, the path beginning to angle up slightly. I was approaching the gardens. As I cut right onto the main road, however, the stitch in my side woke up with the effort. And started to burn.

That wasn't all that was burning. I adjusted my tank to get some air to my chest, wincing as the material brushed against my branded skin. Only I would get zapped in the shape of a *frog*. Seriously, it couldn't have been a wolf? Or maybe Hello Kitty?

I saw a mansion-esque house ahead, which seemed promising enough until I realized it was locked down tight, with security fencing along the entire front of it. *Crap.*

"Okay, you wanna be helpful? Be helpful. How do I get in here?"

More silence. Rolling my eyes, I swiped off the phone. "Fine, whatever. Crawl into my brain. But only the front part—"

"That's more than enough. For now."

The sensation of hearing the Magician's voice inside my mind was entirely different now that I'd experienced it in real life. It was fuller, richer, filling up my skull.

"Earn your keep," I murmured aloud. "How do I get in?"

"Go past the house until you near the end of the fence. You'll see the opening. The cave is thirty meters back, along the outer rim of the lower walkway."

"Meters. Yards, you mean. Great." I shuffled past the mansion, just another tourist out for a predawn stroll. When I'd nearly reached the end of the pathway, I saw it. As Mr. Magician had indicated, there was a break in the barrier, a small fissure where the two types of fencing didn't quite meet—the gorgeously ornate wrought iron of the front fence, and the sturdier chicken-wire-reinforced screen that kept the jungle at bay. I slipped into the break and onto the other side.

"I don't have to worry about dogs or anything, do I?"

His chuckle sent sensations shooting into places that had no business being shot. I shook my head, unslinging my pack. "And is my laptop going to be safe here?"

"I don't predict the future, Miss Wilde. I believe that's your specialty."

"Everyone's a critic." I dropped the bag behind a large bush with bright white flowers visible despite the gloom. Hopefully, there weren't another sixteen bushes exactly like it on the way to the cave, or I'd never be able to find it again. Unburdened, I bent low and racewalked through the darkness. I wasn't too late, I knew instinctively. But I also didn't want to announce my presence any earlier than I had to.

I found the cave without another word from my psychic phone-a-friend, which worked for me. Even his silence was starting to feel patronizing. The hole in the rock looked scrubby and not all that deep, but as I ducked inside, I caught the scent of fresh air, crisp and cool, unlike the heavy forest I'd left behind me. Where was it coming from?

I moved forward into the darkness, trying to hold on to my Zen. I could turn on my phone *at any moment* to get more light. I was *not* spelunking in the middle of the wilderness. I was exploring a nice little hole in the rock beneath one of the most heavily trafficked monuments of modern times.

The cavern came to an abrupt stop, but of course that couldn't be right, because there was still the breeze. And the breeze was coming...

I frowned. There was nothing but solid rock in front of me.

Since Mr. Magician wasn't providing any clues, and I didn't feel like asking, I reached inside my jacket and pulled out a Tarot card. I flashed my phone light over it for a second, then winced.

Well, that was never good.

The card I'd pulled was the Ten of Swords, which didn't make a lot of sense. I mean, yes, I'd been betrayed—multiple times—tonight. Both times by men, as it happened, though I was pretty sure the Russian wasn't a big fan of mine either. But none of this card's traditionally negative vibes resonated with me. I imagined it in my mind's eye to avoid flashing my telltale light again. A man collapsed at dawn, face down on the ground, with ten giant swords sticking out of his back. Cheerful, but not particularly...

I glanced at my feet. Facedown.

Great. "This had better be worth it."

Grunting with the effort, my body beginning to balk at any movement that didn't involve climbing into a soft bed, I squatted to the floor, inching my fingers down the wall for guidance. Sure enough, about ten inches from the ground, the stone gave way to open space. I waved my hand inside the space—and smacked against more rock. The opening was about two feet by ten inches, then. Good thing I hadn't had that second serving of pie.

I stretched out my full length on the cavern floor and shimmied forward, trying to see ahead of me. Beneath me was all solid bedrock. But unless my eyes were deceiving me, the gloom appeared slightly...*less* gloomy on the far end of the narrow passage.

Or at least I told myself that. The prospect of getting stuck in this hellhole wasn't terribly appealing.

Focusing on wide open spaces beneath sunny skies, I flattened myself beneath the rock overhang. I turned my head and screwed my eyes shut as the narrow passageway pressed downward over my neck and shoulders, threatening to crush me.

Merely a trick of my own paranoia and claustrophobia. But it was a very effective trick.

Propelling myself forward with fingernails and toes wasn't a superefficient mode of travel, for the record. But I eventually got to the other end. I stood tall, slick with sweat that was equal parts cold and hot. The amount of fresh air was much stronger here. A glance skyward told me why.

An oculus had been carved into the side of the mountain. This narrow, perfectly round portal seemed tailor-made to view the moon, which, though currently in its waning stage, nearly filled the entire opening. It was nearing the half-moon mark. Which probably meant something to Fernanda, if not to me.

As if summoned by me thinking her name, an all-too-familiar shuddering moan sounded from beneath me, loud enough to vibrate the stone floor.

Relief washed through me. Where Fernanda was, the amulet would be too.

I shifted toward the wall, then frowned at the twinge in my side. A quick check confirmed that my skin was still whole, but the attendant ache of the wound was resurfacing. Apparently, Mr. Magician's narcotic powers were a limited-time offer. In addition, whether due to my exertion or my proximity to the frog amulet, my exhaustion and pain were coming back in waves. Working along the wall, my eyes finally getting accustomed to the darkness, I crept down the tunnel. Along the way, I listened to Fernanda's wails, which changed in cadence in a decidedly non-fun way as I got closer. As if what should have been a joyride had suddenly hit some very bumpy road.

The cavern trail angled steeply down, and unless I was mistaken, my feet were registering actual stairs cut into the rock. Stairs meant civilization, which should have made me happy. Civilization meant there had to be more than one way out of this cave.

But the closer I got to Fernanda and her cries—which mounted in genuine pain and distress, not passion—the worse I felt. My chest where the amulet had lain against me was so hot, I would swear my skin was about to crackle, and my legs seemed made of lead. I trudged on, willing myself forward until I reached a bend in the rock. There were still no guards in sight, but I didn't know if that was a good thing or bad. Probably neither. Not too many people would be arriving at this party from a ten-inch crack in a cave wall.

As I approached, the darkness lessened, replaced by flickering light. Torches? Campfire? Would there be s'mores?

Then Fernanda burst forth in another wail, loud enough to make my spine ache. I straightened against the rock, becoming one with the wall, and dared a peek around the edge.

Visible through the doorway at the far end of the corridor, Fernanda lay in a heap by a fire, moaning pitiably. She didn't look damaged from what I could tell, or at least no more damaged than she'd been the last time I'd seen her. I edged forward carefully, pausing in front of a door cut into the rock. I glanced quickly into the chamber to my right... then stopped short.

Well. This was unexpected.

11

Nigel Friedman lay flat on a pallet in the middle of the stone chamber, apparently asleep. His hands were bound, his mouth gagged. Worse, he was once again completely naked except for a kind of ornamental loincloth that would probably have looked amazing on some Brazilian fertility god.

On Nigel, it looked vaguely ridiculous.

I stared at him hard, but apparently, my supernatural skills didn't extend to remote wakey-wakey. And the Brit's feet weren't bound, which meant his captors expected him to move at some point, so chances were good that nothing was seriously broken. Then again, they could have simply hobbled the insufferable asshat. Nothing like a quick slice to the Achilles to take a man down.

I winced but faced forward again, slipping past the open doorway. I couldn't fix Nigel's problems yet. Not until I fixed my own.

Nevertheless, I crept more slowly along the passage. Fernanda had gone quiet, reduced to whimpering sobs, but I could no longer see her. The crackling of the fire grew louder as I approached, but oddly, the corridor remained empty. There wasn't even a watchdog to sound the alarm.

That...suddenly didn't feel right.

A movement to my left registered a moment too late. I jerked back, but wasn't fast enough to evade a large troll-like guard who lunged at me from a crevice in the rock.

"Hey!" I tried to twist away, but the guard seized my upper arms and hauled me forward into the chamber. A quick recon revealed a second guard standing beyond the fire, then an opening for another chamber guarded by yet more burly men. I had a feeling that second chamber wasn't exactly empty, based on my last experience with Fernanda in a dark place.

As for the princesa, she was on her feet again, now dressed in a white, filmy robe thing. She glared at me haughtily from across the room.

She wasn't crying anymore. Nor was she mewling.

Frankly, I preferred the whimpering Fernanda. This one scared the crap out of me.

I sagged in Thug the Guard's hold, seriously too tired to put up the pretense of a fight. If Fernanda remained pissed at me, she could take a swing at any time. Now that I was in her presence, all the strength I'd been storing to get me here had fled. I'd probably tip over onto her fists and call it a day.

As it turned out, the high priestess of the Icamiabas appeared to be in more of a mood to talk. She pointed at me with a flurry of Portuguese that included one word I'd never forget: princesa. Since my princesa-ing was done for the night, I focused on the fire.

Bingo.

The frog amulet was lying on a white satin pillow, cushioned above a two-foot-high pile of stones banked up around the flames. The stones were carved in all sorts of figures, from fish to snakes to monkeys to birds. As if sensing my interest, the guard helpfully shoved me to my knees, putting me eye level with my frog prince.

As the amulet and I exchanged a meaningful glance, a shuffling to my right betrayed the arrival of another set of feet. A moment later, Nigel crashed to his knees beside me.

"Oh good," I muttered. "I was getting lonely."

He snorted. "That's not going to be a problem from here on out, love. There are about a dozen blokes ready for action in the next room. More on the way."

Nailed that one, so to speak. "When'd you lose the amulet?"

"About thirty seconds after you did. I never planned to give the thing to the git who contracted me locally—the man you saw bracketed with all the headlights."

"Galanis's bagman?"

"Mhm. I had a bigger fish on the hook. But *my* client wanted to make sure said git was out of the running permanently, so I set him up to get his hands on the amulet for ever so brief a moment, fully intending to relieve him of it at the earliest possible opportunity. Before he got smoked by the princesa's goons, the man was quite spooky, wouldn't you say? What with all the lights and shadow? Bloody diabolical."

"Terrifying," I said drily. I didn't have reason to doubt Nigel, though. This sort of double cross was par for the course with artifact hunting. Side deals happened all the time. "So what happened?"

Nigel sighed. "The princesa is nothing if not resourceful. She had agents in the crowd at the Sambadrome who realized that you weren't her, and they tracked you and the professor. Then they bagged me during the crossfire on the street. They figured you'd be back, though, which is why they kept me around."

Before I could puzzle through that one, Fernanda stalked toward me. With one sharp command, she directed Chief Thug to take off my jacket. I wanted to put up a fight, I really did, but the closer the woman got to me, the worse I felt. She was like Princesa Kryptonite.

Taking advantage of my passivity, the guard pulled me away from the fire, then hauled off my jacket. He shoved me hard enough to make me sway as he balled up the jacket, then unceremoniously dumped the whole mess next to the fire. I sagged, watching numbly as the very edge of the pleather curled up and blackened in the flames. The full fire wouldn't reach it right away, but eventually, a stray spark would ignite it. What would happen after that would take the term "burner phone" to a whole new level.

Then I remembered the card reading from my hotel room. The Tower...meant boom. So did the few sticks of fake-looking dynamite still stuck in my jacket.

Uh-oh.

Before I could kick the jacket farther away from the fire, Fernanda positioned herself in front of me and took my right hand, speaking with urgency.

I glanced sideways to Nigel. "She does know I have no idea what she's saying, right?"

He cleared his throat. "That's why I'm still here—I'm supposed to translate for you. And by the way, you've assumed the power of the amulet, apparently. She's preparing you for sacrifice."

"I'm not scheduled for sacrifice today."

"You'll have to take that up with the headmistress."

Continuing to mutter in Portuguese, Fernanda placed one of her jeweled cuffs on my right wrist, then another on the left. I wasn't completely unhappy about my new accessories. Those hunks of metal would go for quite a lot on the open market. Assuming I made it out of here with both my wrists intact.

Fernanda's sudden, sharp words brought my gaze back to her. Her eyes blazed with intensity, and she barked another command that ended with "Princesa."

"She needs to quit saying that," I muttered.

Nigel's snort was cut off as Fernanda finished her rant with something firm and absolute sounding. Thug One hauled me up off my toes, and I hung like a rag doll in his arms. The odd pose let my feet dangle against Nigel's ass. I twitched my foot twice, and the Brit's breath hitched. Despite his bound wrists, his fingers brushed my ankle, and the weight of the knife I'd holstered there vanished. Then the second guard lumbered over and yanked Nigel to his feet. Both of us waited unmoving, locked in cave-troll-fisted grips.

I eyed the fire nervously as Fernanda began some weird and creepy chant. Even though my pleather was industrial grade, we didn't have much time now.

"How'd you get down here, anyway?" I murmured to Nigel beneath her wails. "Because I have to tell you, the route I used wasn't exactly handicap accessible."

"Door directly behind us, to the left of where you came in." He tipped his head toward it. "Narrow passageway, but easy to navigate."

"Guards?"

"Every twenty feet or so."

"Crap."

"Thought you'd like that."

"Despeer-se," Fernanda demanded, waving at my shirt.

Obligingly, Thug One let me go, and I dropped the short distance to the cave floor.

My shoulders slumped. "Do not tell me she just ordered me to strip."

"You *are* getting the hang of this, aren't you?"

"Listen," I said, turning to him. I needed to hurry this along. "Tell them I will not begin the ritual or whatever the hell they're talking about until I have the amulet around my neck. Tell them it calls to me."

"But—"

"Make something up, Nigel. And make it good. I'm not the only liability here, and that loincloth of yours isn't going to help you save your ass if I go down."

Nigel spoke rapidly. His hand gestures were as expressive as his language, and Fernanda's face turned from mulish to intrigued to finally happy.

I glared at him. "That seemed like a whole lot more words than was probably necessary."

"You told me to make it good." He shrugged. "And if we don't get out of this, I'll at least get to see you perform a few acts that defy physics before I die. There's some satisfaction in that."

His spiel had the desired effect, in any event. Fernanda walked up to me, all smiles, and reached past me for the amulet. The moment she touched it, we both winced. The burn on my left breast blazed at the affront of another woman touching the stone this close to me. Grimacing, Fernanda held up the amulet as Thug One forced me to my knees. Again. Canting my head to the left, I saw the calves of another three guards stationed inside the room to the back. Also in there, surrounded by rocks, was the ceremonial bed. And, now that I could see more clearly, at least a dozen men. All of them chained together. And naked.

And looking pretty happy.

After another hard shove from Thug One, I commenced despeer-ing, which was no easy trick since I was kneeling. I handed over my clothes to Fernanda, and she took them from me with her free hand, throwing them promptly into the fire. They joined my pleather jacket, which was now smoking...industriously.

Stripped of everything but my jeweled cuffs and charming disposition, I was apparently deemed ready. Fernanda bowed, then lifted the amulet to place it over my head. When it touched my chest, an electrical reaction shot through me. For the record, electrical jolts hurt.

"Ah... Not to put too fine a point on it, but is your skin smoking?" Nigel murmured.

"Princesa!" I stood abruptly, then twisted toward Nigel. "There must be more. You had dozens more men than this earlier tonight, prepared to do your bidding. I must have more."

Nigel lifted a brow, then gamely translated, his eyes going wide as the amulet began to give off shivery little sparks that were going to be really hard to explain to my dermatologist.

Fernanda blinked, confused.

"More!" I stalked past her into the bridal suite, where the men stood at, er, attention. I dismissed them with a wave of my hand. I pointed to the two guards flanking the bedchamber. "You. Inside."

Nigel caught on, and Fernanda did as well, her smile suddenly knowing as she spoke.

"How many?" Nigel translated her next question.

"All of them." I moved to the guards still blocking the way out, grinning as if I'd been let loose on an all-you-can-eat buffet. "As many as you can spare. The power is strong within me. The men will be prepared for your rites. Bring them."

Fernanda clapped her hands, and two of the guards took off up the passageway. I pushed Nigel against the wall, praying that he'd cut his hand ties. I refused to speculate on where he'd hidden the knife. "You, I want to take last."

"I look forward to it." He winked, then spoke again to the princesa. She folded her arms, clearly well pleased.

The men all piled into the room. I crowded them back more deeply into the bridal chamber, spreading my arms wide.

The telltale smell of sulfur lit the air as the crackling fire ate its way to the live fuses in my jacket lining.

Finally.

I turned and raced for the door. Ever Mr. Chivalry, Nigel surged for the princesa, shoving her out of the way, then peeling out after me a heartbeat before the dynamite exploded from the center of the fire.

I kept running.

The explosion shot straight up into the chamber and connected with the heavy stone ceiling, immediately sending down an avalanche of gravel. It wasn't enough to trap anyone for good, but it was enough to get me a quarter of the way up the tunnel, Nigel on my heels.

"Fernanda?"

"She'll survive. Four guards remain at the top."

"Got it." But as my brain scrambled for solutions, a billowing rush of overheated smoke came boiling up behind us into the narrow tunnel, seeking all the fresh air. The force of it catapulted us forward into the guards at the top of the stairs. I pointed back down the passage and screamed, "Princesa!"

"Socorro," Nigel muttered.

Didn't know what it meant, didn't care. Said it anyway. "Socorro, socorro!"

The men bounded down after their princess. The smoke was already clearing—I'd been packing a few narrow sticks of dynamite, not C-4—but they'd served their purpose. Nigel and I careened out of the cave and down the mountain into a full-fledged jungle. We were nowhere near the mansion, which meant I was nowhere near my pack. Which meant I was nowhere near my clothes.

"You do end up in the most interesting of positions."

"A little help here!" I wasn't proud. I had heavy jeweled cuffs around my wrists and the amulet around my neck, and all of it bounced in frantic counterpoint to my mad dash through the trees.

"Keep heading down. When you reach a street, a car will be waiting."

"With clothes?"

"What?" demanded Nigel behind me, not at all winded. Blasted Brits and their training.

"With clothes, Miss Wilde. It will forever be my pleasure to dress you."

12

————

Sunrise always came too early the first morning after Carnival.

Hunched in my chair, I studied the menu at the Copacabana Palace Hotel like it contained the mysteries of the universe. I had a table facing the ocean. There were already a few couples slumped over tables around me, as bleary-eyed as I was, as if we'd all gone through the apocalypse together.

My client had seemed surprised I'd texted him. He'd seemed less surprised that my price had gone up.

Way up.

Nevertheless, agreeing to meet me at this hotel was a bonus I appreciated. It was the most public spot imaginable, and it afforded a straight drop down onto a nicely land-scaped lawn. If I had to make a run for it, I could. It would hurt, but I could do it.

It was the little things one really appreciated in a break-fast spot.

I nudged the small wrapped gift box on the table in front

of me, which I'd carefully positioned in plain view of the world.

Carl Fellowes was no more nervous than any of my clients: they all had that in common. They wanted to see evidence of the merchandise before they stepped into the open.

I was on my fourth cup of coffee in ten minutes when a disturbance at the hostess-stand door caught my attention. I readjusted the supple leather Versace jacket that was so far out of my league, it was in another stratosphere, then slid my hands down jeans that were of a brand I'd never heard of, Earnest Sewn. They sure felt like they'd been sewn in earnest—they fit me better than my own skin.

Mr. Magician hadn't been kidding when he'd told me he'd send clothes.

The mad dash through the jungle had landed us on a narrow access road to the top of the mountain. Down had seemed like the best direction, and it wasn't five minutes later that a black SUV had cruised along, its lights on low, its illuminated license plate reading MGK MN.

I'd rolled my eyes, but declared the vehicle safe. Nigel and I had clambered inside. The back of the SUV had been set up more like a limo, Mr. Magician apparently taking pride in his transportation. After the vehicle had navigated a tight turnaround, we'd hurtled down the mountain. Nigel and I had struggled into leggings and tech tops, then I'd discovered a second duffel for my own use. With my laptop and its own set of weaponry.

Including a loaded tranq gun.

I'd shot Nigel twice for good measure. He'd stared at me, dumbfounded, and had dared to ask why. He'd passed out before I could explain the finer points of my reasoning, but I'd send him a text later. With that amount of drugs in his system, he wouldn't be caring about anything for the next twenty-four hours or so.

More than enough time to get me out of Rio.

And with any luck, I would soon have a couple of additional fistfuls of money to show for my trouble.

"Ms. Wilde?"

As if on cue, Carl Fellowes made his way toward me, all smiles. It really was too bad that he was so hung up on needing the amulet to give him some sexual mojo. He was handsome enough on his own. Probably in his late sixties, true, but virile and sharp eyed, his smile enough to turn the heads of women generations younger than him. He aimed that engaging smile at me as he took the seat opposite mine.

"You had quite the adventure, it would seem."

"It was a busy night."

He accepted a delicate demitasse of espresso from the hovering server and sipped it, clearly savoring the warmth. I clasped my hands around my own giant tasse of blessed java. This morning, there was no indulgence in the world I was going to deny myself.

"I had a chance to review your report on my drive over." He nodded, still not going for the box. "You didn't learn from the British hunter how he came to be part of the search?"

"Yeah, sorry about that. He got a bit tuckered out."

Carl shrugged amiably. "I can tell you, if you'd like."

I steadied my hand on my coffee, as if I hadn't just consumed my body weight in caffeine. "You know?"

"When you get to be my age, there's more at stake than the thrill of acquisition, even for a prize as special as this. There are four such Icamiabas amulets that belong to Amazon death cults. You were lucky to escape alive with this one. You and Mr. Friedman."

"There was also Miss Russia."

"Ah, yes. Her name is actually Camilla Asker. She came quite highly recommended, I assure you. Not as well recommended as you did, of course."

I slid him a glance. "You hired her too?"

It had happened before. Clients often wanted a fail-safe to ensure that the McGuffin they were paying so much to acquire was actually acquired, one way or another. The practice generally served to piss me off, so to my relief, Carl shook his head.

"I did not, nor the other one, Nigel Friedman." He chuckled with that air of self-deprecation that the rich learned to affect in the cradle. "Unfortunately, I'm afraid my actions are watched somewhat closely by my compatriots, and when they determined my interest in the amulet, they decided to get into the game as well."

"So one of your buddies—David Galanis, maybe?— hired Nigel, and another one tapped what's her name, Camilla, to follow me? That's what you're saying?"

Carl Fellowes curled his lip. "Mr. Galanis is *not* one of my friends, and I assure you he didn't hire Mr. Friedman or Ms. Asker. Not directly, anyway. It's not his style. Any agents professing to work on that man's behalf are the dilettantes and bottom feeders of the arcane black market, whose marker Galanis has called in. He doesn't pay in cash for the artifacts he collects, he pays in favors rendered or debts resolved."

I thought about Mr. Silhouette, Galanis's ill-fated bagman. "What kind of favors?" I asked, genuinely curious.

Fellowes scowled. "Not the kind for polite discussion. David Galanis is in deep with the New York syndicate, and his magical interests are...unsavory, to say the least. You should avoid him."

"Yeah, well. Maybe he should avoid me." I took another deep drink of coffee, knowing it was time to change the subject. "You know, that amulet might have a bad reaction to your, um, skin. Watch out for that."

"But of course. You must have read the same articles I have." He waved off my words, clearly relieved to be refocusing on his treasure. "Fear not. I'd never put it against the skin. The old books say a silk bag is the best container for it, and that seems like a good place to start." He smiled at me warmly. "I'm glad you are so thorough with your research."

"I try." I slanted a glance at the box. "You think it'll meet your needs?" Not a question I usually asked, but I felt off-center, unwilling to let the amulet vanish without knowing more about how it would be used. Because Carl didn't look like he needed it, it had to be said.

"Oh yes." He lifted the lid of the box to see the jadestone frog inside, nestled on its coiled leather cord. "It will go in my private collection, or perhaps more accurately stated, into my wife's."

His wife's? The frog's scar sizzled against my chest at the mention of another woman touching it. "She's, ah, going to love it, I'm sure."

"I know she is." His expression, for once, seemed slightly worn. "I met her about five years ago—here in Rio, as it happened. She too was a Carnival princesa. She too was a member of an underground society, until she was usurped by a younger, more beautiful leader."

Whoa. Hadn't seen that one coming. "Fernanda?"

He didn't answer directly, instead continuing on with his reminiscences. "She didn't go willingly but couldn't stay in the city once power had shifted. I came along and—well. There is an advantage to my position in society." Again with the self-deprecating smile. "But separating my wife from the power of her ancient beliefs has taken its toll on her heart. It's my hope that this small gift will return a light to her eyes that has been gone for too long."

"Yeah...I'm sure it will." I thought about everything I had experienced while the amulet had been around my neck. The power that had coursed through me, and the physical ache that had nothing to do with my chicken-fried skin. "It might return more than that to her, though. If you haven't had your heart checked recently, now would be a good time."

Mischief twinkled in Carl's blue eyes along with obvious affection, which made sense. He'd just dropped seventy large to buy a stone frog for the woman, so it was reasonable that he liked her. "I'd thought of that as well. I guess we will see."

He nodded at the waitress, who was hovering nearby. "Please order anything you'd like. I've arranged to cover the check, and I've also arranged for the remainder of your fee to be wired to your account. My congratulations on your successful endeavor. In addition, not that you haven't defended yourself admirably, but I've asked my compatriots to please call back anyone they had sent to recover the amulet and to trouble you no further."

"Um, thanks." I thought again of Nigel. We'd dropped him off at a hotel off the main drag of Rio. Mr. Magician's crisply suited chauffeur had carried him into the hotel, then returned a few minutes later, quietly informing me that "Mr. Friedman" would be taken care of most excellently, and that I needed no longer to worry about him. Hopefully, his client wouldn't hold Nigel accountable for the loss of the amulet. Not that the thing had ever been his to lose. I'd scored it first.

Speaking of no longer worrying, there was one more

loose end to tie up. "What about Will Donovan? Was he part of your friends' little competition?"

And had he survived?

I don't know why I cared, but I did.

Carl grimaced. "I'm afraid so. I was shocked when I read that in your report, but it only took a few inquiries to run it down. It hadn't occurred to me that an associate of mine would commandeer a civilian to his cause, but the professor appeared to be expertly chosen. He also nearly helped my friend pull off a coup too. It's the closest he's ever gotten to doing so."

"So there were no casualties?"

"None at all. Frank actually paid Mr. Donovan for his services and assures me the professor will no longer require any additional funds to cover his former business choices. He did his job, getting you to where he said he would, with the amulet intact. The attack from the princesa's guards was simply unfortunate timing for everyone involved. You didn't give up, though."

I shrugged. "Job wasn't finished."

He smiled. "Well, it is now. I hope you can take some time to enjoy the fruits of your labor."

I raised my mug to him, thinking of little Michel back in Paris. "Something like that."

Carl took his leave of me then, and I lingered, eating about four pounds of eggs, bacon, and some kind of pastry that was like a truffle on steroids. When I finally rolled out of the restaurant and down the short stairs to the ocean, I weebled more than walked.

I needed to get out of there, though, to plan my next steps. I needed to do some cleanup, get on a plane—probably to Miami—to start. But the food in my stomach and the money in my bank account were combining to lull me into a momentary lapse of—

I whirled so fast that I hit the man's arm at an awkward angle, expecting him to be chopping at me from above instead of from the side. Reacting just as quickly, he backed a step away, his hands going up in a soothing reaction. But I'd already learned what I needed.

The jolt of psychic awareness seared through me, quick and hot. This asshat was a Connected, but not just any Connected. He was way high up the food chain.

"Back off," I practically snarled.

The man who belonged to the hands took another long pace away from me, allowing me to get an entire view of him.

And...well. He was a work of art.

Golden eyes stared at me from an impossibly aristocratic face that looked like it had been hewn out of old gold. His hair parted over his forehead in blue-black waves, framing high cheekbones, full lips, and a chiseled jaw. He was tall, sleekly muscled, well dressed in a deep gray suit and crisp white shirt, and he practically oozed money.

There was also not one single doubt about who he was. "Lemme guess."

Those sensual lips twisted. "You could always draw a card."

I shook my head and continued up the walkway, the man stepping into stride beside me.

"Though I might add—it's just 'the Magician,'" he advised, in rich, caramel-smooth tones. "No additional honorific needed."

I shrugged. "Hey, you can call yourself whatever you want, it's all good." I leaned into the sneer maybe a little too hard, but I couldn't help myself. Now that I'd met him in the flesh, the Magician—or whatever his real name was— freaked me out so much, I was surprised I'd kept breathing. Energy sparked and skittered between us like a live current looking for something to electrocute. There was something about the man I found wildly, blood-poundingly attractive... yet something else that made me feel like a rabbit caught in the sights of a sniper. I had an instant and enduring aware- ness of the Magician as predator and me as prey.

I wasn't a fan of being prey. Prey tended to get eaten, and I had too much I needed to do.

"Your work is very impressive, Miss Wilde," he continued after a moment. "I have need of someone with your skills, assuming you have an equal need to be compen- sated handsomely."

Well, okay. Handsome compensation made up for a lot. But questions? I had them. I squinted at the guy briefly, then looked away before my eyes were permanently seared. "And who would you be, exactly? Besides a creeper who should be paying rent to my head?"

"For now, it's enough that I belong to an organization that eagerly desires to acquire several artifacts over the coming months."

"Eagerly, huh?" That was the second financial reference in as many minutes, and my nerves were already jangling. I thought about Carl Fellowes and the games rich people played. The Magician looked about as money as they came. "Anyone else interested in these artifacts? Maybe David Galanis?"

He glanced at me so sharply, I knew I'd hit pay dirt.

"You really don't like him, do you?" I smirked.

"My personal opinion of Mr. Galanis is irrelevant. I represent the interests of the Arcana Council."

"Never heard of it."

"You're not meant to."

That jacked me up a bit, and another whiff of predator-prey slid through the air around us, with me on the decidedly wrong side of that equation. I made a note to ask Father Jerome about this fancy Arcana Council the next chance I got. Because if these guys were another bunch of upmarket asshats who preyed on the weak and vulnerable...

Apparently not following my thoughts this morning, the Magician kept going. "We are in need of an artifact finder, and we have enough work to employ you exclusively—"

"I don't do exclusive."

"To aid with your acceptance of the arrangement, we will ensure that, as Mr. Fellowes indicated, you are no longer concerned about those immediately in pursuit of you. Nigel Friedman has already been paid and will be sent on his way. Camilla Asker will be monitored, and if she gets personal, so will we. As to Mr. Donovan, his role in this affair was quite minor. And quite complete."

Was it my imagination, or had the Magician's voice gotten a little snippy at the mention of Will? I decided to test that theory. "I don't know, Will and I go way back. I might need to follow up—"

The Magician glanced my way almost casually, but his gaze flat-out pinned me to the wall. Caught in that snare, suspended in time, I had no choice but to stare deeply into his hypnotic golden eyes. They looked otherworldly. Like seriously otherworldly. Like other-side-of-the-universe other—

His words were low, intense, and to the point. "In three days' time, you will receive information about your first assignment, if all my calculations are correct, which they are. Complete that assignment to my satisfaction, and you'll have a hundred thousand dollars wired to your account.

Complete it without drawing undue attention to yourself, and you'll receive an extra twenty thousand. Since financial terms appear to be the only salient information you require from your clients, is that satisfactory?"

I drew in a breath and released it. It sounded suspiciously like a squeak. "Sure."

"Good." He leaned a little closer into me. His looming intimacy made me nervous—but not nervous enough. Which was a dangerous thing. "There is something about you I cannot place, Miss Wilde. Your ability to close your mind to me is a mystery I do not understand. And I have walked this world long enough to know most of its mysteries."

I peered at him. "You're sounding really Syfy Channel now. You know that, right?"

A smile barely creased his lips. "I look forward to our partnership. And to learning everything about you there is to know."

His lips hovered over mine, not near enough to kiss me. Maybe this was still a dream, and he wouldn't get any closer. Maybe...

But no. Without any further hesitation, the Magician leaned in, brushing his lips across mine. Energy shot through my body, not at the same caliber as when the frog amulet had nearly fried me, but close enough. I drew in a sharp breath, reaching for him—

And he was gone. Poof.

"Oh for *the love of Kansas.*" I rolled my eyes as expressively as I could to communicate my disdain, then glanced around. Unfortunately, there was no one in view who could corroborate whether I'd been talking to someone in the flesh, or if I'd just been treated to some really, *really* great tech. I was no newb to the arcane black market, after all.

With today's brain-scrambling technology, there were a million ways to appear and disappear into thin air. I could easily have been drugged at breakfast, then treated to projection VR, my eyesight fried on a frequency undetectable by me, you name it. Nobody just *disappeared*—not even powerful psychics who fancied themselves the incarnation of the Tarot Magician. That was way above everyone's pay grade.

Still, it was a neat trick.

I shoved my hands into my pockets and turned toward the ocean. My fingers scraped against a hard edge, and I frowned, pulling out a crisp business card on heavy cream stock. A mere two words were printed on the card in sharp aristocratic letters.

Armaeus Bertrand.

No number. No address. The inference was clear—he'd contact me. I simply needed to be ready when he did.

Well, Armaeus Bertrand could get in line. After this weekend's job, I'd be getting more work. More notoriety. More everything, if I played it right. I didn't need the generosity of Armaeus Bertrand, and I didn't need his money. I sure as hell didn't need—

The wind picked up, drifting through my hair, a brush almost like a caress floating against my cheek. The words in my ear were so faint, I might have imagined them, but I somehow knew I hadn't.

"Three days, Miss Wilde."

13

"Pretty sure you can count better than that."

I muttered the words under my breath, but I figured they'd be heard by the guy I intended them for. His radio seemed specially tuned to Air Sara.

I'd been intensely aware of the Magician's arrival the moment he'd blown through the diner's foggy-paned door. This had less to do with my keen powers of observation than with the fact that I was sitting in a Waffle House about thirty miles north of Miami, Florida. The worn vinyl benches and peeling Formica tables were a balm to my senses, a necessary shot of normality, as was the tepid yet exceptionally strong coffee that was currently eating away at both the insides of my esophagus and the base of the scarred, well-washed cup I'd just had topped off. I fit in a place like this.

Armaeus Bertrand did not. This morning, he rocked a sleek dark suit that hovered somewhere between indigo and sorrow, the white shirt beneath open at the neck, revealing a hint of bronzed skin. His hair gleamed black and luxurious underneath the fluorescent lights. His shoes fairly glowed.

Even his eyes sparked. He was altogether far too bright and shiny for five o'clock in the morning.

"Coffee?" the waitress asked him from behind the counter, and he nodded, surprising me. I wouldn't have picked him for a Waffle House coffee kind of guy.

He stalked over to me, and I suddenly wished that I wasn't the only other patron in the restaurant at this hour, though I'd chosen the place specifically for that benefit. After a week in Rio and the red-eye flight that had gotten me out of the country, I'd had enough of people pressing in on me for the time being.

The sun wasn't even close to rising, and I was hunched over my plate of pancakes and eggs like someone was going to steal it from me. Given the look of aristocratic disdain on the Magician's face as he surveyed my meal, I didn't think I had anything to worry about from him.

"I have it on good authority that your financial resources no longer necessitate the frequenting of such an establishment," he observed drily. "Which means I am forced to conclude that you chose it on purpose."

I sat back in my bench seat and gestured magnanimously to the space opposite me, where the vinyl was about three families away from splitting entirely.

"You're in luck. My last client just left. How can I help you?" I asked as Armaeus slid into the bench seat opposite me, somehow managing to still look elegant.

He nodded graciously as the waitress approached. It was a testament to his real magic that she placed what I suspected was the restaurant's only chip-free mug in front of him and filled it expertly with coffee that seemed remarkably fresher than what she had served me. She turned to refill my mug as well, however, and I caught the concern in her eyes. She held my gaze a moment longer than necessary, and my heart tugged hard. This stranger was worried about me. Worried that I had drawn the attention of someone who looked like the Magician, someone who'd clearly tracked me down in the middle of nowhere. As quickly as she had begun pouring, she retreated. Leaving me to meet Armaeus's amused smile.

"You don't get out and mingle much among the people, do you?" I asked him as he glanced around the coffee shop, then nodded at my plate.

"By all means, continue your meal. I would hate to keep you from whatever that is."

I shrugged, but weird rich potential client or not, I wasn't about to let good food go to waste. Because Mr. Bertrand was right. I was making money now, loads of it, but it hadn't been all that long ago when breakfast at the Waffle House had been a treat reserved for special occasions.

"You said three days. It's been less than forty-eight hours. What's the hurry?" I asked around a mouthful of pancake, studying the play of emotions across the Magician's face. I expected contempt to be among them, an acknowledgment of my poor etiquette if nothing else. But his primary expression seemed to be bemusement, along with a whiff of academic study, as if I was wholly unexpected to him. I got the impression that he wasn't used to much being unexpected.

Good for him. I stuffed down a renewed spurt of almost primal fear and forced myself not to flee the Waffle House and disappear into the humid Florida morning. Cocky or not, Armaeus Bertrand had money, and he was ass-deep in the arcane black market. He was exactly the kind of mark that I needed. Nothing more, nothing less.

He didn't answer right away, so I went back to my meal, which I realized a few seconds later had been his intention. What was with the solicitude I was garnering this morning?

I didn't like it. When I reached for my coffee cup and lifted it, Armaeus finally spoke, but only to issue a warning. "It's hot."

I snorted. "Trust me, it's not."

But I wasn't completely stupid, and I slowed my roll long enough to notice the steam rising off the mug before I completely scorched my tongue.

I scowled at him. "Okay, buddy. I can put up with you crawling around my head, making me feel things without being there, and even appearing to go poof into thin air with the VR trick of the century. But you screw with my coffee and you're going too far. Who are you, really?"

Armaeus Bertrand arched one of his impressively manicured brows and regarded me with even more satisfaction.

"Do you still believe that I'm merely altering your perceptions through some sort of mental manipulation?"

I shrugged. "I'll go you one better than that." I'd also given this a lot of thought. "I'd say you're a very accomplished tech wizard, chock-full of products that legit *do* change the perceptions of the people you target. Not exactly magic, but transformational all the same. The arcane black market is filled with guys like you."

Again with the raised eyebrow. "You've done research to bear out this hypothesis?" he asked, and again, there it was. Not annoyance. Certainly not concern. But an amused curiosity, as if I were a new species of butterfly he was looking forward to pinning to his board.

"I've done enough," I snapped, which of course was a total lie. Because the truth was, there was virtually nothing out there on Armaeus Bertrand. Not on the regular web, the dark web, *or* the arcane web, and my multiweb Google Fu was strong. It was as if the man didn't exist. "So cut to the chase already."

The Magician didn't hesitate, though I picked up his flash of interest in continuing to spar with me. Instead, he gestured to the window of the Waffle House.

"You acquired your rental car under an alias, choosing to travel by vehicle the moment you reentered the US. You also chose a secondary highway out of Miami versus a primary thoroughfare. Who is it you're avoiding, Miss Wilde?"

"Okay, so when I said cut to the chase, that specifically meant, why are you here? I don't need to answer your questions. That's not what this process is about."

He smiled. "This *process* could prove to be very valuable to you."

Another zip of panic sliced through me at his emphasis on the word, and this time, I decided maybe I should pay attention to it. After my artifact-hunting abilities had evolved into the garnering of objects with a very distinct provenance, I'd learned there were a lot of creepy guys in the arcane black market. It looked like they'd just welcomed a newcomer to their rolls.

I carefully put down my mug and edged ever so slightly toward the aisle. The guy was big, and probably fast, but I was no slouch in the escape department.

Opposite me, the Magician stiffened, clearly intuiting my thoughts, no mind meld required. "I am no threat to you, Miss Wilde," he informed me derisively. "At least not in the way you suspect. I merely wish to point out that if *I* noticed your furtive behavior, chances are good that whoever it is you are seeking so assiduously to avoid has noticed it as well. I could help you evade unwanted scrutiny, should you wish."

"Well, gee. That's very nice of you." The truth was, I wasn't on the run from anybody specifically. I simply liked to keep myself to myself. Jobs seemed to find me anyway, and the competition was never far behind. My stature had not grown so much in the arcane community that I was a target, at least not so far. I was merely a sought-after hire. I preferred to keep it that way.

Which brought me to my next problem.

"I don't know how much you work with artifact hunters, but it's not like we have a lot of downtime between jobs." I waved at my backpack beside me, which contained my laptop and, well, everything I traveled with. I didn't like leaving anything in my car if I could help it. My life just didn't work that way. "I've got three other assignments I need to knock out before I can find whatever it is you're hot for. I'd offer you a recommendation of somebody else, but anybody worth their salt is going to be just as busy as I am. It's kind of a weird world we're living in right now, so there are lots of people looking for lots of strange things."

"Yes, well, I'm afraid my requirements are highly specific, and my timetable has escalated." The Magician dipped his hand inside his jacket and withdrew two cards, which he laid out with a flourish in front of me. Business cards with the names of my next two contracted clients.

I squinted at the cards, then lifted my gaze to meet his golden eyes. "What's this?"

"These two gentlemen have quite unfortunately become engaged in an altercation which is going to necessitate their removal from activities on the arcane black market for the next few weeks. Should you wish to seek them out to confirm, I encourage you to do so, but, regrettably, you will find that there will be no opportunity for communication with them in the immediate future. I presume you receive tacit confirmation before you engage in any activities on behalf of your clients, yes? You don't strike me as the type to waste your time."

"Yes, I do receive that confirmation, and no, I haven't received it from either of these clients yet," I agreed, while renewed anger bubbled beneath the surface. I glared at him. "You took them out so I could work on your job first?"

"Only temporarily."

"Well, then I'm only temporarily going to be increasing my price to do whatever job you have in mind."

Something shifted in the Magician's eyes, the flare of interest turning almost sensual. Another zip of danger arced through me, like a lanternfish cruising by in the depths of the ocean, warning of trouble right behind. But Armaeus's next words were almost insultingly bland.

"Name your price, Miss Wilde. You will find the opportunities I can afford you are worth accommodating me, and I can assure you that the assignments I will give you will be far more interesting than whatever these gentlemen sought to procure."

"You think so?" I took another swig of coffee as dollar signs danced in my head. I hadn't known what the payoff was going to be for the first client in particular, but I honestly hadn't been looking forward to meeting the guy. He was in deep with the DC elite, and those asshats almost always wanted something to do with finding an ancient national treasure. If I ever met Nicolas Cage in person, I was going to need to punch the man in the throat.

The Magician was clearly waiting, however, so I shrugged. "Okay, hit me. Whattya got?"

"I need you to draw out David Galanis's patron. The person for whom he is amassing so many artifacts."

"And pop goes the weasel once again." I studied Armaeus, newly intrigued.

Over the past day and change, I'd made it my business to track down Mr. Galanis, and what I found wasn't inspiring.

He was a Class A antiquities nutjob, parlaying a respectable adjunct antiquities position with the New York Metropolitan Museum of Art into serving as some kind of arbiter of all things arcane in the city, the darker the better. It didn't surprise me Armaeus didn't like him—not too many people did, from the sound of things. Nevertheless, taking out random douche nozzles wasn't my jam. The world was full of them. "I don't do murder for hire, not even if people deserve it."

"Murder won't be required. I simply need a name. The information is barred from me, which shouldn't be possible. Now that Galanis has lost his bid for the Icamiabas amulet, he knows who you are, and so does his patron. We will be gathering a few choice artifacts over the next day or so that are of a level to pique their attention. By my calculations, though Galanis is the front man of their operation, his patron will want to meet with you personally. Once that happens, I can do the rest."

"Right." If Armaeus was looking for me to scoop up a few baubles to dangle in front of some avaricious collector he didn't like, the job was technically once more within my purview. It still didn't mean I was keen on doing it. I let my gaze drift lazily over the Magician's shoulder and out the pane glass windows. The sun still hadn't bothered to rouse itself, but the Waffle House's parking lot was illuminated by several floodlight style street lamps. Which was how I noticed the man slinking along beside my rental car, right before he crouched down. Someone squatting beside your rental car was never good. Score one for hauling my pack into the diner.

"If you'll excuse me for a minute..." I muttered, but Armaeus lifted his hand.

"My offer will include transportation, as it does appear

you'll need it." He leaned forward. "But who is it that's hunting you, Miss Wilde? Specifically. It's important for me to know."

I wasn't in the mood to explain who was after me or why. The truth was, there were several options, up to and including Mr. Galanis, if Mr. Silhouette had blamed me for his failure to secure the frog bauble in Rio. The guy snuggled up to my rental car was spending a little too much time to be simply dropping a bug on my vehicle, though, which was admittedly kind of weird.

Artifact hunters didn't usually waste their time trying to take me out. There was plenty of hustle to go around. And the more formal agencies who had taken note of my activities in the past generally didn't skulk around in Waffle House parking lots. Despite my best efforts, my hands got a little clammy at the idea of my rental car blowing up. I didn't like it when things blew up around me, at least when I wasn't the one lighting the fuse. I'd had enough experience with unexpected explosions to last a lifetime.

"Why don't we stay focused on the job at hand." I refocused on Armaeus, shoving my hands into the pockets of the fancy leather jacket he'd given me in Rio. The fingers of my left hand brushed reassuringly over my pack of Tarot cards. It was a new deck, purchased before my trip to get the frog pendant and kept as a spare. I was hard on Tarot decks and I hated to be without them.

"Very well," the Magician conceded. "There are two artifacts we require to ensure we have Galanis's full attention. Regrettably, I cannot be directly associated with the first assignment."

"Oh, that is a pity," I deadpanned, sneaking another glance out the window.

All seemed to be quiet in the space around my rental

sedan. But as I watched, a second vehicle entered the parking lot, a minivan with a couple of bikes lashed to the back. It parked right beside my vehicle, and two stiff-legged adults in short-sleeve T-shirts exited, opening the sliding door to release a scrambling pup. The travelers were either local or not yet dressed for a trip home. February in Florida was beautiful, but the farther north you got, the grosser the weather became.

"The artifact I require first is an ancient reliquary crafted by a wealthy French family," Armaeus began.

I squinted at him. "You're sending me to France?"

"Not exactly," he allowed, and I returned my attention to the scene unfolding in the parking lot. I had to admit my curiosity was blunted by the emergence of a child plucked out of its incarcerating car seat from the van, the toddler sleepy eyed and docile, as the gamboling pup was locked back inside the van after its brief walk. My gaze strayed back to my sedan with its potential bug/bomb, and I watched with dismay as the young family made their way to the Waffle House.

"Yo, does your percentage calculator indicate what that guy did in my car?" I asked, my fingers fanning through the cards in my pocket. I pulled out the deck, weighing it in my hand, while keenly aware of the Magician's eyes on me.

"In this particular case, I suspect you are being targeted for bodily harm."

That got my attention. I flicked my gaze back to him.

"Why? I didn't do anything. Not recently anyway."

"I think you underestimate the number of interested parties in the fertility artifact you recently recovered. Your search for it elevated you to my awareness, and to the awareness of Mr. Galanis, or at least his proxies. It's reasonable to believe it raised your profile with other members of the arcane black market as well."

"I bet that freaking Russian chick sold me out," I muttered. I'd found Camilla on the arcane web, but not her current employer. Still, there was a dog in that minivan, and that was not cool. I spread out the deck on the table in a blunt arc and pulled three cards in quick succession.

Fool, Tower, Five of Wands.

I scowled at the cards. The Fool could ordinarily mean adventure, but there was that daggone dog again, which was mostly why I cared. The Tower was one of the deck's favorite cards to indicate things going boom in a big way, and of course the Five of Wands was a perennial go-to for a fight.

Armaeus leaned forward slightly, almost despite himself. "You are, of course, aware of the many possibilities for interpretation of such cards?"

I slid another card free as the young family entered the Waffle House, the dad handing off the kid to the mom after a quick scan of the place. The restrooms were behind me, and he headed our way.

I flipped the card over. Seven of Swords. Strategy and deception. I flicked a glance at Armaeus. "Do *you* have any enemies I should know about?"

Outside the Waffle House, my rental car exploded.

14

Several things happened at once. The man heading toward the restroom pulled out a gun, ignoring the explosion outside, while the little boy and the waitress screamed in unison as the mom swung toward the door. A second later, the window next to my table shattered in a spray of glass.

I paid no attention to any of that. The guy had almost brought his gun level before I'd gotten out of the booth, but my shoulder was down and I was driving hard, hopped up on caffeine, sugar, and a healthy dose of carbs. I piled into his midsection, knocking him backward as the gun went off, the bullet punching through my heavy jacket. But what I lacked in size, I made up for in sheer pissed-off energy as I brought all my frustration down on the guy—frustration and the blunt edge of a knife that I'd yanked out of my pocket at the last second, with a specially weighted hilt. It amplified my strength by a factor of ten. I cracked down on the guy's temple, my sight going red while his eyes rolled back into his head.

"Not yet," I growled. I collapsed on the guy's chest, my

knees over his shoulders, as I cracked him the other way, shaking him back into woozy sensibility.

"Who sent you? And what the hell did you do to that dog?"

"I—ugh," the guy managed, and I flipped the business end of the knife around, pinning it below his chin. There was somebody shouting now close by, and I dimly heard the sound of a vehicle peeling away, the wail of sirens following.

"Who sent you?" I demanded again.

"I don't *know*—it was—just a job," the man groaned. I jerked back, my gaze shooting to the now-empty Waffle House booth. A thick envelope was all that remained of the Magician.

"What about the dog?"

"The dog is *fine*," the guy muttered. "Fuck, get *off* me, lady. The dog got out. Like I'd kill a fucking dog."

"Congratulations. You get to live." I flipped the knife again, butt-side down, and clocked him out cold. "Asshat."

The sirens were louder. I surged up, grabbing the thick envelope and stuffing it inside my jacket, then retrieving my deck of cards and pocketing it as well.

I hauled my pack onto my shoulder. Without sparing a glance to the screaming chaos in front of the building, I ran through the opening between the counter and the wall and bolted through the kitchen, now emptied of any cooks. Worse, due to the early hour there wasn't even a single strip of bacon frying. This really wasn't my morning. A second later, I was through the back door, skidding to a stop at the sleek limousine that awaited me. The door had already been opened, and I could see a to-go container of four cups of coffee emblazoned with the Waffle House signature sitting on the back seat. I piled into the car.

"Sara Wilde, right?" chirped the early-twenty-something

driver in the front seat as the vehicle peeled away from the Waffle House, bumped over a heavy concrete curb up a short grassy embankment, and onto the street. We were heading away from the highway, but I hunkered back, well aware of the thick aroma of expensive coffee—no way was that Waffle House's usual brew—and even more expensive leather.

"What is going *on*?" I demanded. "Is this how you guys always do business?"

"Brand-new to the job, so not sure," the guy countered, sounding far too delighted to be a contract killer, or even a contract driver. "I'm Sam Haskins, by the way. Pleased to meet you. And all I know is a guy showed up at my mom's house four hours ago while I was working in the garage, practically the middle of the freaking night, telling me he needed an Uber. I told him he had the wrong guy. I race stock cars, I don't drive people around. He said a race car driver was what he needed, and me in particular. Plus, he was driving this car, and it is *suh-weet*. And we're going to New York, did you know? Or at least you are. I'll probably be dropping you at an airport along the way once he gives me the all clear, 'cuz we'll never make it otherwise, even in this amazing ride."

I pulled one of the coffee cups free from its holder and popped the lid. "New York," I muttered. "That's interesting." I glanced down at the envelope, noting the crest insignia without a location, some place called Prime Luxe. Sounded like a steakhouse.

"How much is he paying you for this?"

"Fifty *thousand*," Sam Haskins informed me, sounding positively gleeful. "He already gave half of it to my mom, telling her some story while she was standing there in her bathrobe, that he was sponsoring me in an upcoming race.

Said the rest would be sent to my account after I got you safely up north. And that speed was not a problem." He grinned, tapping something hanging from the rearview mirror. "Apparently, this baby tracks cops in a three-state radius."

"Four hours ago, huh?" I thought about the cards I'd pulled, presaging a fight, strategy, and the Fool and his damned distracting dog. But if Armaeus wanted to send me to New York, he would have flown me. Unless there was some good reason not to.

Exactly how far into the future could the Magician see?

Sighing, I flipped over the envelope, then slid my finger beneath the envelope's flap. The bulky package opened easily, and my eyes widened at the thick sheaf of bills inside. There was a card tucked into it as well, its rich creamy stock emblazoned with the same steakhouse logo.

The handwritten note on the card was elegant, almost old world. *Sargov Volkov hired your intended assailant, a local contractor, by all accounts.*

"Volkov." I curled my lip. A different dickhead than I expected, but a dickhead all the same. Russians never did know when to leave well enough alone.

I will ensure neither troubles you again, the note continued.

"Yeah, well, you might need to pay the rental car damage fees while you're at it," I quipped derisively, half expecting to hear the Magician's arrogant reply in my mind. I felt it start anyway, a subtle push of pressure, but out of sheer perversion, I pushed back, mentally willing my mind to remain impervious to his assault.

Silence. The barest echo of annoyance slid through me, but even that was only a faint hint of the pressure I'd felt before.

I leaned back, grinning as I riffled through the money. I

did appreciate a man who paid in cash, I had to say. Then I turned the card over. There was a New York address, a name, a time for later this evening—a deadline we'd never meet by car, Sam was right—and instructions.

Cocktail party. Clothes will be waiting for you. Your first expense allocation is included herewith. There will be an intermediary assignment as well to gain the artifact I mentioned, which will be helpful in New York. Those details will follow.

"Sounds good to me." I tried to remember the piece he'd referred to right before everything went boom, but the explosion had shot it clean out of my head. Resolutely, I pushed the vague, years-old memories of another explosion out of mind, and settled deeper into the thick leather seat. A few more miles slipped beneath the wheels of the limo, and I finally allowed myself to relax, feeling better than I had in a while.

If I was going to be taken for a ride, at least I'd be going in style.

15

Despite the tray of coffee, which I applied liberally to my exhaustion, it didn't take long for me to start nodding off. My helpful chauffeur pointed out the small compartment that contained a blanket and pillow, and it was all over for the next four hours. I awoke to the plaintive beep of my cell phone, indicating a text. Momentary confusion—this was a burner phone—was replaced by sharp alertness as I came fully awake and reached for the device.

I scowled down at the text.

Your assignment, Miss Wilde. Please complete it by nightfall, if you would. Remember, the artifact is the most important piece, and do be discreet. Events are already in motion in New York.

Before my annoyance fully coalesced, another text came through.

You're in the US?

This message was from Father Jerome. He, of course, was always the first person to get the telephone number of whatever burner phone I ended up with. The only person, as it happened. A realization that should have made me sad but mostly made me relieved. I didn't always make the kind of choices that were conducive to friendships, as my run-in with Will Donovan amply demonstrated. I texted the affirmative and waited.

I already knew that Father Jerome had received the payment I had wired to him with the completion of the Rio job, and he could have had no way of knowing about my new association with the Magician. He also would not have caught word of the troubles befalling my other two clients.

Father Jerome had worked in the arcane black market for a long time, but he was no longer a young man. He made a show of staying out of day-to-day operations, both for his own safety and, more importantly, for the safety of the children and families he protected. He wasn't contacting me about a client, at least not one of mine. The first message to come across was an address in Savannah, Georgia. I glanced out the window, taking in the position of the sun.

"How far are we away from Savannah?" I asked as the short row of dots on my phone screen indicated there was more to come. It was taking its sweet time. Father Jerome was based in Paris, serving one of the venerable old churches in the city. I tried to tamp down my impatience as his message made its way across the Atlantic.

"Another hour, tops," the chauffeur said. "You got friends there? Mr. Bertrand said your plans might change, and that I should just, you know, roll with it. I figured out pretty quick that he's...not your average employer." He said this last with such deliberate offhandedness that I squinted at him, mildly surprised. He glanced back at me, and for the first time, I felt a faint shiver of awareness. Not the shiver that might sometimes happen between a man and woman, but the recognition of a kindred soul.

I'd been roaming around the Connected community, especially in its darker fringes, for long enough that I was starting to pick up the telltale signs. That said, I didn't exactly know what to do with such information. It wasn't like we had a secret handshake or snappy lapel pin indicating years of service.

Fortunately, the chauffeur put me out of my misery by chattering on. "I checked the vehicle after Mr. Bertrand left. He all but invited me to do so. It doesn't have a VIN number. Not like it was scraped off, but it never had one to begin with. It's a prototype."

"Really?" I glanced around the limo, but it looked...sort of limo-like to me.

"Yep. I don't just race cars, I'm kind of obsessed with them. This manufacturer, the insignia on the vehicle looks a lot like a lot of things, but it doesn't exist. There is no Luxe brand of vehicles, at least not in common circulation."

Luxe. I made a face, but I wasn't surprised. I'd only known the Magician for a few days, but I already knew humility was not one of his talents.

"So you're saying the guy is loaded," I acknowledged.

Once again, he surprised me. "I'm saying the guy's got magical powers. You don't just make a car appear out of nowhere in the middle of Miami without a trail. It's a city known for being an entry point for a metric ton of shady shit, so there's lots of ways to get in and out of the city, but they're all established ways, and as it happens, they are ways that I know. I think Mr. Bertrand knew that too. By showing up at my doorstep with this car, he was giving me a message that I heard loud and clear."

"Oh yeah?" I asked, intrigued despite myself. "What message is that?"

"There's a bigger world out there than I had allowed

myself to believe. A bigger world even then my mama and her Tarot cards hinted at, though they've been doing plenty of hinting."

At the mention of cards, my brows shot up, and I glanced at the rumpled jacket beside me. Sure enough, the cards remained intact.

"Your mom reads?"

"Oh yeah. She's kind of made a name for herself in my neighborhood. But she doesn't have this kind of flash."

I snorted. "Well, to be a hundred percent clear here, neither do I."

"But you've got access to it," he said with such intensity that I blinked. This man was a low-level Connected. Maybe his psychic abilities manifested in his exceptional driving, maybe they hadn't even fully manifested yet, but they would now that he knew to look for them...and it had been the Magician who'd tipped him off that it was a possibility. Why had he done that?

My attention was distracted by a flash of color across my screen. I looked back down at my phone and took in the earnest face of a young girl, maybe sixteen years old. Her skin looked spray tanned, but expensively so. Her eyes were large and unadorned by makeup, though shaped in such a way that she could easily make herself look several years older with a few swipes of mascara and a heavy hit of eyeliner. Even through the thumbnail picture, which became instantly grainy as I enlarged it, I could feel the same shiver of awareness that I had with the driver. Then again, Father Jerome wouldn't be sending me this girl's picture if she wasn't both Connected and in trouble.

More text followed.

Maria Ambrose, 16, disappeared from a school dance this

weekend, hasn't been seen since. Her grandparents were members of my congregation. The family is exceptionally wealthy and Connected. They moved to Savannah from Paris when Maria was born, to hide her and her siblings from outside attention. But Maria is a teenager who loves nothing more than music, singing, and drawing attention to herself. She's a remarkable young girl.

I made a face. I'd only been through Savannah a couple of times, but it wasn't a place I'd go to hide. Creepy old trees, grand mansions, and lots of Civil War history attracted a heck of a lot of tourists. That kind of traffic was trouble for someone trying to stay out of sight.

There was another problem with this information too. Father Jerome didn't let the question hang.

The resources of the Ambrose family don't matter here. They can't act at all, because the arcane black market is watching very closely. If pieces of the unfortunate young woman start appearing for sale, it will be a win for the wrong kind of people.

I curled my lip. If there was one thing I'd learned about the arcane black market, it was that they were eager for anything new. New drugs, new magical potions, new uses for ordinary things. If news that the blood of a Connected had unique and magical properties leaked out, everyone would start preparing bloodbath. And by preparing, I pretty much meant drooling.

You don't think she's already dead? I typed.

This time, Father Jerome's response was immediate.

I don't think that poor girl will die for a very long time if those who have taken her can help it.

A familiar rage burned in my stomach. It was always the children who suffered the most when it came to the arcane black market. The idea of Connected ability being transferred by an object, bones, or a kidney wasn't new. Rare species of animals had been used in various forms of medicine since the beginning of time. But with the advance of technology and the ever-growing need for power, especially among those who had or aspired to have magical abilities of some sort, the lure to appropriate the magic embodied by a child had proven to be too great a temptation. As sick as it was, those who had abilities were convinced that others' purpose in life was to help feed their own.

You think she's still in Savannah? I texted.

I do. A vial of Maria's blood was hung from a tree in front of the Ambrose mansion this morning. They could have flown it in, of course, but there is a personal nature to the attack that leaves Mrs. Ambrose to think they will keep the girl close. I have circulated warnings to the families local to me who fit the profile. They are watching closely. And they are now more motivated than ever to assist. If you could recover Maria...

Got it, I typed back. And I did. I had funneled a lot of money toward Father Jerome, but I was only one person, and I didn't have generational wealth. If his cause to protect the most vulnerable Connected could be augmented by the cash of those who had more money than they knew what to do with, I was all in.

"So, are we going to Savannah?" Sam asked brightly, and I roused myself to take in his eager face.

"It's more or less on the way, yeah?"

"It is. And my mom's got family there. If we end up spending the night, you wouldn't need a hotel."

I lifted my brows, feeling a now-familiar twinge of annoyance. *Goddammit, Armaeus...* I knew there had to be a reason he'd pulled in Sam to be my driver. "You have family in Savannah?"

"I know Miami doesn't seem like the South because it's kind of a city unto itself, but we're not originally from there.

And Savannah *is* the South. Most families who've been there for any length of time are spread out all along the seaboard from Florida to the Carolinas, but not any farther. We tend to stay close."

I nodded, taking it in. The coincidences were piling up, but I got the message, and that was part of the point. The Magician was no idiot. He'd known why I'd increased my level of work in the arcane black market. My ability might have bubbled me up to his awareness, but ability wasn't a lever, while the reason I wanted to amass this much money was. Enter the Magician, with plenty of money and not only connections, but the ability to see connections I couldn't. The ability to tap resources and to manipulate them into place for bigger paydays that benefited me and, I was sure, benefited him as well.

He'd known Father Jerome would be contacting me, and why, and he'd decided he wanted me to respond to the priest's call for help. Not because he gave a flying leap about Maria Ambrose, I was sure. He wanted the artifact I'd uncover while searching for her. An artifact that would help him take out this David Galanis.

"How long have you had family in Savannah?" I asked, tapping a quick confirmation to Father Jerome.

"Oh sheesh, probably for the last hundred years or more anyway. Hell, at this point, they're part of respectable society. Why?"

"Next time we pull over, you need to text your mama. I need to know everything she knows about a family called Ambrose."

And as Sam heartily agreed, I texted Armaeus too. I could just have thought my annoyance at him, but I wanted a record of this.

You suck.

Not surprisingly, an immediate response flashed across my screen. *I have every faith in you, Miss Wilde. Please focus on obtaining the artifact.*

16

We didn't stop after that for more than a quick break, especially since Sam insisted that the food would be way better in Savannah. I scrounged in the limo's fridge and found fresh fruit and some crackers, so that worked for me.

Once we neared the city, I contacted the matriarch of the Ambrose family using information provided by Father Jerome. While waiting for her to respond, we tooled down the cobblestoned River Street, which was choked with cars and tourists—and roughly four hundred and seventy perfectly serviceable places to eat and drink. When Mrs. Ambrose finally contacted me, I was about to break down and fall face-first into a platter of prawns. Instead, she asked me to meet her right away...at a cemetery.

Not any old cemetery either. According to Sam, the most famous one in the city. He didn't have any problems redirecting us, and we made the four-and-a-half-mile trek to Bonaventure in less than twenty minutes. Which was impressive, since it appeared that any tourist in the city who *wasn't* at the riverfront taking in the sights could be found at Bonaventure Cemetery.

"Shouldn't they be selling tickets?" I muttered as Sam turned into the line of vehicles. There was a steady stream of cars in and out of the place, most of them rental sedans or SUVs. Because nothing said vacation getaway like a trip to a crypt.

"This place was always popular, even before the movie," Sam informed me, still chipper as all hell. I vaguely remembered the movie he was talking about, something about a garden, but that'd come out well before my time. "Granted, it did pick up quite a bit with the movie. Not so much the book, though I'm told there was a burst of attention then too. It's been kind of a problem for the oldest families who still have a presence here. According to my aunt, the Ambroses have their crypt in an area of the cemetery that's constantly closed for repairs, if you get my meaning."

I snorted. "With this many grave gawkers, sectioning off an area without a good explanation would be like posting a big flashing sign saying, 'Hey, come check this out.'"

"Yup," he agreed. "But we'll get you there quick enough. There's a break in the action up ahead."

I took advantage of the slow crawl of tourists to pull out my cards. I'd waited until I was officially on the hunt before consulting them, because the cards enjoyed nothing more than presenting information that could be construed multiple ways depending on your circumstances. It paid to have your eye on the prize when you asked a question, or at least your eye moving in a concerted direction toward the prize. But something about this job smelled off from the start, in a way that was reminiscent of the Magician's faint aroma of citrus and cinnamon.

"What do I need to know?" I murmured, feeling more

confident that I'd get a straighter answer from the cards than from the Magician. Not that my new client would try to deceive me, exactly. There was no money in that. But I hadn't quite figured him out yet, while the cards were usually on my side.

They could still be a pain in the ass, though.

I drew the High Priestess first, a card not out of place in a city as old, venerable, and steeped in psychic lore as Savannah. The second card was more interesting—the Four of Cups, featuring a young man sitting under a tree, ignoring the three cups before him as he fixated on the cup floating in the air. Depending on the circumstances, that card could signal ennui, boredom, a desire for a new adventure—or the hint of something special and possibly supernatural in the wings. Given that we were dealing with the kidnapping of a young psychic female, I was being put on notice that the supernatural was definitely going to be in play here. I quickly flipped over the third card. The Ten of Swords.

Yippee.

Unlike a lot of psychics, I wasn't given to inherently negative readings of the cards. First off, my use for the cards was usually more practical. Secondly, there was enough negativity in the world, and I didn't need to be adding to it.

That said, the Ten of Swords in this particular situation wasn't good no matter how you sliced it. Somebody felt betrayed, and chances were it wasn't my kidnapped target. Betrayal wasn't something children felt as keenly as their older counterparts. They hadn't lived long enough to have expectations of the world, so when bad things happened to them, most of the time they thought it was their fault.

But if young Maria wasn't the one feeling betrayed, who was? Had her purported psychic abilities proven not to be strong enough? Had her kidnapping not resulted in the desired outcome for her captors? Either way, that Ten didn't bode well for the girl's long-term safety.

I noticed another card sticking out of the deck and pulled it before I could think better of it. Card decks could sometimes be overly chatty, but I hated walking into a situation blind.

The last card was interesting—another ten, this one of Pentacles. Traditionally a money card, the Ten of Pentacles was specifically a family money card, the card of generational wealth. Considering I was about to walk into a whole pile of generational wealth, the card made sense...but I suspected it held an additional clue as well, one maybe a little darker than I preferred.

Most domestic violence struck close to home. In the case of the Ambrose family, psychic violence might be following the same pattern. Even among the Connecteds—especially among the Connecteds—people could be horrible to each other.

No one blocked our way into the section of the cemetery reserved for the Savannah elites. The gate had been pushed open wide, without a guard in sight. A situation I was sure wouldn't last.

We reached the mausoleum of the Ambrose family a few minutes later, nestled between two imposing oak trees hung heavily with Spanish moss. There were two cars parked in front of the small, squarish building, both of them sleek sedans that made a good attempt at looking as expensive as the one we were arriving in. No one stood near the vehicles, so I told Sam to wait and watch as I slid across the leather seat and liberated myself from the limo.

I stumbled a few steps to regain my land legs. The comfort of the Magician's limo couldn't make up for the fact that I hadn't moved in way too many hours. Still, with gradually steadier strides, I crossed a short distance of manicured lawn to the Ambrose mausoleum.

It wasn't exactly an imposing structure. Built about ten feet wide and fifteen feet deep, it was composed of what looked like concrete brick plastered over with a thin layer of stucco. Small windows had been cut around the roofline. They couldn't let in any appreciable light, I thought, but they were arguably decorative.

Most of the effort in the mausoleum's design had been spent on the front of the building, where a graceful span of angelic wings spread from an orb atop the doorway all the way out to the edges of the building. The doorway itself was a two-part affair, with an ornately filigreed wrought iron screen softening the thick metal door that made up the business end of the security arrangement. Both stood open, and I peered a little uncertainly at them as I passed through them. The heavy metal door in particular struck me as a little overkill to protect the dead, but rich people were crazy.

My arrival did not go unnoticed. Not surprising, given that the interior room was about the size of a tribble.

"Sara Wilde?" a woman whose face I couldn't quite make out in the gloom asked imperiously, no doubt Mrs. Ambrose, who Father Jerome had advised me was the matriarch of the family. But her voice was far too thin to be the mother of the lost girl, a suspicion I validated as soon as she stepped forward into the light. This would be Grandma Ambrose, an appellation I was sure the slender woman in her crisp business dress never, ever used.

"Yes," I confirmed. "And you must be Mrs. Ambrose. I'm sorry to interrupt you, but I've had a close associate suggest you might need help—Father Jerome at Saint-Germaine-des-Prés."

At the mention of the priest's name, the old woman's

face softened. "He told me I couldn't hide my family away forever. But he underestimated the tenacity of my desire. It was kind of him to send you. I also understand you're in the employ of Armaeus Bertrand."

I nodded, unreasonably annoyed as I realized I hadn't asked Father Jerome about the Magician's mysterious Arcana Council. I needed to follow up on that. "I'm currently working with him, yes. I don't expect it to be a long-term assignment."

"Wise of you." Mrs. Ambrose lifted a slender, pale finger, devoid of any rings. "Our family has known the Bertrands for centuries, but Armaeus has not been as helpful as he could be. He did, at least, contact us to advise he was allowing us to borrow you for this task, as well he should. He owes us."

I swallowed a smile, not surprised that Armaeus seemed to have temporarily abandoned his attempts to hitch a ride in my mind. Nobody likes to be called out by old ladies.

"I'm sure he does," I offered mildly. "And I'm also sure you would like to get your granddaughter back as soon as possible. I'll help you do that."

"This is highly irregular," huffed a second voice from deeper in the mausoleum.

I squinted past Mrs. Ambrose, waiting a beat for my eyes to adjust to the deeper gloom. It didn't help much. The man who slowly came into focus looked like he preferred the shadows. A slender figure with a slight stoop to his shoulders, perhaps to overcome his height, regarded me with dark, somber eyes that were nestled in a hangdog face. His overcoat and suit were gray, his tie was gray. His underwear was probably gray.

"You did not advise me that we were expecting company," Mr. Gray (probably not his real name, but still) informed Mrs. Ambrose.

"Forgive me, Milton. We're expecting company," she said drily. She skewered me with a glance. "You're here because this is a safe space. Safer certainly than my house or the country club, or wherever it is that spies have clearly learned our secrets. Milton, shut the doors, if you would. I have no interest in continuing to talk in the dark."

I tensed as the man moved to the doors and shut them, but my Spidey senses weren't going off in an imminent-threat kind of way. Mrs. Ambrose was Connected and definitely pinged my eccentricity radar, but Mr. Gray—Milton—whoever he was, seemed mostly to resemble an exceptionally mobile lump of clay.

The moment the doors on the mausoleum were secured, Mrs. Ambrose banished the darkness with a flick of a decidedly modern light switch. I blinked around in surprise. The walls were smooth marble, with nary a single shelf cut into the surface. "This isn't a mausoleum?"

"The Ambrose family is French. *That* is our home," Mrs. Ambrose informed me crisply. "We came to Savannah to protect our family, not to bury them."

I frowned. "Then why have a mausoleum at all?"

"Appearances." She flicked a dismissive hand. "And, of course, William's family, the Manchesters, had their mausoleum elsewhere in the cemetery. It was important to look like we were committed."

"Oh. Of course," I murmured. I suppose it sort of made sense. Nothing said commitment like a crypt, right?

Mrs. Ambrose didn't give me any more time to ponder the idea. "Do you have any expertise in recovering kidnap victims?" she asked me.

"I generally hunt artifacts, not kids, but you don't need to worry about that. I can find her."

Mr. Gray let out an unhappy sigh. "Ophelia, I really must advise against utilizing someone outside the family. This is a delicate situation, I should think."

"It's not a delicate situation, Milton, it's a dire one," she shot back. "And it's not your place to think. Maria's already been injured—probably more than once. There's every likelihood that she will be again. What's more, I'm tired of having my decisions prescribed by anyone. William, God rest his soul, took great delight in controlling me throughout our life together, and I allowed it with grace and gratitude. But he's dead now. I have served my time."

"*Ophelia,*" the hapless Milton tried again as my eyebrows lifted.

She waved him off and focused her steely eyes on me. "My second-born granddaughter has been kidnapped and drained of at least a pint of her blood, probably more, in the past week. We know this because we've received a reliquary filled with it."

I made a face, but the word pinged a synapse in the back of my brain. Reliquary. This was the artifact Armaeus had mentioned...though artifacts didn't usually sport freshly spilled bodily fluids. *Gross.* "You know it's her blood? You're certain?"

"We matched it against samples we had in storage."

This time, I managed to keep my face blank, for which I deserved an Academy Award. "In storage?"

Mrs. Ambrose's mauve-tinted lips thinned, so clearly I wasn't doing that great a job with my attempt at impassivity. "Yes. Against this very concern. You see, there is an old fable about the members of my family. Our blood—or at least the blood of those members who display psychic abilities—is said to be able to transfer psychic ability to another person. You drink the blood of an Ambrose psychic, and your own powers will flare to life. A foolish, dangerous tale, and one that persisted far too long. It took me years to convince William that the curse had long since left us—and I should know. I was the last surviving daughter of the family, and I, of course, was blessedly spared from any psychic curse."

I stared hard at Mrs. Ambrose, but I couldn't deny what I was seeing. My Connect-o-detector wasn't merely bubbling with awareness, it was throwing its own parade. The woman was so full-on psychic, she practically vibrated with it.

"So you, ah, don't believe your granddaughter has psychic abilities either?" I offered cautiously.

Something in my voice must have given me away, because Mrs. Ambrose's snort was rich with derision.

"My second-born granddaughter is *overflowing* with psychic abilities," she confirmed with grim certainty. "Flagrantly, obviously, deliriously. The curse has well and truly returned. That would be dangerous enough, of course, but it was made all the more so because my dearly departed William was adamant that his precious Presbyterian bloodline would not be besmirched by such a foul taint. He could not abide the idea of Maria possibly having abilities and took steps to punish her for it—punish all of us. Though I had no way of knowing this because I was not *informed* by his trusted legal *adviser*."

Mr. Gray flushed as she glared at him, but didn't offer any counter.

She plowed on. "It was only after William's death that I learned that my husband had changed his will. Apparently, if there is any hint of psychic impropriety in my bloodline, the children will be cut off—all of them, including beautiful, foolish Maria."

She grimaced, lifting a hand to rub her forehead. "I knew that having three grandchildren was going to be trouble. One or even two children, you can manage. Three, they get out ahead of you and you never catch up. But none of that is your concern. I simply need you to find my grandchild and bring her back to me before she is entirely exsanguinated—and also before the entire arcane black market has learned that the Ambrose blood is once again flowing with power. You do that, Sara Wilde, and I'll believe that *you* are magic."

17

"Do you know anything about who might have taken her?" I asked. I had my Tarot cards at the ready, but it was always a good idea to get answers from real live people when you could. As if a conversation in the crypt wasn't a good indication of what I was walking into.

Mrs. Ambrose shook her head. "If you mean specific families, names, and locations, ultimately, I could provide you those, but they would be rather useless. The list is regrettably long. Prior to our relocation to the United States, my family had developed a reputation—among only the politest of circles, mind you—for psychic gifts. Specifically, the gift of making money."

My brows arched. "Through a sound investment strategy or literal alchemy?"

It was a testament to Mrs. Ambrose's personal presence that the question was not a rhetorical one. The woman practically reeked of old wealth, its aroma wafting even higher than the smell of moldy stone.

"A bit of both, I think it would be safe to say. Among

other holdings, we had a sizable stake in an experimental mining operation. That mine did its job pulling precious stones and metals out of the earth, but we sought a more specific treasure."

She held out her hand imperiously to Mr. Gray, snapping her fingers when he didn't respond quickly enough. With a sour expression, he fished in a pocket of his long overcoat, then pulled out a small gallon-sized plastic bag. In it were the shards of what I could only assume was the glass canister that had held Maria's blood.

Mrs. Ambrose took it and gestured me forward, while Mr. Gray flipped on a flashlight he had produced from the same serviceable overcoat. The canister looked like your garden-variety reliquary. About six inches long, it was crusted with gemstones, though its gold-framed leaded glass was now mostly shattered. Inside was a cushioned bed of dark fabric, now empty of what looked like it had been a three-inch vial.

She angled the canister toward me and tapped one of the gemstones through the plastic, a milky-green stone.

"Jade?" I hazarded.

"A form of it, very rare, very unique. My family owned mines in South Africa, where it was discovered. We coined it Ambrosia, because of course we did, the nectar of the gods. Wear a piece of ambrosia jade and any psychic powers that you possessed would grow more acute. All well and good, until one of my ancestors stumbled on the discovery that if you ground the crystal into a fine powder and consumed it —not too much, mind you, as it is quite poisonous in large doses—but if you consumed the correct portion of it, you would develop not only the psychic powers you previously laid claim to, but a whole litany of others as well. And the coup de grâce? Once Ambrosia was in your body, it was in your bloodline."

I winced as she shook the reliquary at me. "It didn't take long for elixirs of the drug to be mixed with actual blood to give the transfer of power more punch. Pour it into a container studded with Ambrosia, and the powers magnify once again—and then anyone can drink it and be augmented."

"Got it," I said. "I bet you guys are really fun at parties."

"This reliquary is, of course, one of our own," she continued, giving the bag an authoritative twitch. "My family's insignia is etched into the base. We confirmed it had been stolen from our own collection—along with several others—a theft that went completely unnoticed. But now, far worse, whoever took those reliquaries have stolen Maria as well."

Something about this wasn't tracking for me. "But if they have Maria and the reliquaries, they've got everything they need, right? Why taunt you with it? If putting Maria's blood in that thing somehow renders her blood more effective at transferring psychic abilities, why would her kidnapper return any of the canisters to you? I mean, for one thing, that reliquary's gotta be worth some money. Even as distinctive looking as it is, it could be sold—especially on the arcane black market. But they didn't sell it. They gave it back to you. Why?"

"Being rich doesn't preclude you from being foolish," Mrs. Ambrose pointed out.

"No." I shook my head. "There's something more here. As soon as your granddaughter turned sixteen, she was kidnapped at a high school dance. Your older granddaughter presumably passed both of those milestones without being afflicted. Neither granddaughter knew of their supposed psychic abilities, though I have to think Maria suspected."

"She did more than suspect. She announced it to anyone who would listen. She was a continual trial to her older sister, though Elizabeth had no idea how dangerous Maria's game was. Neither of the girls did. Their mother, who is about as psychic as my magnolia tree, didn't see fit to inform me of what was going on until after Maria had been taken. Apparently, attempts to silence the child only made it worse, and the decision was made by her parents to simply laugh it off. I, of course, had no idea about the provisos in my husband's will, which *cannot* be legal." She said this last pointedly to Mr. Gray, who remained predictably stoic.

"Okay," I said, knowing we weren't going to get anywhere further on that topic. "So you don't know who specifically would have done this, but chances are good that it's somebody related to your family, either by blood, not to put too fine a point on it, or social standing. Is there a community of your long-time friends in the area?"

"No," she said, surprising me. "When I married William Manchester and left France, I agreed to settle in Savannah specifically for that purpose. I let it be known that we needed the isolation from our own social network, that William and I would see them on our terms. That's not to say there aren't wealthy and even families vaguely related to me in the area. Some may have had the opportunity or occasion to acquire an Ambrose vial, even steal one, but I doubt quite seriously any of them would use it in this way. This reliquary is worth perhaps a few hundred thousand dollars. Hardly a concern for the top echelon of our social group, but rather an investment for most of our neighbors."

"Gotcha," I said. I handed the bag back to her and she

flicked it toward Mr. Gray, who seemed resigned to his role as pack mule.

"What else aren't you telling me?" I asked, and Mrs. Ambrose's lips thinned.

"A great deal, as you may imagine."

I couldn't help it, I had to laugh. "Fair enough. Then what else haven't you told me that I actually need to know?"

The distinction gave her pause. She considered me more acutely. "I'm not sure I understand your meaning,"

"I do," Mr. Gray put in. He regarded me with a somber gaze that spoke less of approval than resignation.

"There is a deadline in play for this to get resolved to Mrs. Ambrose's satisfaction, not to mention the safety of Miss Maria."

Mrs. Ambrose turned to stare at him, not in horror, merely in resignation. "Mother of God. I knew it."

Mr. Gray pushed on. "William's dismay at the less expected elements of his wife's family's history was regrettably quite profound. Perhaps all the more so because he should have seen the signs. While Ophelia here did her level best to live a circumspect life, she did not outright deny her heritage, and rightly so. Had William not been so swayed by other factors, he would have conducted more research, I have no doubt."

"Other factors," I mused. "He needed money?"

Mrs. Ambrose snorted. "He had money. He wanted the legitimacy of an old European family. He simply got more of a family story than he wanted."

Mr. Gray huffed a quelling breath. "In any event, upon finding himself in the unexpected position of having his line questioned now, at this late date, he made certain decisions that he did not have time to rescind before his recent, unfortunate death."

"Oh for God's sake, speak plainly," Mrs. Ambrose said as I blinked. William had kicked it recently? That was...potentially important.

"What is this deadline?" she demanded. "What are you talking about?"

Mr. Gray offered me a pained smile. "If you are unable to recover Maria within five days' time of her abduction and she is found to be alive and in good health, her captors may extend an offer of marriage into their family in exchange for keeping the Ambrose family's secrets close to home. In that event, the offer must be accepted, and the bulk of William's wealth will flow to Maria and her new husband."

"*What?*" Mrs. Ambrose gasped, nearly speechless for the first time.

I scowled. "How does that make sense? In order to hit the incredibly specific deadline to enact that highly weird codicil, somebody would have to know the terms of the will. Somebody who *wasn't* Mrs. Ambrose."

Mr. Gray's lips thinned. "Somebody almost certainly did know the terms of the will, somebody who was not Mrs. Ambrose, and that someone is now enacting those terms for the dual benefit of accruing a great deal of wealth and prestige to their family, and ensuring that William's untimely death is avenged, if in fact it was improper in any way. Which, of course, it wasn't." He slid a cool glance to Mrs. Ambrose. "Because that would have been foolish to the extreme."

My eyes shot wide as I stared between the two, Mrs. Ambrose's face now gone fully pale, while Mr. Gray studied her with a suspicion only barely visible under layers of civility and experience with working for the eccentric rich.

"I didn't kill him," she finally managed, sounding credibly aghast. "Is that what you think? That I killed him?"

"It is not my place to think," Mr. Gray reminded her, his tone ever so slightly icy. "However, there would be no obvious reason for you to do so. Your children were happy, your life was set, you had managed William's concerns for the entirety of your marriage, and there was no indication that that was going to change, other than Maria's precocious outbursts, which her parents had done a good job shielding William from. So, you could say it was just a poor happenstance of timing that William's heart stopped while he was at the club with his friends and you were with Maria in Atlanta. Certainly, no foul play was ever suggested. But the terms of his will were quite specific. I had hoped quite sincerely that such codicils would never be invoked, because of course, you will appeal them and of course, you will fail, but you'll spend a great deal of money in the process."

"Oh my God," Mrs. Ambrose said faintly. "This cannot be happening."

"Five days, huh?" I put in. "How much of that is left?"

"Less than twenty-four hours," Mr. Gray said grimly. "So in all sincerity, I wish you Godspeed."

"*Milton,*" Mrs. Ambrose pleaded. I glanced back at her, startled by the sudden shakiness of her voice.

Milton apparently shared my alarm.

"Ophelia," he said, turning to her. "Are you all right?"

Ophelia clearly wasn't all right in the slightest, but as she faltered a light step, causing Mr. Gray to step hurriedly toward her, she flicked an imperious hand my way. I got the message loud and clear. She would handle the lawyer and try to work things out that way. I needed to go find her granddaughter and do my part to fix this mess.

I wheeled around, escaping the mausoleum and emerging with profound relief into the sunlight. As I strode back through the cemetery, I reviewed the job. A teenager, desperate to be special and different, discovered that she most definitely *was*. She told anyone and everyone who would listen, and likely put it out on social media to boot, which pretty much meant that the suspect pool now included the entire world. I had twenty-four hours to recover the girl, unmask her kidnapper, and nick one of the reliquaries for Armaeus Bertrand while I was at it. Because there was no doubt in my mind that he was jonesing for an Ambrose special, with or without fresh blood.

I shuddered. The cards had better not fail me.

Sam was waiting for me back at the car.

"You got good stuff?" he asked.

"Oh yeah. I think I need that drink now."

"Well, you're in luck, because Aunt Trulia is ready for us, and before you say anything, this isn't going to be a distraction. I told her a little bit about what was going on, and she says she can help."

I eyed him a little narrowly, surprised that I wasn't surprised. How much had the Magician known about this job before it fully came together, and why did I think this was going to be another test?

Either way, he now not only owed the Ambroses, he owed me. Rich people were crazy. Connected rich people? The worst.

18

Aunt Trulia's house was overrun with people. Small people and large, young and old, healthy and sick. Some in clothes that looked fresh from the dry cleaners, and some that looked fresh off the floor. And all of them appeared to be hungry.

"Well, come on in, the food's not gonna eat itself." A statuesque woman with an expansive smile and forearms that meant business waved in newcomers through the door of a deceptively simple-looking two-story stone building. Boasting eight windows and a door on the front and completely obscured at either side by a thick overgrowth of the Savannah verge, the building made short work of the formal rooms and then expanded backward. It attached to a smaller building and then a larger kitchen, which dumped out into a broad covered patio with built-in stone fireplaces and easily a half dozen picnic tables. Then it petered out into conversational seating of Adirondack chairs around multiple firepits.

"Whoa," I said as we emerged out of the tidy but un-lived-in shadows of the main house and into the bustling backyard.

Sam practically rubbed his hands together in glee. "Nobody does backyard barbecue like the Lowcountry," he said, his accent dipping perilously close to the Deep South. "Now let me just introduce you to Miss Trulia, then you can come get me when you're ready to leave."

He turned as the bright-eyed matriarch from the front door bustled into the space, her voice pitched loud enough to hear in DC. She was tall, red-haired, and sturdily built. Dressed in a soft green linen tunic and dark leggings, she wore gold earrings that peeked out from her swept-up hair. "Now, I don't want any of you to go away hungry, and I don't want to be cleaning up a bunch of leftovers. So eat all you can. Anyone wants to help me clean up, there's more for you to take home."

A convivial cheer rose up at this, and I slanted a look to Sam. The house, for all its size, was modest; the food was anything but. Huge steaming pots of boiled shrimp, clams, and God only knew what else bubbled over at three different locations. Platters of cornbread and savory beans and rice graced nearly every flat surface. There were other options too, something that looked like a room-temperature coleslaw and more grilled hunks of meat that I couldn't quite identify at this distance, which smoked and crackled on farther grills.

Sam just grinned. "It's not much to look at from the front, and she keeps it quiet, but Miss Trulia has always had a knack for getting what she wants. And what she wants more than anything is to feed people. Works out, because most of the people around her want nothing more than to eat her food. It's good for the body and the soul."

"Now, Samuel Haskins, don't you go telling tales I'm going to have to live down."

My attention was drawn back to Miss Trulia, whose appearance had changed in the short time it had taken her to cross the floor to us. Her smile had softened, and her eyes had grown quieter, more contemplative. Even her body seemed smaller, as if the need for bombast and good cheer had passed. I felt the familiar prickle of electricity dance along my skin as she closed in. This woman was Connected with a capital C. And here she was, tucked away in a tiny little square of property in Savannah, Georgia, keeping her light not quite under a barrel, but at least confined to her own backyard.

Her thick russet-gold brows arched in amusement as she studied me, apparently well aware of my assessment.

"You do a fine job of blocking your mind, but your face is another matter, dear. Don't change. It's actually to your advantage for people to assume that you're judging them. It prompts them to play their cards that much more quickly. You've got me wanting to trip over myself explaining my every little decision that brought me here, and of course, none of that is necessary."

She turned to Sam. "Now you go on and eat something, Samuel. I swear my sister does not feed you anywhere near as well as she should."

He grinned. "I gotta fit into the cars I drive, Aunt Trulia. I can't eat too much, or I'll slow them down."

Her lips thinned with disapproval as he wheeled off, heading for the nearest grill. "There will come a moment when that unstoppable force meets an immovable object, and he will be forced to reconsider his life choices. That'll be a dark day."

I blinked at her, shocked. "You think he's going to crash? Shouldn't you warn him?"

She scoffed. "Now, what good would that do? He knows every time he gets behind the wheel he could crash, whether he's racing around a little bitty track or heading to the country store. No point second-guessing when it's going to happen."

Still... "But you know when it's going to happen? Like specifically?"

She eyed me with amusement. "It's not so much a knowing of the actual fact as knowing elements that have to come into play to make that outcome an absolute. I know some things about you too, child—and you are a child too. Don't you start bristling at me."

I barely stuffed down the need to assert my own questionable hold on adulthood, but I wasn't a child. I hadn't been a child for a very long time.

Miss Trulia merely nodded. "Oh, I know, I know. You only have to look around to see souls who've had a raft of pain to endure, and you're not alone in that. We can't choose our parents, though yours are stranger than most."

I opened my mouth to protest as irritation sparked, then shut it. *Stranger,* she'd said. I suppose that was as apt a description as any for my mother, the only parent I'd ever known. She'd tried her best, but trouble had a way of following her. One day, it had caught up when she wasn't looking, and everything had changed for me.

But I wasn't the lost soul who needed finding today. "You know why I'm here?"

"I knew the Ambroses' trouble was circling close. That old battle-ax of a grandmother did the best she could to keep her brood safe. But sometimes there's no help for it."

"Maria Ambrose is Connected?"

"They all are in their way, but she's opened herself up to it, taking the natural tendencies of the bloodline and willing it to be more. It's hard to resist a mind that won't stop pushing."

She slid her gaze to me. "She's done, for now. They won't take more blood from her for a while."

"What?" I blinked at her. "What the hell is wrong with you people? How are the police not involved in this already? How is it you're not talking to Mrs. Ambrose, and where the hell is Maria?"

"All good questions, though they're sort of naïve, but you can be excused. You're not from around here. Yes, yes, I know you grew up in Memphis. That's what Aunt Adelaide said anyway, and she's quite good."

"Aunt Adelaide?" I asked a little faintly. I was never going to remember all these names.

"Great-aunt, actually. She's back inside. She likes knowing all the people are close, but not too close, if you know what I mean."

I did, and I followed Trulia back into the house, bracing myself for a woman who had to be as old as the four horsemen of the apocalypse.

I wasn't wrong. A small, wizened female, her head crowned by a puff of white hair, peered our way from a mound of crocheted blankets as we entered a room stuffed with antiques and hushed grace. Threadbare elegance was evident in every corner, whispering from the furniture and the ornate picture frames. But Adelaide eyed me with an intensity that belied her ancient appearance.

"You're the one who's supposed to save us?" the old woman croaked, clearly disgusted, her comment taking me off guard.

"No, ma'am, I am not," I assured her with absolute

certainty. "But if I can help recover Maria before all her blood drains out of her, I'd like to try."

She snorted. "All about the money for you, hey? You won't get money out of old Ambrose, though. It's the only thing that battle-ax loves more than her grandbabies or even her own self. Now that she's offed poor William, she'd mortgage her soul to that sad sack of a lawyer if she thought it would keep her comfortable."

I was getting the impression that living in the South would suck. "Do you people know everything about each other down here? Or is all that purely psychic premonition?"

The woman uttered a harsh cackle, making her dentures clack. "You can't survive in the South without being somewhat Connected, child. It's just the way it is. But Ophelia Ambrose and her family came to our town when I was a young woman looking for work and able to hide my own true nature far better than she was. I worked in that great house for going on ten years before I decided I knew enough to make my own magic, settle down here, and start a family."

My brows lifted. "This is yours? This house and all that's in it?"

"It's Trulia's now, and she's kind enough to take care of me in my old age. But I can answer the questions that are still burning on your face."

I frowned. I really needed to get a better face around these people.

"Our family used our Connected abilities to coerce, manipulate, and make a tidy fortune, all without anyone paying much attention. We didn't apologize for that, and still don't. Trulia here is a godsend for those who don't have what we do. In turn, we keep quiet and don't draw attention to ourselves, and it all goes merrily along."

A strange movement rippled beneath the blankets, exactly as if she were waving off my next question, only her hand couldn't escape its crocheted prison.

"The mess the Ambrose family is in has been building for years. Ophelia could have sought help. She didn't. I waited, and she didn't come. And it's not the obligation of the Connected to save fools, even of their own kind."

"You're wrong," I blurted. "There aren't enough Connecteds in this world to have an everybody-for-themselves kind of attitude. There are those who need to be saved, their magic protected."

Adelaide shrugged, a ripple of pink and purple squares, her bright eyes narrowing a little beneath their delicate white brows. "Maybe yes, maybe no, but I guess you'll find out. I don't mean to be rude, but Maria does need rescuing, I'm here to tell you. You might want to get a move on."

"And you're not doing anything?"

"Of course I'm doing something. I'm talking to you now, aren't I? Now you'll find her, in the way only you can, and you may be in time, but honey, you may not. That's not the sum total of this game, though. The dark forces in play with young Maria are something you need to see to understand. You think you've seen the worst of the worst, running around the world and making your money by finding things that need to be found. But the darkness of the Connected community is a real thing. It runs deep in each of us, bound up with the brightness that is our power. You'll need to leave the boy behind, by the way. If he sticks with you, he's dead, and his mama...well, that would break her."

"What?" I blinked. "You mean Sam?"

She huffed. "Oh, he'll be fine once you pass this spot of

trouble you're about to get into. I just think you both should sit out that particular crash."

"Um, *yeah*," I agreed, a little shook despite myself. Something about this old woman had me believing everything she said, and I wanted to edge out of the room carefully. "What else do I need to know?"

"You need to know that not everybody thinks the same way you do," Adelaide informed me. "And you need to think about why, exactly, you've caught the attention of the most powerful psychics in the world."

I rolled my eyes. "I mean, is there anything I need to know about Maria?"

She snorted. "Sweet girl, but not terribly bright, I'm afraid. You can save her once, but not twice, okay? She's got to do the second bit on her own. Remember that."

"But I do save her, right?" I pressed.

Adelaide bumped her hand out again, punching unsuccessfully through the blanket. "Well, she's surely not going to save herself. Eat something before you go. It'll help."

19

I found Sam engaged in a boisterous game of cornhole, his jacket casually flung to the side to take advantage of the burst of February sunshine. I boosted the keys to the Magician's souped-up limo without anybody noticing and was behind the wheel with the engine running in less than five minutes. Before I swung out on the street again, I pulled the cards from my pocket, selecting three in quick succession and tossing them on the seat beside me. I might play life a little dangerously, but it was never a good idea to read and drive.

Sometimes I had a sense for what the cards would report, and in this case, I expected the trail to lead back to Maria's school. She'd been taken after a dance, she'd apparently been vocal about her burgeoning Connected capabilities, and she was by all accounts rich, pretty, and flighty. The girl was going to have friends.

The cards had other ideas. The first one up was Death, the second Judgment. I snorted, not being a stupid rabbit. "Back to the cemetery, huh?"

The third card made things even clearer. The King of

Pentacles. Not Ophelia Ambrose's fake mausoleum, but the final resting ground of William Manchester's family, who'd produced a wealthy son who still felt the need to borrow someone else's name to feel legitimate. William Manchester had paid handsomely for his pride, it would seem, but it looked like he'd set his own game in motion at the end, complicated though it might be.

I pondered that truth, trying to smooth its odd edges without success. Why would a good, God-fearing WASP disavow his own children and grandchildren for something they couldn't help? It was like cutting them out of the will because their hair was blond instead of brown. What was the point?

Unfortunately, Google wasn't forthcoming on where the Manchesters' final resting place lay. I tooled around the cemetery for several minutes as a soft, brief rain shower drifted down, barely speckling the windshield, and waited for an inspiration that never came.

"This is stupid, and the clock's ticking," I muttered aloud. "Just tell me already."

The voice that emerged from the dashboard was immediate. "Continue driving on this lane until it splits, Miss Wilde, then take the right fork and drive for approximately two more minutes at your current speed. The Manchester mausoleum is a rather subdued affair, but still quite prominent."

I eyed the dash. "Have you been listening in this whole time?"

"I regained access to you only after you returned to the vehicle." A beat. "And only then because you allowed it. Again, all this is...highly irregular."

I grinned, happy to have the upper hand in our relationship, if only in this small way. "Yeah? And have you figured out why I'm so special?"

The Magician's response was a soft chuckle. "I suspect it will take some time to discern that, Miss Wilde. But what is clear is that you have a rare psychic strength, which, frankly, should not exist on this plane. And a remarkably small footprint from a genealogical standpoint."

I frowned down at my phone. "You looked me up online?" I deadpanned, but I wasn't truly surprised. If some backward fortune teller from the Deep South had something to say about my mom, chances were good the Magician had dug up the old newspaper articles as well. "I'm not in the mood for any smart comments. My mom did the best she could."

"She did quite a bit more than that," the Magician offered, irritating me anew.

"You got anything else that's actually helpful? You could have mentioned the deadline."

"I needed you to complete this task within twenty-four hours regardless," the Magician reminded me. "Sooner would be better. And to answer your question, this might be useful. William Manchester instructed his will not to be read for three months after his demise, unless in the event of a family crisis. Which they are now in."

I frowned, once again taken aback by the complexity of the scheme. "Seriously? That seems a little specific. Almost prophetic."

"Indeed. In this case, I understand that William presented the distinction as a formality, yet I agree it is somewhat coincidental."

"It's more than that," I insisted as I pulled up to the mausoleum, yet another creepy box of moldy stone. "Did you check out that lawyer of his? He looks like he's three months dead himself. If William was worried about something, I don't know that he'd trust old Milton."

"It would be a simple thing to ascertain the presence of a second will, if anyone still living knows of its existence," Armaeus said thoughtfully. "Fortunately, the minds of most humans are not closed to me."

I shot my dashboard an amused glance, not missing his use of the word "human." Who was this guy, really, if he didn't count himself among the people of earth? Or was he simply that arrogant? At this point, my money was on arrogant, but that didn't make me feel much better. Crazy was crazy, no matter how attractive the packaging.

"Why don't you go focus on that, and I'll see what I can find out around the comfy crypt? By the way, I don't suppose you've had any luck tracking down Maria?"

The Magician uttered what might have been a scoffing laugh. "Despite my interest here, embroiling myself in the affairs of individual Connecteds is not in my job description."

"Yeah, well, when it comes to individual Connecteds getting hurt simply because of how they're made, it's part of mine."

"So I am beginning to understand. I look forward to your next report, Miss Wilde."

I grabbed my phone and stowed it in my jacket pocket, making sure it was turned off. I didn't think the Magician could infect my technology the way he did his own vehicle, but I preferred to control what I could.

I also idly plucked a few cards from the deck as I shoved the main pile back into my pocket, noting that a fourth fluttered to the ground. First, I scanned my haul: Six of Swords, Six of Cups, Six of Pents. That gave me pause.

The cards had many ways of sharing their information.

For me, especially when I was on a hunt, it was the imagery that mattered most. In this case, the Six of Swords likely indicated a body of water, maybe a stream, maybe a culvert, maybe a lake or a pond somewhere on the property. When dealing with a kidnap victim, none of those options were great, but something to keep in mind. The Six of Cups was more interesting. The theme of that card was childhood and could often indicate a school or kindergarten or someplace where children gathered. Not really a lot of options in a cemetery. My immediate thought was a section of infant graves, but I deeply, deeply hoped that would not be in the offing.

Then there was the Six of Pentacles. A man distributing his wealth to the poor, while additional coins rained down on his head. The card of the philanthropist, the benevolent provider, or simply someone who was about to get hella rich. It also could indicate a loan coming due. But the cards in this case weren't content with that layout, I didn't think, because they'd served me up three sixes. Setting aside the obvious demonic ramifications, which I didn't think were in play here, sixes implied balance, health, and harmony. They also were an attaboy from the deck saying that I was closer than I thought I was to a goal.

While I appreciated the vote of confidence, none of those really resonated quite yet. Out of sheer perverseness, I drew another card and was rewarded with four of a kind, another six, this one the Lovers from the Major Arcana deck. I didn't even consider the Hollywood depiction of the card. Lovers was rarely about sex, more about a choice after trial. At least with four sixes instead of three, the question of demons faded into the background. So, that was a bonus? Hard to tell at this point.

I leaned down to pick up the card that had fallen to the

ground and muttered a curse. The Devil. I could wax eloquent about the interesting juxtaposition of the figures in the Lovers card compared to the figures in the Devil card, but I was mostly annoyed that demons seemed to be back on the table. Either that or crazy sexy love times were taking place somewhere close by, which didn't quite feel right.

This area of the cemetery was hopping with people in light rain jackets roaming around the gravestones, staring at the moldering statues. I took this as a good thing. Probably not a lot of demons hanging around.

I shoved my hands in my pockets and moseyed up to the mausoleum, just another tourist taking in the sights, and was unsurprised to find it locked up tight with a suspiciously new, bright, and shiny lock. I wasn't sure how long ago William had kicked it, but when it came to interring your loved ones inside a concrete box, there generally weren't a lot of moving parts. Most mausoleums I'd seen were lined with shelves the depth of which indicated whether the dead would be buried intact or in ash form.

I suspected William had been cremated. Not because it was what all good Presbyterians did, far from it, but if this was a man who was worried about the magical makings of his in-laws, he wouldn't want to leave anything around for them to mess with.

Come to think of it, maybe he wouldn't want to leave anything at all.

I squinted hard at the mausoleum, then shifted my gaze past it, my gut tightening at what I saw. Beyond several more markers, there was an ornately fenced-off plot with miniature statues popping up like gnomes at a picnic.

I sometimes hated it when the cards were right.

I changed my trajectory from the mausoleum and made

my way back through the musty stones and the surprisingly well-kept plots.

When I reached the children's graveyard, I realized I wasn't alone. An older woman in a light rain slicker and boots stood with her arms crossed, her eyes trained on two children poking among the gravestones with little pails. She glanced up, alarmed and embarrassed as I approached.

"Honestly, they don't mean any harm," she said hurriedly. "They're just fascinated by this little graveyard, and I didn't want to stigmatize the passing of children, not in today's world. I hope you don't mind."

"I don't mind at all. What are they looking for?"

"Magical river stones," she said with a chuckle. "There's an old story about this cemetery, that the stones in it can serve as coins in the netherworld. There's a creek just beyond—an offshoot of the main river—that the kids drop the stones in and wait to see what happens. So far, we've had no magical boats or Swan Princesses show up, but hope springs eternal."

I smiled, though my mind was already racing. "Um...is this a local story? I'm not from around here."

"Oh, that I don't know. It's just one of those things that bubbles up around cemeteries I guess, and to be fair, it would be hard to find a cemetery prettier than this one. Is one of your relatives buried here? They say all the plots were purchased by the Manchesters—the ones who own that mausoleum right as you come up. Did you see that one?"

"I did."

"Well, they donated all that land to the cemetery between their mausoleum and the river, but insisted it be used for children. It's considered some of the holiest ground in the cemetery, thrice blessed to ensure that anyone who rests here goes straight to heaven. I think that's a sweet story as well."

"It's a great story," I agreed, scanning the small cemetery again. This time, it wasn't difficult to find the signs of freshly turned earth, no matter how artfully it had been designed and covered over to replicate three small graves with appropriately weathered headstones. Had William Manchester decided he couldn't take any chances? If so, unless I missed my guess, it looked like he was buried in the thrice-blessed children's cemetery, safe from anything that might go bump in the night.

"Mommy, it's happening again!" One of the children, a little girl, stood at the edge of the child cemetery looking away from us, flapping her hands excitedly. "She's singing. She's singing!"

20

The woman beside me groaned softly.

"I think maybe we need to take a break from the cemetery," she muttered. "The last few days, Anna's been convinced she could hear another child singing. I haven't wanted to make a big deal out of it, but it's starting to creep me out, I'm not going to lie."

In silent accord, we began strolling casually toward the little girl, but I wasn't picking up any sound other than the excited chatter of Anna's brother dragging his small bucket of angel coins to the stream that I could now see winding its way along the edge of the cemetery. The stream flowed down a gentle embankment and looked more like a culvert, more rocks than water unless there'd been a good rain. I watched the water babble over the rocks as we reached the little girl, who looked up with shining eyes to her mother, then handed me a smooth river stone.

"Can you hear it?" she asked, and I tensed. I couldn't hear it, and what was more, I wasn't picking up that this child was particularly Connected. Whatever she was hearing, it could have been made up, or it could have been a test for her mother. Children were strange creatures with their own mystical ways. Being a parent was not for sissies.

"I can't hear it, honey," her mother said, surprising me. "But that doesn't mean you can't hear it. Is it a happy song?"

"No. Um, yes. Um, I don't know," the little girl said, appearing to give the matter careful thought. "It started out as happy, then it got sad, and now it just seems, like, happy mad."

I kept my face carefully blank, waiting for whatever the mom might say to this. I didn't speak fluent child, but she clearly did. Either way, I immediately snapped back to something Father Jerome had said. Maria liked to sing, to sing and dance.

But if she was singing, how come only a little girl could hear her?

"Happy mad is sometimes even better than happy," the young mother assured the child, earning her a smile from her daughter. "It means you're not gonna give up no matter what, because you feel safe or at least strong. Maybe we could come up with our own happy-mad song."

"Maybe," the little girl said, then she frowned, squinting back toward the cemetery. "She stopped. I think she's done singing for today. She probably needs a nap."

"Oh, naps are the *best*," the mother said, though from the look on the face of the little girl, I could tell she didn't necessarily agree.

Nodding at me, the mom took the little girl's hand and jollied her along toward her brother, who remained dutifully pitching stones into the creek bed. The plop-plop-plop of his offerings didn't appear to stir up any wrathful nymph, so I figured we were safe from the supernatural another day. I watched them go at it for a few seconds, drifting forward, then stopped at the soft, plaintive cry that seemed to bubble up from the ground. I looked down, unnerved despite myself, then squatted. I could hear the sound more plainly now.

Brushing aside the thick layer of leaves and pine needles, I could see a metal grate embedded in the ground and hinged at one side. Sitting back on my heels, I noted that we were at the very edge of the cemetery plots, and no gravestones rested nearby. Chances were good the root system of the tree that overlooked this section of the cemetery didn't allow for the easy placement of graves. So why was this grate here? Why would somebody put a root cellar here on the banks of an old cemetery up against a creek that flowed out to the main waterways of Savannah?

My vote was a smuggling hideaway. Maybe a smuggling hideaway known only to an old, respected Presbyterian family who had purchased the land all the way from the river to their mausoleum...then donated it to the cemetery for children's graves.

I waited for the young family to leave. After that, it took me only a few minutes to clear the grate entirely, aided in no small part by the fact that I hadn't been the first person to open it recently. Someone had been coming in and out of this hole in the ground on the regular. As recently as in the past few days? I wasn't sure, but it was looking likely.

No more sound emerged from the hole as I pulled up the creaking grate, and I peered inside. If there were guards, they didn't seem to be overly concerned with my impending approach. More concerning, this seemed legitimately like a hole and not something you could climb down. Considering the issue, I shoved my hands back in my jacket pocket and worked another card free. I spared a glance back toward the creek, grateful to see that the young family hadn't returned. Nobody else was back this far in the cemetery. It was just me and the dead kids and whatever lay in the bottom of this pit.

I glanced down at the card that I'd pulled out of my pocket and shoved it back, grimacing. The Three of Swords. Not one of the most pleasant cards in the deck, it depicted a heart pierced by three different blades. It was the card of necessary cutting, of grief, and of bloodletting. A little too on the nose, frankly, but readers couldn't be choosers.

Leaning forward, I dropped the stone the child had given me into the pit, gratified to hear it clatter almost immediately. It wasn't a far drop. More concerning was that no sound accompanied the rock falling. Either the angry-happy singer had passed out, or she was being held quiet.

Time to find out. I sat at the edge of the hole, braced myself on the metal barrier, and grabbed the lid of the grate, pulling it over me as I dangled in the open air. If the bad guys were watching, I was already screwed.

The lid of the grate clattered into place as I dropped.

No more than nine feet later, I collapsed easily to the ground, bracing myself with my hands in a move I'd perfected during way too many similar drops in the past few years. There was no shortage of pit drops in my repertoire as an artifact hunter, but at least in this case, it wasn't onto a pile of bones. I pulled out my burner phone and switched on the flashlight app, waving it around. Again, I hadn't been quiet about my entry into this space. I didn't think I was going to be startling anyone into sudden awareness.

I was right, but totally not for the reason I expected to be.

The place was insanely dry and clean for what I had expected to be little more than a grubby hole in the ground. The walls had been reinforced with mortared stone, the floor was concrete, and a sizeable drain had been cut into the ground—I hoped merely to redirect rainwater. I wasn't sure exactly what this Manchester cave had been used for over the years, but right now, the room was set up like an arcane laboratory, with a long bench covered in tools, vials, and sophisticated bloodletting equipment, including hoses, syringes, and tourniquet materials. Stacked in a jumbled pile were easily a half dozen glittering reliquaries, each of them as long as my hand, and two of them filled.

All that would have been creepy enough if it weren't for the two teenagers having flailing sex in the bed beyond it, totally oblivious to my arrival. I'm not sure if the sex had been songworthy, but I didn't want to think about that too much.

"Freaking cards," I muttered, remembering the Lovers I'd drawn topside. They'd tried to warn me, but seriously, I could get a pass for this. That said, enough was enough.

"Yo!" I shouted as loud as possible, and predictable chaos ensued. Squeals of surprise, indignation, the flurry of sheets and clothes being drawn up. The charging of the young guy, bursting out of the shadows with a knife.

"Zach!" a girl screamed as I batted the boy back and added a shove that sent him sprawling into the arms of the young woman, who could only be Maria. I was grateful for the thick material of my leather jacket, which took another injury that had been intended for my forearm.

"Oh, give me a break," I groused as the boy attempted a second surge forward. "You come at me again and I *will* beat the crap out of you. I don't have time for this."

I waved my phone light at the very disheveled girl—definitely the same young woman from Father Jerome's picture, complete with spray tan. "You want to explain what's going on here?"

Maria opened her mouth, apparently eager to tell

someone—anyone—about her newest adventure, but the boy stepped in front of her.

"No," he blurted. "Who are you? You're not supposed to be here."

"You okay, Maria?" I asked levelly, speaking over the guy. I thought about invoking the grandmother's name, but thought I'd shoot closer to home. "Your mom is worried about you."

"She is?" Maria asked, her voice wavering, but once again, her boyfriend bristled.

"Who are you?" he demanded again, his arms going around Maria to cradle her close. Protective, possessive, or both? Too early to tell.

"I've been hired by the family." As I spoke, I moseyed over to the operating table and flipped on a few gooseneck lamps. The lights played across the reliquaries, which, like far too many arcane artifacts, were both tantalizing and vaguely unnerving. "I don't think they know about you, Zach, but they're about to."

I could practically hear his chin go up. "I'm not afraid of them."

"That's a relief." I turned back to the hapless young couple as my hand drifted into my pocket again. There was no way I was to get the full story from these knuckleheads, and now that Maria was clearly still among the living, I needed to wrap up this little drama as quickly as possible. I pulled out a card and quirked a smile.

Justice. Well, *that* was interesting. Sometimes, Justice meant balance, getting what you deserved, the epitome of fairness and righteousness.

And sometimes, it meant lawyer.

I leaned against the table. "So tell me, Zach, when did your Uncle Milton tell you all about how you had to save

Maria? Recently, or have the two of you been working it out for a while?"

"Shut *up*," Zach growled as Maria clung to him. "He's not my uncle. He's my godfather."

"Uh-huh." I waved my phone. "So do you want to call him, or should I?"

There was a long, heavy pause. "That won't be necessary, Ms. Wilde."

Mr. Gray stepped out of the shadows.

Unfortunately, Mr. Gray was holding a gun.

21

Maria yelped in alarm, but Mr. Gray never wavered. "I confess you have me at somewhat of a disadvantage, Ms. Wilde," he said coldly.

I snorted at both his unintentional echo of the Magician and the patent falsehood of the allegation. "Based on visual evidence, I'm inclined to disagree."

My attempt at humor netted me only the thinnest of smiles. This guy needed a joy enema in the worst way.

"When it became clear to me what Ophelia had planned for William, I felt I had to act. William had always cared for his wife, rescuing her from an awkward situation in her youth and giving her the support and seclusion that she required. Yes, of course, he benefited from this arrangement in his business endeavors, but no more than was his due. Mrs. Ambrose was not always the easiest of personalities."

"Fair enough," I said. "So what did he do to piss her off?"

"Oh, that's very much as she indicated," the lawyer allowed. "He truly did not approve of the psychic dilettantism of his wife and had rather enjoyed the idea that his bloodline had been strong enough to eradicate its negative effects. In the meantime, over the past thirty years, he had contributed quite handsomely to the family's wealth and no longer felt quite so beholden to his wife. That said, he did love his children and his grandchildren, with the love of a patriarch who wishes to see them have an easy path through society."

"Well, that's super gracious of him."

Milton's lips thinned. "Regrettably, once Mrs. Ambrose discerned Maria's psychic abilities, she came to her own conclusions about how events should proceed. She decided to use Maria's blood for her own gain. That is why they had it in storage, you should know. They have had quite a lot of it drawn, over the past year in particular. Apparently, Ophelia had long suspected Maria's gifts. William discovered the stash about six months ago. He gradually began moving the reliquaries to his safety deposit box—but there were still too many left for Ophelia to use."

"Grandma?" Maria asked, her voice sounding a little wobbly. I winced. She was a little young to have her trust broken, but...had to be done.

Nevertheless, something about the lawyer still grated. "So, William came to you with his concerns."

"He did. And when he abruptly passed, well...I knew that was no heart attack. I made some discreet inquiries and learned that she had been speaking with some rather unsavory parties about potential artifacts for sale."

"Let me guess. Did one of those parties owe a debt to David Galanis?" It was a shot in the gloom, but Milton's jerk of surprise provided satisfactory confirmation. No wonder the Magician was on board with this side trip to Savannah. Galanis knew about the reliquaries, and about the augmenting powers of the blood they contained. And we were going to bring one right to his door.

"Naturally, I felt it appropriate to bring these rumors to William's attention, confidentially, of course," Milton said. "We've been lifelong friends."

All this storytelling would have been suspect if I'd been the only one in the room. Despite what I'd been taught by Scooby-Doo cartoons and old James Bond movies, most villains didn't share their well-laid plans out of a sense of misplaced hubris. A quick glance at the rapt faces of Maria and Zach bore out my suspicions.

Milton was still selling them on the lies he needed them to believe. These poor kids were underage, and they were surrounded by assholes. I could blow up Milton, but then Maria would suffer at the hands of her grandmother. I could blow up the grandmother, but then Milton would have these kids' futures on a string that he could tug whenever he wanted.

And then there was the question of the grandfather. Buried in a thrice-blessed children's cemetery.

Something about that poked at me, but I didn't have time to suss it out.

"So where do we go from here?" I asked. "Because, not to put too fine a point on it, I was hired for a very specific job, to find the girl before she died, and I did that."

"I would never have let her die!" Zach announced with all the impassioned fervor of an eighteen-year-old.

"No, right, you were just willing to bleed her out in a freaking hole in the ground where she could have gotten infected with God knows what and ended up in the hospital. That would have been a way better outcome of your little plan," I said pointedly, pointing out the pointy things on the table. "I'm not sensing a hell of a lot of advanced planning here, is all I'm saying."

Once again, something about that struck me as wrong, but hey—not my circus, not my monkeys.

"Okay. We can play this any way you want," I said to the lawyer. "If you've done your research on me, you know I can keep a secret, and I know you have the trust of Zach and Maria. I'll happily keep your secret too, so long as I get paid."

"Secret?" Maria asked for the first time sounding a little more focused. Glad to have you back with the program, Maria.

"That's all very good and well," Mr. Gray said, satisfaction adding some warmth to his words. "The terms of the will still hold. Zachary and Maria have mixed blood according to the ancient rites, and Mrs. Ambrose is bound by the strictures of her arcane belief."

I peered at him. "Let me get this straight. You knew about the peculiarities of William's wife and her family from way back, but both you and William thought that was all blood under the bridge. Then William comes to you, worried that the curse is back. He starts fretting about the sanctity of his bloodline. He begins ferreting away reliquaries—out of sight, out of use by the arcane black market. Why didn't he destroy them?"

"They're priceless," the lawyer blurted, and I grimaced. Money may not have been the root of all evil, but it sure was the root of all stupid.

"Right. So he sets aside the reliquaries to sell at a future arcane yard sale and changes his will to cut out the grand-kids if this Ambrose curse can't be smothered. Meanwhile, you suggest adding the codicil to protect Maria, what, out of the goodness of your heart? Something like that?"

Milton didn't shift his glance to the teenagers huddled in

the corner, but the tightening of his jaw told me I struck a nerve. Dickhead.

Had William realized the trap he'd neatly set himself while he was updating his will under the careful supervision of his counsel? Had he figured out he was worth more dead than alive at this point?

"You have found Maria, and you will be paid," the lawyer reminded me, but I held up a hand.

"I'm not finished yet. When did you tell Maria about her blood properties?"

"He didn't." Maria spoke up, stepping away from Zach in a show of spunk that warmed me to my toes. She'd need a hell of a lot more of that if she was going to survive being a golden goose. "My grandmother did, last year. She told me the story about our family, about what we used to do and how much money we'd made. She drew my blood for testing months ago, but warned me not to talk about it. But how couldn't I?" She smiled, and the wattage of her expression could have fueled the lights in this room for a couple of weeks. She was Connected capital C, no question. "I'm special. I can *help* people."

"You're special even if you don't help people," I corrected her, then swung my gaze back to the lawyer. I didn't know for sure whether Ophelia had taken out William or if the lawyer had. But dead was dead.

"This is how this is going to go," I informed him. "I've worked with a lot of Mrs. Ambroses in my time, and she's not getting the better end of this deal. You are. So *you're* going to pay me, right now, with money wired into my account. If you don't, all this unravels. How about that?"

The kids were watching us with wide-eyed surprise, and Milton was no fool. He could kill me easily enough, and we both knew it. Unfortunately, that would threaten his hold on the kids. Murder tended to do that. He nodded, slid the gun into a holster beneath his suit jacket, pulled out a phone, and made a call.

He slanted a glance at me. "It will take some time."

"No, it won't. You know it and I know it. Besides, I've got an account number with its own mobile app."

The fact that the lawyer conceded so quickly tipped me off to just how much Maria's blood was probably worth on the open market. I hated everything about this, but to show more of my hand would be to risk the girl too soon. Milton wasn't about to kill his golden goose, and neither was Mrs. Ambrose. I had time—I might even force the Magician to get involved. Screw owing the Ambroses, he owed *me*.

Or at least, he was about to.

While Milton chatted on the phone to his minions, I eased back toward the table. The reliquaries looked every bit as expensive as the one Mrs. Ambrose had been wielding, some new, some old. Once again, this part niggled at me, and I quickly pocketed the smallest of the jeweled canisters, filled with gleaming blood. With all the drama, I knew Milton wouldn't ask how many new reliquaries had been filled, not right away, and Maria and Zach were making out again.

My phone chirped a few minutes later, and I read the screen. Milton had even given me a tip. Whoever said doing business in the South was difficult?

It didn't take long to dismantle any incriminating pieces of the makeshift phlebotomy lab and depart the underground lair with Romeo and Juliet. By now, Milton was paying more attention, and he supervised the collection of vials and reliquaries with murmured assurances that everything would be okay now. I grimaced, eyeing both him and the hand-holding teens, trying to figure out what was still bothering me about all this.

We emerged from a door cut into a low arched bridge that spanned the stream. The perfect smuggling hole for the Manchesters of old, transformed into a tidy modern hideaway. Once all this blood business was done, they could put it up on Airbnb.

"Zachary?" Milton asked, and his godson hastened up to his side as I hung back with Maria.

"How are you doing?" I asked, lightly touching the girl's arm. She had started shaking the moment that Zachary had stepped away from her.

"My grandmother really did have my grandfather killed," she said dully. "She told me she was going to do it when we were at lunch in Atlanta, and then she actually had it done that *day*. I didn't believe her at first, but after I heard about Grandpa's heart attack...I knew that if that was true, then the rest of what she said last year had to be true too. That my blood was rare and powerful."

I slanted her a glance. "She told you how your family used that blood?"

"Yeah," she sighed. "I was actually okay with most of that until Grandma gave me all those little glass vials. They were pretty, but..."

My whole world slowed down. "Um, you got that stack of reliquaries from your grandmother?" I asked carefully. *Ophelia, you conniving bag of suck.*

"Some of them, yes. And then Zach's godfather found more—and Zach and I, well...we saw the possibilities." Maria smiled, her light jumping from within her, plain for anyone with eyes to see. "We knew we could sell them without Grandma ever knowing—and really help people.

His godfather did too. He said he would help me—and help Zach and me get free of all this."

I grimaced. "I'm sure he did."

She fluttered a small, delicate hand. "I didn't like getting my blood drawn, though," she confessed. "And I don't know what we'll do now."

"Well, for starters, you should smash all those canisters to bits," I informed her, resolutely ignoring the vial I'd scored for my own client. That blood was already out of the bag, as it were. It wasn't going to do Maria any good anymore.

She gave a stunted little giggle. "When I told Zach about my blood properties, I was scared, but he told me it was gonna be okay. We weren't really that close before then. We ran in the same groups, but he hadn't really paid that much attention to me."

"Wait, you and Zach weren't close before?" Another piece of this screwed-up puzzle slipped into place. I glanced ahead to where Zack and Milton were hunched together, my eyes narrowing a little bit. "You guys looked pretty chummy back there."

She laughed, sounding like a young girl for the first time. "He's super cute," she acknowledged. "And he really does seem to love me. No one ever loved me like that before."

"No one?" I asked it as a question because I wasn't sure, but Maria's smile said a lot.

"Oh, well, I mean Grandpa did—but differently, you know. Like a grandpa. I tried to warn him about Grandma, but he wouldn't believe me. He said that Grandma liked to scare people with her tall tales and hocus pocus, as he called it, but she was a good woman. I even told him about my blood." She bit her lip.

"Yeah?" By the time Maria would have screwed up her nerve to do that, William had to have already known about the truth. Known about it and changed his will to screw over his own kids and grandkids. "How'd that go?"

"He...he hugged me," she confessed. "He looked like he might cry. He thanked me for coming to him and said he loved me no matter what, and that no matter what, he would keep me safe. And if I ever doubted that, I just needed to dig a little deeper." She glanced away. "He looked so tired after that day. I remember that now. I should have done more to stop Grandma. Something. Anything."

"He said to dig a little deeper?" I grimaced, another connection firing in my brain. "Those were his exact words?"

"They were," Maria said. "They stuck with me because he made me repeat them back."

I thought about the children's cemetery, and I thought about William and all his rigid ways. Working with Connecteds wasn't always easy, especially when they were in your own family. Especially when you didn't *want* them in your own family. But in the end, family was family, and children needed to be taken care of.

I pulled out my phone and checked the text stream again, sent another couple of texts, and waited for the chime. Then I pocketed the phone. By then, we'd made it back to where Milton had parked behind my own limo. I gestured for Maria to follow him. There was no reason for me to play a part in their pageant any longer, at least not in person.

"You'll come to the wedding?" Maria asked me, glancing a little shyly to where Zach stood waiting for her. "Will I ever see you again?"

"I probably won't be at the wedding, and I suspect you

won't see me again, sweetheart. Because if you do, things probably aren't going too well for you," I said, as kindly as I could. "But I'll do my best to make sure things *do* go well for you okay? How about that?"

"Okay." She sighed happily and turned away toward her future.

I waited until they left, then I pulled out my phone again. Sam picked up on the first ring.

"You ready to roll?" he asked. "Mr. Bertrand contacted me, but he wants me to take you to the airport next, not all the way to New York. Says it's too dangerous to do that now."

"Mr. Bertrand worries about the wrong things," I said, scanning the children's plots behind me, but for once, I didn't mind the Magician's heavy-handedness. I didn't want Mrs. Ambrose to start counting reliquaries anytime soon, and I didn't think she'd be too happy with me after this day was through. "But yeah, I'm ready to roll. I'll come get you."

Over the course of my drive back to Aunt Trulia's house, I eventually rejected my initial theory of William Manchester's body taking up space in the children's cemetery. A separate burial site was far too obvious, complicated...and not very restful. William had undoubtedly been cremated and tucked into his own family's mausoleum under its newly updated lock and key. But I more than a little suspected that a very recently executed will and testament, dutifully signed and witnessed by someone *other* than his bestie Milton, was buried beneath that freshly turned dirt. At some point, William must have realized that he couldn't beat the various agents around him looking to take advantage of him and his granddaughter, but he'd decided he could outwit them.

And maybe—just maybe—he had.

I didn't know what to think about Maria and Zach or

how their fledgling relationship would survive the crap-storm that was to come, but that was their problem to figure out. As for Maria, she'd be safe. I'd clue Father Jerome in to her unique condition, and of course, the Magician was now fully aware, even if he didn't like to involve himself in the messy details. If Ophelia or anyone else tried to turn Maria into a pincushion against her will, I'd be back.

Sam was waiting when I pulled up, his grin broad as I turned the limo over to him and gamely returned to the back seat. "You found her?" he asked brightly.

"I found her," I said. "And more trouble than I expected along the way." I gave him the shortened version of the story as he drove. His brows climbed his forehead, and his mouth dropped open.

"And you let them all get *away* with it?" he finally asked, aghast. "They're all just going to walk?"

I smirked at him. "For now, that's the safest course for young Maria. Unless, you know, we can find another will left by Maria's grandfather, giving him the chance to get in the last word. I don't suppose you happen to know any good gravediggers around here, do you?"

"Ha! Darlin', this is the South," Sam assured me, his grin turning as sly as mine. "We are uniquely skilled at digging up dirt."

22

As Sam headed out of the city, he transacted a half dozen phone calls, then entertained me with updates on his cousins, his cousins' cousins, and stories of the small, covert army that planned to descend on the children's cemetery that night. Eventually, he angled the car into a private hangar, where a small, sleek jet awaited me —apparently, Armaeus's updated transportation of choice. We pulled to a smooth stop and sat there for a second, admiring the view. No one greeted us. No TSA lines, no pat downs, no problem. Okay, I could get used to this.

I couldn't help but smile as Sam popped out of the driver's seat and opened my door, beaming at me as I stepped out with my backpack. It was a foregone conclusion that he'd be keeping the Magician's car, which made me like Armaeus Bertrand more than I should. I suspected that was quite possibly my new client's intention.

"Are you going back to Florida tonight?" I asked Sam.

"Are you kidding? I'm not missing tonight for anything." He shook his head. "An entirely new will. I hope old Mr. Manchester takes them all down."

"I think he might." I nodded, shouldering my pack. Now that the excitement had passed, fatigue was dropping over me like an anvil. These last few days had been a lot of a lot... and another job waited in New York. "As long as Maria's safe —and the rest of her blood stays inside her body. That's really the game."

"Definitely," Sam agreed, then he finger gunned me. "Aunt Trulia was right about you—you care even when you act like you don't. You let me know if you're ever back in Miami, and you've got a ride set."

I grinned at him. "I will."

A subdued flight attendant greeted me as I boarded the sleek little jet. Murmuring something soothing and vaguely airline-security-ish, she showed me to a seat that was so comfortable, I began nodding off almost as soon as I sank into it. I stayed awake just long enough for us to lift off the ground, then curled into the overstuffed captain's chair masquerading as airline seating, and passed out.

What felt like thirty seconds later, I jerked awake out of a deep and disorienting fugue—just in time to be advised of our impending arrival in New York. I pulled myself upright, an unusual anxiety ripping through me, and spent the next few minutes accessing every bank account I had encrypted across multiple platforms, some of which were even legal.

In every case, the numbers matched what I expected. Not as high as they needed to be, but enough to cover the regular and frequent deductions I funneled to Father Jerome. Eventually, I'd need to work out a 401K plan, but it was kind of difficult to think about securing my own future when kids were getting picked up on the side of the road and killed for their eyeballs.

Even after assuring myself that no one had drained my accounts, I couldn't tamp down the dread. I shot another text to Father Jerome to check on Michel's status as we landed and to fill him in on Maria and what might be happening next with her. His response was immediate and reassuring, though he nagged me to return to Paris. I tapped back another question regarding his safety and let the other issue alone...opting to table my questions on the Arcana Council for the moment too. No matter how many times I told him that I could do far more for the kids by accumulating money and sending it to him, Father Jerome never seemed convinced. I knew he worried about me, but he shouldn't. I'd been through the fire a few times already. I knew what I was doing.

There was no immediate reply coming from the priest, so I poked through my emails—but there was nothing there. As the Magician had indicated, my clients weren't upset at my delay in finding their next most-coveted baubles. They had their hands full with issues that could in no way be traced back to me or to one heavy-handed Connected billionaire. None of them wanted to cancel my contracts, but neither did they have any interest in seeing me for least another week.

Fair enough. I set my phone aside, letting myself sit with my low-key panic.

Why was I resisting the idea of working with Armaeus Bertrand so much? He was everything I wanted in a client. Rich, generous, and also rich. I could find nothing about him beyond surface information on the arcane web, and even that was carefully curated. He was reclusive, he owned a ton of property across the world, and he bought commodities from the arcane web. Bought them, never sold them.

I didn't know how he made his money or if he literally conjured it out of thin air, but he'd latched on to me as his newest finder and seemed to take a particular interest in putting me through my paces. Why did it bother me so much? Still unable to rejoin the real world, I pulled the deck of cards out of my pocket, shuffling them idly.

As I passed the cards through my hands, I could feel the energy spool off them, but that was nothing new. What was new was the renewed spurt of apprehension that riddled me as I considered my question and its portents.

What did the universe want me to know about the Magician? Who was this man to me, and why did he trigger equal parts anxiety and excitement in me? It went beyond the feeling of getting onto a roller-coaster ride. It was more that the roller coaster might leap off the tracks and go soaring over the broad ocean at any moment, with no indication of where or whether it would touch back down. I had encountered some pretty high-end psychics in my time hunting artifacts, but something about this guy just seemed off.

Before I could talk myself out of it, I pulled three cards in quick succession, laying them upright on my seat tray.

The first was the Magician, which I appreciated. Always good to know that the cards were paying attention. The second was the Ten of Swords, and the third was the Two of Cups.

I blew out a long breath. The Ten of Swords, of course, was betrayal, destruction, and a forced ending, usually with a sharp, pointy thing sticking in your back. I was already up to my eyeballs in betrayal today, so it was touch and go as to whether that card was about the Magician or my most recent job. However, the Two of Cups indicated a contract, a love match, and a bonding of two like souls. The cards of the ten and two could not be more opposite, so of course, they showed up next to each other in my reading.

"You guys are pretty funny," I informed the cards, then

darted my hand into the deck for a final card, like a seagull snatching a fish out of the ocean. I flipped it over.

Justice.

"Okay..." I muttered, but I couldn't deny that I felt better. The Justice card of the Major Arcana could mean many things. Still, when it wasn't guiding me to an official building or pointing the finger at a dastardly lawyer, it generally meant balance and validation. That which was given would be paid back, and to spare. I would be treated fairly. Best of all, no matter what happened, I could handle it.

All those thoughts flooded through me at the sight of this card, and I tapped a finger against it with bemusement. No matter what the Magician dished out, I could take it. No matter what I brought to his table, *he* could take it. All this still didn't make me feel all that great about the Ten of Swords, and relationships were not really my skill set, as my experience with Will Donovan bore out.

I scanned the line of overturned cards and pulled another one, because I never could leave well enough alone. I smiled. The Ten of Pentacles—the Tarot card for money, money, money. Well, okay, then. There was no doubt that a whole pile of money lay behind the Magician's door. I might get the crap beaten out of me along the way to securing that money, but I would end up well paid. That alone made everything worth it.

I bit my lip, my nerves jangling as we banked toward New York. All of this *would* be worth it, right? I'd be okay in the end?

The cards had spoken, but the cards didn't always tell me everything I wanted to know up front. They were super handy that way.

We landed a few minutes later, shuttling onto a private

landing strip just outside JFK. A car was waiting for me on the tarmac and I kept my mouth shut and my eyes sharp until I was dropped at my destination—an upscale boutique hotel just north of Midtown. No sooner had I walked in the front door than I was greeted by a slim, blonde concierge who whisked me through the lobby and up the elevator, assuring me that my every need would be met while I stayed in the hotel. I managed to keep my weirdly escalating anxiety tamped down until she finally left me, and tossed my pack on the enormous bed of the suite Armaeus had booked me into. There were two bedrooms, both with ensuite bathrooms, but I didn't want to think too much about the ramifications of my way-too-spacious accommodations.

Because right now, more than anything, I needed a shower.

Old-world or not, the hotel boasted some seriously impressive plumbing fixtures, and after throwing my clothes on the floor, I surrendered to the pounding streams. Jets shot out at me from all directions, and I sagged against the tiled wall, whimpering in gratitude as my muscles were pounded into jelly, a faint aroma of jasmine in the air. My mind started drifting, so I wasn't all that surprised when the voice murmured in my ear, sounding slightly strangled.

"Why are you allowing me access to your mind now?"

I smiled.

"One, I'm relaxed enough not to keep up my shields," I informed the voice in my head. "But two, if you chose this hotel because of the showers, I wanted to let you know I appreciate you."

The Magician barely skipped a beat. *"There are breaks in your bones that have never been professionally tended, Miss*

Wilde. Torn muscles, dislocated joints. What did you do to your toe?"

I sighed, my eyes still closed. "You've got a future at the carnival with a skill like that." But I didn't mind the inspection, honestly. The Magician could see me. Truly see me, not just my figure and features, but literally the poorly fused bones and shattered cartilage that were going to haunt me one day down the line.

He was also waiting for an answer. It was an answer I didn't mind giving.

"I don't go to hospitals. And I generally work alone. That makes setting bones kind of tricky."

"You've healed yourself?"

"I mean, not really. I just haven't been hurt all that badly."

"What happened to your right femur?"

I frowned. "Is that the lower or upper leg?"

"Upper," the Magician informed me drily. I shrugged against the cool tile, tracking the injury back in time. "I jumped. There were ropes that should have broken my fall, something I could tangle my hands in. That was in Tanzania. Really awesome mines down there. The ropes broke, and I crashed into the side of the cliff. It wasn't a smooth cliff."

I groaned a little as a new spigot of water somehow opened up in the wall beside me, this one pounding between my shoulder blades. The water had turned scented, the smell of exotic spices rising up around me.

"That particular landing hurt a lot," I murmured. "But this is nice."

"Do you trust me, Miss Wilde?"

I snorted. "I do not. You're going to stab me in the back, not once but several times. That's going to hurt a lot too."

The scent of jasmine lessened somewhat, but didn't fully go away.

"How do you know this?" came the question, this time more carefully asked. I shrugged again, unconcerned. I suspected the Magician was nearby, even though a quick glance over my shoulder confirmed that he wasn't standing behind me in the shower. He wouldn't assault me without my permission, not sexually. He posed a threat to me, but not a sexual one. Still, I was willing to see how this played out.

"Do you trust my motivation?" the Magician tried again.

That answer was easier.

"I do." I leaned more heavily against the wall, savoring the fall of water. "You want to know more about me."

"And will you let me learn?"

I could have said no. I should've probably said no.

I didn't. "What's in it for me?"

"This, to start. With your permission."

The pressure against my right leg was soft and cool at first, not cold enough to make me jump, but I still gasped as waves of deep healing flooded through me. The break that Armaeus had referenced was three years old, and I'd remembered at the time thinking I might not be able to walk again, but I'd still managed to drag myself out of that Tanzanian hellhole with my tanzanite wands intact. Now it was as if each crumpled bone shard lifted away from each other, then fit seamlessly back together in the space of a breath. My leg shimmered with a sense of rightness that it simply had not had in longer than I could remember.

"Oh..." was all I could manage, and then the pressure moved up my waist to my rib cage.

It was the Magician's turn to breathe out a long, somewhat tortured sigh. *"What have you done to yourself, Miss Wilde?"*

"Nothing that can't be undone," I murmured, but in truth, I wasn't paying too much attention to the Magician's words. My mind was delirious with the pleasure his hands were giving me, once again not sexual, or not entirely sexual, though there was no denying the charge that flowed from his fingertips as his hands pressed against my waist, then slid up toward my breasts.

Before he reached them, his fingers paused, tracing the long gashes in my side.

"Gunshots?" he offered.

"Mmmm." The ripping pain of those memories didn't even bother resurfacing in my mind. Everything was lost in the haze of cool redemption. "That's why I wear jackets now. Hoodies catch a lot of bullets."

The Magician's laugh was soft and warm, and a moment later, a new pressure nuzzled against my ear.

"You do not seem concerned that I am in your room and in your shower. You should be."

"Yeah, well. That's not how you're going to destroy me," I murmured.

I always did know how to ruin a moment.

23

The energy of the Magician didn't just ease off, it completely disappeared. Without the counterbalance of his weight, I staggered a little in the shower, feeling incredibly alone as my hands went out and connected with the reassuring sides of the shower stall. I braced myself, grateful that the water at least remained hot, and my mental barriers slammed down out of self-preservation.

I hadn't asked for the Magician's insidious and alluring touch, but I hadn't protected myself against it or rejected it either. Not even in the end. He'd withdrawn from me as swiftly and completely as he'd come. The crazy thing was, though, I couldn't remember exactly what I'd said to piss him off. It hadn't seemed that dramatic, and now, in the face of his abrupt departure, I knew it had to have been. And yet —the memory was gone.

I narrowed my eyes beneath the spray of water. I hadn't been *that* befuddled by his sensual massage.

"What did you do?" I asked aloud. There was no reply.

Had the Magician wiped my memories somehow? In my

open and receptive state, had he manipulated me mentally the same way he'd been manipulating me in a very clear and physical way? I mean, there was no disputing that my ribs felt hella better, and I suspected an X-ray of my leg would display a near-miraculous healing. The Magician had skills. He'd made me forget my pain, but could he make me forget my words too?

When no clear memory was forthcoming, I gritted my teeth, annoyance washing through me, followed by outrage at the unfairness of being duped, and then outrage at myself for expecting my employer to treat me fairly.

What the hell was wrong with me? The multimillionaires of the arcane black market were little more than marks to me. They couldn't be anything more, not when I was trading them priceless objects potentially imbued with psychic properties for stacks of cash. Because some of those artifacts were little more than well-crafted hunks of gold, while others were so powerful, I couldn't hold them without feeling my cells dance around in shock. I handed the booty over with equal speed in both scenarios. It wasn't my place to judge; it was my place to take these people's money and run on to the next job. I was useful to my employers for one reason. It was not to my benefit to complicate that equation.

The Magician was no different. I needed to remember that.

I finished my shower and was unsurprised to find packages of clothing fresh from the dry cleaners and laundromat waiting for me on my bed. My own clothes had been whisked away, or they possibly could have walked off on their own. That thought made me smile as I pulled on the fresh underwear and barely there bra, then turned to the designer jeans and silky pullover. The perfect clothes for lounging on a cold February day in New York City. But the dress hanging on the back of the door suggested that my time in the city would not be spent entirely at my ease.

I snuck glances at the garment as I pulled on the other clothes and even gave the material an experimental tug as I passed by the door. The dress shifted and rustled, and my fingers prickled. Something was up with this dress. Something not necessarily normal.

The actual flesh-and-blood Magician was waiting for me in front of the fireplace as I exited the bedchamber and stepped into the main sitting area of the suite. I hadn't really seen him in the shower, which was probably a good thing. He'd been impressive that morning—had it *really* only been that morning?—striding into the Waffle House in his expensively tailored suit and gleaming shoes. But here, in what was probably a five-thousand-dollar-a-night room, he seemed far more imposing. Worse, he looked like he belonged. His latest suit was a rich midnight black, with just a faint indigo overtone. His shirt was an electric blue and open at the collar, exposing a shallow vee of burnished skin. His hair, nearly as dark as his suit, was brushed back from his forehead and fell to his collar, thick and luxurious. His gaze was assessing, golden eyes raking over my own simple attire with satisfaction.

He'd chosen these clothes for me, and that pleased him. Mentally, I catalogued this as a potential leverage point, but my heart still wasn't in it. Armaeus Bertrand had made me forget my own words. If he could make me forget that, what else was he capable of? I steered away from the question like it was a group of thugs on the sidewalk, praying it didn't follow me to the other side of the street.

"You must be hungry," the Magician said, and honestly, nothing could have distracted me more. I followed his gesture to a table tucked into an alcove I was sure was supposed to approximate a kitchen, though nobody ever cooked for themselves in a place like this.

Then the aromas of his offering hit me. Barbecue and cornbread, beans and rice. My mouth watered as I approached.

"Sam informed me that you didn't eat much at his aunt's. She wasn't offended, she knew you were preoccupied, but she still thought you should eat."

"She was right," I moaned as I filled a plate, not missing the fact that my hands were shaking. I didn't try to miss meals, not on purpose. I wasn't trying to fit into designer anything. I was just busy.

The loud growl of my stomach echoed in the room.

"Are you going to join me?" I asked, fully expecting him to say no. At this point, my money was riding hard that the Magician was some sort of vampire, though I was pretty sure those didn't exist, not even in the screwed-up world of the Connecteds I was quickly cataloguing.

To my surprise, however, he nodded and moved forward, elegantly assembling a plate of food and gesturing me to the table. I took a chair, eyeing him as he sat opposite me, the intimate assembly of two people having dinner vaguely triggering for me. This was an illusion, which I needed to remember. Even if it was actually happening, it was still an illusion. I couldn't trust any of this.

"What's the job you've got lined up for me, specifically?" I asked, my words a little harsher than I intended. I didn't miss the soft arch of the Magician's brows. "And what's up with that dress in there?"

That last bit made him smile. "I wondered if you would notice before you put it on."

"Yeah, well, it practically had a conversation with me.

Was the material infused with Connected properties from the get-go, or did you do something to it?"

"You asked two questions. The dress is by far of secondary importance, but I'll address it first. The garment is made of a silk first cultivated in ancient Egypt, used to make the ceremonial gowns of a sect of priestesses. It provides the wearer with bodily protection and augments their psychic abilities to whatever degree they are willing to endure. It also has pockets."

"So it really is magical." I chewed on the rest of what he said as I swallowed my next bite of Miss Trulia's Southern culinary masterpiece. "Egyptian. Relatives of yours?"

The question was a stab in the dark. I wasn't the best at figuring out bloodlines, but one thing I had noticed about the hyperrich of the arcane black market was that they tended to put a high stock on their heritage. In addition to their breathtaking ability to be assholes in other ways, racial supremacy was a thing, though it didn't so much matter what race it was.

"My mother was Egyptian, my father French," he said.

I didn't miss the fact that he spoke of them in the past. Had only his mother died, or both of them? The Magician looked to be about in his late thirties, maybe early forties, the titular prime of a man's life—though his eyes seemed like those of a far older man, assessing and amused, as if he'd seen everything in the world at least twice. And let's face it, the guy was loaded. He probably spent a lot of time at the spa.

But back to the silkworm at hand. "And what exactly do you expect to happen when I put that thing on? Will it improve my ability to find stuff? Is that what the game is here? Because you could just as easily have given me a pair of snappy silk tights and a turtleneck and that probably would have been a little more useful."

Again with the smile. The Magician leaned forward, passed me another plate of food, and picked up a tablet I hadn't noticed was lying there, mainly because I was fixated on the plates of food. He propped it up and, with little more than a gesture, fired it to life.

A man's image filled the screen. His face was foxlike, with bright, small eyes, prominent nose, and pointy chin, under a thick but close-cropped thatch of silver hair. The image zoomed out, and I saw the picture had been taken at some sort of gallery showing, with artifacts under glass, and what looked to be museum donors all standing around, holding cocktails and chatting. As I watched, the image moved, a video now playing that showed the man walking around, mingling with a range of well-dressed guests.

"What is this feed?" I asked. I hadn't seen this video in any of the recon I'd done on the flight between Rio and Miami, and I'd scoured every version of the web I could get my hands on. "Because that's Galanis, but I can't place the museum."

"It's the private collection of a New York donor, one with deep ties to the antiquities community. Galanis was invited to give credibility to the showing. With him in attendance, all the high-end antiquities buyers made sure they were there to see and be seen."

"Well, that sounds fancy," I mumbled around my food, snagging a piece of cornbread for good measure. Mr. Bertrand's fancy dress had better come with a built-in girdle or I was going to be in trouble. There was no way I was letting this food go to waste a second time.

"What do you notice most about him?" the Magician asked, sounding like a professor quizzing his slow student. I slanted him a look, annoyed, but his gaze was fixed on the image. Maybe he just was that curious.

"People don't like him," I offered. "They respect him, and they don't fear him, exactly, but they don't like him. He makes them nervous."

The Magician chuckled, a warm rolling laugh that set off a wash of awareness deep in my body. I froze, my heart stutter stepping as he continued, apparently oblivious to my physical reaction to him.

"A fair assessment, I would agree. He is very well respected, even admired. But he's also set the antiquities community on edge—particularly those collectors who favor arcane artifacts. His role in ensuring the provenance of the artifacts held in the Met's public collections—as well as, it is rumored, the private collections of many of the art world's most prominent donors—makes collectors of all types desperate to curry his favor. Mr. Galanis has no official dominion over them, yet he terrorizes them all the same."

"And the Connected collectors, they let this guy come along to their arcane artifact swap parties?"

"Not directly, no. But as is the case with most criminals, they have worked very close with the official and respectable channels of the profession. In other words, those who hold the most secret treasures have also donated to fill the coffers and the galleries of museums throughout New York."

"Interesting," I allowed, eyeing the well-dressed partygo-ers. At least the gown in the other room made more sense now. "You think they're currying his favor? Why?"

"Protection. If Galanis anonymously tips off the right agency that a private collection contains artifacts that were originally sourced illegally—the collectors are forced to give them up. No one can say for sure he was the source of the intel...but everyone suspects. Bear in mind, these properties were in all cases stolen. Often through the auspices of someone with your unique skills."

I smirked. "Well, that is a bite, isn't it. I hate it when I steal something that gets restolen."

"Yes. My interest in Mr. Galanis is more direct. He is looking for artifacts of greater and greater power, I believe for a specific benefactor. I want to know who the benefactor is. Furthermore, I believe Galanis is using these arcane artifacts to augment his own Connected abilities, perhaps in service to that benefactor. If so, he's amassing an exceptional amount of power without the discernment or control to manage it. I can't allow that to happen."

Now it was my turn for my brows to lift. "Why not?"

He smiled, a world of misdirection in the expression. "Let's just say it goes against the interests of my organization."

24

Before I could choke my way past the spoonful of barbecue I'd just inhaled to ask my questions—of which I had many—Armaeus cocked his head like a dog who'd just caught a particularly interesting scent.

"There still remains the second artifact we need to secure. We can do so now."

"Oh, really." I studied him skeptically. "You know, this isn't usually how I work. Most of the items I recover require research. Preparation. At least a Wiki article or two."

He smiled. "Your imagination is ever to your credit, I'm coming to learn, Miss Wilde. I assure you the task at hand is far less exciting. There is a home nearby that is rumored to have an unusual effect on some of its visitors, particularly those with Connected abilities."

I quirked a glance at him. "You mean it's haunted."

The Magician dismissed that with a disdainful flick of his fingers. It was a move he excelled at. "Haunted is not a term I would have expected from you. There are several more nuanced options."

"Yeah, well, there's also no need for nuance most of the

time. Haunted is haunted. I don't care if it's the spirit of some dead man's grandma or an idle shade taking up residence for an extended weekend, ghosts are a pain in the ass. They're usually grumpy energy balled up around... Wait a minute." I peered at him. "Is there an artifact in this house that you want? Something with enough mojo that it's flipping out the residents? What is this, some kind of Ripley's Believe It or Not situation? Because that could be fun."

"Not exactly. The Morris-Jumel Mansion is one of the oldest mansions in New York City still standing. It is now a museum, currently closed to the public for renovation, which makes it an opportune time for us to make our acquisition and depart. The museum does not generate money from its supernatural occurrences and in fact considers them nuisances. Something to entertain the children, little more."

"Hmm. Most kids I know don't find ghosts all that entertaining. Children tend to be a lot more sensitive to that kind of crap. If kids are routinely freaking out in this place, you've got something going on for sure."

"As you say." He nodded at me. "I have arranged for a private tour of the building. Quite private, in fact. If you're ready?"

Private turned out to be self-guided, but it wasn't as if we were skulking up to the back door. Armaeus's fancy limousine, a new vehicle driven by a quiet young man who didn't engage with us, brought us around the drive to the museum and parked a short distance away in the fading afternoon light. Armaeus turned and offered a solicitous hand to me, the gesture so unexpected that I narrowed my eyes at him and stood my ground.

"There's going to be cameras around this place. You can't just walk inside without somebody seeing you."

"Arguably true," he conceded, but reached out and tucked my arm into his despite my hesitation. He turned, and we strolled up the steps, my senses prickling the closer we got to the house.

"You say there's an artifact inside here? Because there's certainly something setting off my alarm bells."

"The most famous proprietress of this home was Eliza Jumel, but she was not the first woman of note to live here. That was the wife of Roger Morris, who was himself a respected colonel of the British Army. There are some rumors that Mary Morris had an affair with George Washington, but those rumors were never proven. When Eliza arrived with her husband and stepdaughter some thirty-five years later, she brought her lavish lifestyle with her. Eliza made several rash decisions of her own, some more successful than others. After her first husband's death, she was married for a short time to the notoriously unlucky vice president of the time, Aaron Burr."

"Oh! You've seen the musical?" I asked, earning me a withering glance from the Magician. "Well, you've got to do something when you're not counting your money or stirring your cauldron, or whatever it is you do when you're home. Where is home, again?"

"A place I've grown quite fond of," the Magician said mildly. "I look forward to receiving you there so that you might see it for yourself."

I snorted at his suave evasion. "I'll make a note."

"As you say."

By now, we had reached the front door of the Morris-Jumel Mansion. Armaeus leaned forward, opening it as if he owned the place. Never mind the very obvious electrical lock that flashed all to green as his hand neared the door handle.

He gestured me inside, his voice sounding only slightly strained. "The electronics are rather a bit more sophisticated than necessary, wouldn't you say?"

I understood more fully what he meant a second later. We stepped past the doorway and the door swung shut behind us, but that wasn't the end of the protections the museum afforded. Small rays of red light crisscrossed the floor, barely discernible to the eye in the shrouded gloom. The mansion looked like a Georgian dollhouse, with richly papered walls, gilded finishes, and a sweeping grand staircase off the front door. It was impressive and oppressive at once, and not just because it was shut up for renovations. "Was it always this creepy?"

"I only had the occasion to visit one other time. I was not making my home in the US at that point, but Paris. I had business in the city and even then, New York was a magnetic pole for all things arcane. I had heard rumors of this house and its strange effect on women and decided to see for myself. At the time, I determined there was no reason to alter the course of history that was unfolding here. But now I have a greater interest in, shall we say, making sure no loose magical accoutrements are lying about for idle hands."

"And what is this accoutrement, specifically? Did you see it the first time you were here?" I looked around, but didn't move. I had a hard time believing Armaeus had taken a five-dollar tour to see this place, but I could see him coming here for a party, one of those private gigs that were no doubt similar to the event where we'd meet Galanis.

"It is a relic of the One True Cross."

I jerked my gaze back to him. "The *what*? And you didn't think this was something you should pick up? That sounds like kind of an important trinket to leave lying around."

"As it happened, I was not accompanied by anyone with

your unique skills at the time, and the relic proved elusive to my hand in this house. While located here, it would only allow transfer to a woman. Once I departed that night, I could not track it down again. I know that Galanis is interested in the artifact and has made discreet inquiries. But he has also been unsuccessful. I suspect he will be very eager to receive it from you later this evening."

I cocked him a glance. "Assuming I find it."

"I have every expectation you will," he assured me. "Especially since I've arranged for Galanis to learn that you are in the city and have already obtained the item, along with the reliquary."

"You...never mind." Setting aside the Magician's almost breathless levels of arrogance for the moment, I considered the challenge at hand. I had dealt with enough goofy artifacts not to discount what Armaeus had said. Though Jesus was obviously a dude, there were any number of ways that feminine energy could have been applied to the relic. And I didn't even bother with asking if the thing was real. Most of them weren't...but that didn't mean they didn't have power. "So you've got the colonel's wife, who was rumored to draw George Washington's attention. Did he ever come back?"

"He did, and the mansion served as his headquarters for a time. However, the British eventually retook the building."

"Interesting. So that didn't work out too well for him, though he did okay in the end. And then you've got this Eliza chick who married Aaron Burr after he'd fallen from grace?"

"Married, then divorced," Armaeus put in. "Their union was both brief and unhappy."

"That guy couldn't buy a break." I waved at the shooting beams. "So what's this all about?"

"I can assure you, it is not part of the standard security.

As a woman, I suspect you will be able to pass without issue, but I will not. However, I can join you on the other side."

I squinted at him. "What, you think I'll deactivate the security system with my feminine wiles? Seriously?" I glanced to either side of the opulent room. There didn't seem to be any blowholes through which poison darts could fly, but I was definitely getting an Indiana Jones vibe.

"I think in this particular location, nothing is quite as it seems," Armaeus said. "I am advised only that riches untold will be granted to the right hand."

"Well, I like the sound of that." I peered at the red lights, then lifted my boot-clad foot and nudged into the first ray. The wolf trap didn't spring, but I could feel the energy ticking up.

"Hang on a minute…" I shoved my hand into my pocket and pulled out three cards, flipping them over to scan. They didn't make me feel any better. The Tower with its falling people, the Seven of Swords with its furtive, sword-stealing thief, and then my old friend the Ten of Swords, back for a limited-time engagement. "That's a whole lot of sharp pointy things," I muttered, showing Armaeus the cards.

To my surprise, he hesitated. "That's not the first time you've drawn the Ten of Swords."

"Not by a long shot. You're going to betray me, and it's probably gonna hurt."

"Here?" he asked, sounding genuinely intrigued. "I assure you it is the last thing I intend."

"Yeah, well, we can't always get what we want." I tucked the cards back into my pocket. "But I also can't keep standing here. Nobody wins if I do that."

I thought about the Seven of Swords. Strategy, swift action, surprise. I considered the target artifact as well.

"Okay, so we're here to sweeten the pot for Galanis. Why isn't the reliquary enough?"

"Because when it comes to people like David Galanis, more is always better. And, in truth, I do want this particular artifact out of general circulation."

"And then you'll destroy it?"

Armaeus looked at me with genuine surprise. "Not at all. The purpose of the Arcana Council is to ensure the balance of magic, not its eradication. Only mortals follow that path. Any magic that is considered too extreme for mortals to maintain simply needs to be removed from their access until such time that it can be released again."

Arcana Council. He'd dropped that name before. "Uh-huh. So you're gonna go all *Ghostbusters* on me, drop the relic into a trap, and hope that nobody ever crosses the streams?"

"I assure you our storage capabilities are better than that. When magic is removed from common access, it would take the extraordinary act of a Council member to return it. An act I will not be performing."

"Kind of dog in the manger of you, isn't it? If you can't have it, no one can?"

He offered me a thin smile. "When you have seen as much as I have, you will understand."

"Mmm. Doubtful."

Still, I was as curious as the next person to find this relic, if it was somewhere in the house. I stepped out into the foyer, barreling right through one, two, then three narrow beams of light, pivoting back to grin at Armaeus. The old floor creaked with the warm resonance of wood that had lasted for centuries.

Just before it collapsed.

25

The fall was abrupt and jarring, but the scenery didn't change, exactly. It just got...brighter. And louder. Music clashing, people laughing, and everything stank of perfume, meat, and sweat.

"What in the ever-loving—"

"Miss Wilde."

I whirled around, which took some doing as my body was no longer fully my own. It had been encased in a gown that bit into my waist with a grip like a vise, then flared out like a bell.

But that was nothing compared to the man who now stood beside me in a stunningly beautiful colonial costume. I hadn't known Armaeus Bertrand long enough to have any real sense of where he fit in the world, beyond being wealthy, well groomed, and decidedly attractive. But seeing him in a long coat, short pants, and honest-to-God knee-high stockings flat out took my breath away. His hair was swept back and fastened into a short ponytail, and his white shirt with its fluffy cravat contrasted dramatically against his golden skin. The long, heavily embroidered coat he wore over the shirt was a deep midnight blue, and he wore it like he'd been born to a gilded age.

Before I could speak, he reached out and lifted my hand, the simple touch of his skin shocking me perhaps more than anything else.

"I can *feel* that," I said sharply. "I mean, we fell...and now we're here. And there's no broken ceiling above me, so I'm not sure where we fell from. I'm just saying, if this is some kind of VR mind screw, it's a really, *really* good one."

"I remain continually impressed by your colorful observations," the Magician commented, once more tucking my hand into his arm and turning me back around so that we faced the room. I wasn't sure whether he did it to ground me or to keep me from running. Either way, it was effective.

The hallway had been transformed into a bustling center of activity. Well-dressed cosplayers from colonial times were laughing and talking as musicians played a variety of stringed instruments in a distant room. It sounded like some kind of bouncy, cheerful reel that seemed tailor-made to a pre-Revolutionary War cocktail party.

"What the hell is this?" I hissed.

The Magician tightened his hold on my hand.

"It is safe to say that it is something we were meant to see. Or, perhaps better stated, that you were meant to see. The home is reacting to your not inconsiderable energy. Surely you've had experiences like this before?"

"Surely I have not," I corrected him. And I hadn't. Granted, when I came into contact with certain artifacts of evident power, I reacted, like with the frog amulet, which had added a decided pep to my step as I'd raced through the city after briefly touching it. And, sure, I suppose Fernanda had wanted me as part of her postcarnival orgy because she'd known that I still carried some of the amulet's energy.

But there was no artifact in this house that had the kind of energy that the frog amulet had. I would have noticed that. And the mansion itself hadn't struck me as being quite this much a bouncy house of crazy. So what was going on here?

"Do not be alarmed, but I feel like we should move," the Magician said, putting action to words as he stepped forward, dragging me along.

"Why?" I asked warily. "What do you know about this place?"

"The Morris-Jumel Mansion, at this point simply the Morris house, enjoys expansive views of the surrounding hills down to the river, which made it a useful headquarters in the war. But that war has not yet come to New York. The city is still holding its breath in anticipation. There is always a unique energy that builds in a place before such a cataclysm. That energy is driving the unsettled atmosphere of this home. The fact that we were taken back to this time is evidence enough of that."

I stopped cold, forcing Armaeus to stop too. "Hold up there, sparky," I hissed at him. "You're actually serious. Which means this isn't VR, is it? This is real."

His winged brows tented, the effect only magnified by his swept-back hair. He stared down at me with an amused smile, his golden eyes glittering with pleasure. He was enjoying this—straight-up, full-on enjoying this. And that scared me most of all. "You mean, as real as me speaking in your mind, helping you dance, helping you heal, and disappearing into thin air?" he murmured. "Sort of like this?"

I barely smothered a squeak as he poofed out of existence, then reappeared not a hairsbreadth later, about six inches farther away from me. It had happened so quickly that I could have almost believed I'd imagined it...but I hadn't imagined it.

"You can poof," I breathed, my eyes now pinned wide, as if he might do it again at any moment. "That was you, back in Rio. Poofing."

"I excel at poofing," he agreed. "But we really must keep moving." He turned and curled my arm into his, and I let him pull me along again. At this point, I was impressed I remained upright, though I didn't think my dress would bend enough to let me faint. I'd just totter like a stuffed doll.

"What is going on here?" I managed, my voice barely a squeak.

"There are two options," Armaeus responded, as if my question was reasonable. "One is that we were pulled back to this time to secure the relic I seek—the other is that we were brought here to see who takes it. The magic I wrought to bring us to this place is complex, but not infallible—and it is reacting to you, Miss Wilde, creating outcomes I cannot yet foresee."

"Forget I asked," I moaned, my head now spinning from far more than the constriction of my dress. We'd stepped through a doorway to a straight-up ballroom, and I stared around, trying to make sense of what I was seeing.

The ballroom of the Morris house was a relatively modest affair, though the space was large and the art on the walls tasteful. We hadn't walked into the Hall of Mirrors or anything, but what the room lacked in furnishings, the whirling and chatting partygoers made up for. Everywhere I looked there was rich fabric, glittering jewels, and powdered wigs. Some of the men wore their hair naturally long and tied back like Armaeus did, but those who could not, particularly the older men, rocked their hairpieces proudly.

Not to be outdone, their wives favored towering piles of curls and ringlets, from the remarkably natural looking to obviously fake but no less impressive. Curious, I lifted my own hand to my hair, my brows lifting as I felt my tresses piled high. There had to be a mirror in this place somewhere. I'd never worn my hair up in my life.

"I assure you, you look quite beautiful," the Magician said offhandedly, ignoring me as I jerked a startled glance at him.

Beautiful was not a word anyone used to describe me. Usually because if I were that close to a person, I was either stealing from them or about to beat them senseless. Something to consider another time.

"We're not drawing attention," the Magician observed with satisfaction as he turned to me. "Until we catch sight of the relic I require, we should dance."

"I don't know how to dance," I blurted, my voice pitched slightly louder, because new sensations were beginning to manifest that I wasn't too happy about. For starters, I was wearing a corset, and it was affecting my ability to breathe. Secondly, the place seriously *stank*. Heavy perfumes notwithstanding, there was a smell of sweat and body funk that was unmistakable, rising up as the dancing grew more energetic. And meat. It smelled like meat being cooked somewhere nearby. The combination of aromas and my own restricted breathing was making me a little dizzy. I clutched Armaeus's arms tightly to steady myself, not happy that he took the opportunity to sweep me around as if we were, you know, *dancing*.

Fortunately, the music shifted once again, allowing me to catch my breath. This tempo was slower, and couples paired off, moving around the room with almost haunting slowness. Another wave of dizziness swept over me, and as I turned with Armaeus, I glanced at the far doors for movement. Nothing.

"Come on..." I muttered. This was taking too long. At

least the stiff-armed awkward sway I had perfected in the eighth grade still stood me in good stead.

I glanced up to see the Magician studying me with a look I was beginning to know well. "Do you treat everyone like they're your personal science fair project, or am I just special?" I groused, trying hard to remember not to bite the hand that was feeding me—but I really was having trouble breathing.

"I assure you, Miss Wilde, you are quite an uncommon experience for me," the Magician returned. "Even now, I cannot read your thoughts, though you are not trying consciously to avoid my touch."

I blinked, but he had a point. Now that I was focusing on it, I could feel the slight, insistent pressure on my mind, yet I had absolute confidence that Armaeus couldn't pry open the Pandora's box of my thoughts without my permission. "How am I managing that?" I asked. "Is it the residual effects of that frog amulet? Because if so, I need to get another one."

"Possibly," the Magician allowed, and with a soft, murmured word, I felt a jab like an ice pick in the back of my skull.

"Ouch!" I snapped, going rigid with the sudden pain. "Stop it, you asshole, that hurts."

The Magician's elegant brows leapt. "I assure you I'm not—"

"*Seriously.*" The next jab nearly pulled me out of my own skin, and it was only because of the Magician's rigid hold on me that we kept dancing as if nothing was happening. A thin trail of sweat snaked down between my shoulder blades, and I raked my gaze over the Magician's face. This wasn't coming from him. Somebody was screwing with me, trying to get into my brain the same way the Magician was, but being a lot ruder about it.

Armaeus swung me around, and I shot a sharper glance across the room, catching the flash of light at the far end. It corresponded with another stab in my brain. I stopped, jerked my gaze back, but saw nothing but a pleasant-faced woman talking with a trio of older men.

"Who's that?" I asked as the Magician turned me in his arms, taking up the role of lookout.

"Unless I miss my guess, that is the proprietress of the house, Mrs. Morris. There is nothing that indicates that she bears exceptional psychic ability—"

"She doesn't have to. She's the cover. The relic is somewhere over near her. Let's go. This brain prick *sucks*."

The moment we strode toward the corner of the room, another flash caught my attention, this one at a side door.

"Are you *seeing* this?" I growled, but the Magician was distracted by someone with a passing tray of glasses, two of which he secured before turning back to me. His eyes were alight with interest.

"Do you have your cards with you?" he asked, even as he made a show of offering me a glass of some light bubbling liquid, presumably champagne. I frowned down at my voluminous skirts, then patted the thick folds of material for good measure. To my surprise, one of the overlaying pleats hid a small pouch dangling from the embroidered waistband of my incarcerating dress, and in that pouch, sure enough...

"Okay, that's kind of cool." Despite my admiration, I didn't waste any time. I drew three cards in quick succession.

King of Pentacles, High Priestess, Knight of Swords.

I glanced back toward Mrs. Morris, still holding court, but she was no longer my target.

"Who's the richest guy here, besides you?" I asked.

The Magician scanned the room with casual hauteur. "Roger Morris," he said. "No relation to the owners of this home. He will go on to be a key financier of the new Republic after the war."

"Yeah, well, he's our competition. Right up there with that guy carrying the fancy sword in his belt."

I pointed across the room, and the Magician flicked his gaze that way, then huffed an amused laugh.

"That guy would be George Washington, Miss Wilde."

26

I managed not to stare after that unexpected comment, but it was a close thing. The man who stood speaking expansively to a couple of buddies and a small woman in a fancy dress was striking, but I wasn't sure he was *future president of the United States* and *hero of the Revolutionary War* striking. How did you prepare for a role like that?

I wasn't particularly up on my colonial history, but just like my DC clients, I'd seen *National Treasure* enough times that I had a healthy suspicion of George Washington's not so deeply hidden occult leanings. Healthy enough that I'd done a little research on my own and turned up all sorts of fascinating conspiracy theories, so I couldn't really blame the DC guys for their obsession.

"I would ask if I wanted to know what you're thinking, given the expression on your face, but the answer to that is, of course, I want to know your thoughts," the Magician said, asking and answering his own question in such rapid succession that I blinked at him.

"You'd be really terrible on a first date, let me just put that out there."

"I assure you, you're wrong." The Magician's response was so unexpected, I shivered a little...or maybe that was because I once more caught sight of the flash of sparking fire deep in the room. The artifact was on the move again.

"Okay, so here's the deal. We've got this Roger Morris guy, who apparently has a ton of money, and George Washington, also a ton of money. And you. I've got no clue who's selling this little relic, but they fancy themselves a priestess of some sort, and whoever they are, they're flashing it around enough that I'm picking up on it. This is a pretty elaborate illusion that they've got going here too, which is important for us to be aware of as well."

"Is it?" The Magician had angled us over toward a thicker knot of people, and I realized for the first time that he did not tower over the assembly, though he should. Armaeus was a tall man, sometimes seeming almost a giant at well over six feet, but here he was more modestly proportioned. Was he doing that on purpose? I kind of suspected so, which both impressed and unnerved me. If he could change his appearance so easily, could I really trust anything I saw when he was around? Could I trust him?

The answers were no and also no, but the man *did* look good in an embroidered velvet coat, I had to give him that. And nobody in the room rocked knee-highs like he did.

Armaeus leaned closer to me, the scent of jasmine and cloves hovering lightly in the air. "Have you seen the relic directly yet, or merely gotten a sense of its power?"

I grinned. Not only did he have great socks, the Magician was no slouch in the intellect department.

"Just the pretty pop of energy," I allowed. "And I've seen that so many times, we're almost on a first-name basis. Which leads me to believe that what we're about to see once we *do* finally get a load of it is not exactly what Morris and possibly Washington will see. Because they're Connected, but they haven't been fully topped off, if you catch my meaning."

"It appears that we will get the opportunity to prove your hypothesis," the Magician murmured. "I see the relic as well. At the side door?"

"Yup. Here we go." We watched as both Morris and Washington reacted almost viscerally in different parts of the room. They stiffened, turning toward the far doorway where I'd last seen the latest flash of energy. Both men made gracious bows to their compatriots, then turned and began strolling casually toward the far door as well. "You could beat them, right?" I asked. "Get there first?"

The Magician lifted a brow and nodded. "We both could."

"Yeah no, I'm not about to serve as the Magician's apprentice. You do your thing, and I'll follow behind. Try to blend in."

"As you wish." And then poof, he was gone, disappearing in a swirl of smoke that no one but me seemed to notice. He really was good at that, and for the briefest moment, I wondered if I'd ever be able to pull off the same magic trick. If so, I kind of suspected it wouldn't be anywhere near as tidy.

I snagged another glass of bubbly liquid, not quite champagne, but some sort of sweet sparkling wine, and made my way through the crush of people toward the far door. No one paid much attention to me, just nodded and smiled in that offhanded way of parties where you were expected to know everyone and yet couldn't possibly. I noticed one man in particular, a young, too-thin figure bent over a large sketch pad, feverishly drawing the dancers and the extended collection of the rich and socially accepted.

Was he a hired hand for the Morrises? A sketch artist for whatever passed for a tabloid in colonial New York? Either way, he seemed very earnest. Hopefully someone would give him a meal for his troubles.

When I reached the door, I was surprised to find that it didn't lead to a hallway, but yet another room, this one somewhat less well lit, but still cheerfully bright, with only a third the number of occupants as the main ballroom. Men and fortunately some women stood in small groups, laughing and talking in subdued tones. The Magician was nowhere to be seen, but Washington and Morris stood at respectful attention, speaking to an unexpected party—a woman with large dark eyes, and a quiet, almost cloistered sense about her, as if she were a nun on holiday. She wore a long gray gown with a high neck and no adornment, and in her hands, she clutched her velvet pouch.

Hello, High Priestess card.

Armaeus still didn't put in an appearance, so I gave up, reaching out mentally to ferret him out of whatever corner he'd found himself.

Did you get lost? I asked the question in my mind, not trusting myself to mutter it aloud, and the Magician responded immediately.

"I found it more useful not to make my presence known. The woman's name is Dame Edna, and she presents herself as an emissary from France with a tool to help in what she terms the coming conflict."

Has she named her price?

"She is styling it as a gift."

I scowled. *Uh-oh.*

"My thoughts exactly."

In the world of the arcane black market, there was no such thing as a gift. That meant if Dame Edna was planning on unloading a trinket to the richest guy in the colonies and the future leader of the free world, there could be only one of two reasons. One, to give them said strength in such a way that would tip the coffers to her favor—or two, to give them some seriously bad mojo. The jury was out for the moment until—

Dame Edna coughed up the goods.

I didn't need to have much psychic sensitivity to understand what I was looking at. The chunk of wood looked ragged and weather-beaten, stained, and even charred. It could have been rooted out of anyone's cellar or charnel pit. But the wave of menace that exuded from it was palpable.

"The One True Cross," Washington murmured, his voice so filled with reverence that it shook me out of my thrall.

Roger Morris was slightly more suspicious, though he had gone deathly pale. "Where did you get this? How have you carried it safely all this way?"

Dame Edna opened her mouth, doubtless to spout some nonsense about being protected from harm by the grace of God and his only begotten son, but I didn't have that kind of time. The revealed chunk of wood was giving off firefly sparks that leapt up into the air and floated almost lazily toward the two men. Two men who, by all historical accounts, were to direct the future of the United States and, perhaps more importantly, its fledgling finances. I didn't know who was being tested here. Was the Magician trying to see what level of chaos I was willing to allow? Was the artifact itself driving this game, or Armaeus? My money was on the Magician, but he was also the one paying the bills. If he needed yet another test to convince himself I could hang with his crazy, I could afford to be gracious.

"You owe me so big," I muttered aloud, but I didn't wait any longer. I moved forward, striding across the room as quickly as my voluminous skirts would allow. I startled Dame Edna, who was so fixated on her marks that she, like everyone else, had paid no mind to me until it was too late. I didn't bother with small talk. I merely stepped up, dove for the chunk of wood, and wrapped my grubby fingers around it while Edna tried to yank it back.

Someone screamed. It had a very Sara-esque tone to it, but I wasn't the one overreacting. In less than a blink, Dame Edna shriveled into a husk and then a burst of muddy smoke, causing both Morris and Washington to step back in alarm. I turned on them, intending to give them a healthy warning and maybe a few suggestions about how to set up a government, but as I gripped the relic, I too felt my voice thinning out, my body becoming more diffuse, my blood turning to ash.

Out of nowhere, the Magician's arms closed around me, and I felt myself propelled at alarming speed away from the startled faces of the luminaries of colonial New York, back through the ballroom, out into the hallway and finally, with a wrench of sensation that left me queasy, back to the shadowy entryway of the present-day Morris-Jumel House, complete with all its crisscrossing security lights. I sagged against the Magician, not protesting when he produced a bag of black cloth and pried my fingers open, nudging the chunk of wood out of my grip and into the bag while I numbly stared down at my hands as he pocketed the bag.

My palms were burned black.

"*Crap,*" I muttered. I jerked my hands away as the Magician reached for them, but he was faster.

He held my hands in his, drawing in a sharp hiss. "How do you not feel this pain?"

I wanted to respond with something glib. I felt it was my duty, but the nausea that was welling up from deep inside me went to war with any smart words that were trying to get out ahead of it. I managed little more than a guttural groan before tipping sideways, but the Magician still had hold of my hands. He pressed his thumbs into my palms, the pain so immediate and electric that my knees buckled and my head tilted back. What came out of my mouth was not liquid, thank God, but a rush of smoke and ash that burst into the still air as the Magician whisked me to the side.

"What the *hell*," I groaned.

"There was a gap in the narrative, but there were indications," the Magician said. "When I was unable to recover the relic in France, I braced for the worst. The worst never came, but this...this was most unexpected. You seem to have a habit of being unexpected, Miss Wilde."

"Are you saying anything I'm supposed to be paying attention to?" I managed, whimpering with relief as wave upon wave of cool, healing relief floated over me. The Magician murmured something else, and I lifted my chin toward him, meeting his golden gaze and nearly drowning in it.

"Quite...unexpected."

Then he lowered his head and kissed me.

27

Heat exploded through me. Not the delicious slide of sensual pleasure that I had experienced once or twice before while kissing a beautiful man, but a bolt of pure fire that shot along my bloodstream and electrified my nerves. I jolted, instinctively pulling back, but as if my newly healed hands had a mind of their own, they reached toward the Magician even as he attempted to release me, my fingers twining in his long hair, pulling him toward me while I sighed against his mouth.

He obligingly deepened the kiss, and I felt myself approaching a precipice, galloping, leaping, *striving* toward it as if everything in my body needed to fling itself over the edge and into the abyss. I wanted nothing more than to taste, to feel, to be with this man, to be consumed by him, overtaken, made one—

Then a new set of sensations rocketed through me, as devastating as the first and far less pleasurable. Fear. Panic. Flat-out horror. I gasped, and this time, I did pull away, violently, barely registering my own scream as if my eyes were being ripped out of their sockets, and maybe they were, because blackness slammed into me like a pair of meaty fists on Fight Night.

I vaguely heard the Magician's cultured but undeniably startled shout—then there was the faintest rush of cool air —and then there was nothing at all.

I awoke to being carried in Armaeus's arms, sprawled out like a six-year-old after a rainbow-themed birthday party with too much cake. As I scrambled to awareness, he swung me lightly down, letting me stumble away from him to stare, disbelieving, at the elegantly appointed sitting room of our suite.

"What the *hell*?" I demanded. "Did you poof me too? How long have I been out?"

"You've sustained quite a shock," the Magician answered, which was no answer at all.

I reoriented my attention on him as he moved gracefully to the sidebar, lifting a carafe of water and pouring the clear liquid into a large crystal glass. The water seemed to dance and shimmer, and I blinked, squinting hard. It was as if each molecule was separate and unique, glittering far beyond its natural limits.

"What is going *on*?" I pressed my hands against my temples, watching as the Magician walked back to me, not missing, in my heightened awareness, that his steps were slightly tentative. He didn't know either, I realized with sudden clarity. And that sent a fresh wave of panic slithering through me.

I accepted the glass of water, eyeing it dubiously as it bubbled and fizzed in the glass. "What's wrong with it?"

"It's reacting to your energy," Armaeus said calmly, almost but not quite condescendingly, like a professor encouraging his star pupil. I had surprised him, but I wasn't sure exactly how. "It is quite safe to drink. Any sustenance you take in will bolster your own energy and serve to strengthen you."

"That sounds like a lot of bullshit," I grumbled, but in truth, I was parched. For all its unexpected fizz, water seemed like exactly what I needed. I tipped the water into my mouth, relishing the quick pour of cool liquid. It was too cool, actually, considering the carafe had just been sitting out in the open air, but I wasn't about to argue. I could feel it slide down my throat and chill my superheated organs. A trick of the mind, probably, but it worked for me just the same.

And the Magician was right. I did feel steadier when I handed back the glass. He took it, setting it down on one of the little carved tables, but didn't gesture for me to sit. We stood facing each other, our arms loose, our stances wide, like two boxers unsure of whether or not we were the next fight card.

"I blacked out after I kissed you?"

"So it would appear." He nodded, eyeing me closely.

"You do that to all the girls?"

"It has happened, but very rarely. In fact, perhaps less than five times in all the years I have walked this earth."

That made me smile, albeit a little wobbly. "Okay, Grandpa." Armaeus always spoke as if he were a thousand years old, but to my eye, he was barely pushing forty. "When it's happened before, why did it happen? Do you, like, make a habit out of kissing people when they're exhausted?"

"I suspect your fatigue is partly to blame for your response, yes. But only partly." He lifted a hand, not moving otherwise, but I felt the corresponding leap of awareness within me. Half trepidation, half recurring desire. My brows lifted.

"Are you doing that? Are you causing that reaction?"

"I would contend that you are causing the reaction. I assure you, I do not coerce any mortal into bodily responding to me in any particular way. My province is in the manipulation of the mind, true enough, but even that has proven to be of limited value with you. Your barriers hold fast against me."

I gritted my teeth as he lifted his other hand, curving it slowly with a slight outward flare, as if he were tracing the line of my rib cage to my hip. My body responded with a surge of heat along my waist, as real as if he were touching me.

"Well, I can feel *that*," I advised him. "And I can assure you, I'm not trying to do it to myself."

"And yet you are allowing it to happen," the Magician said. "Miss Wilde, there is nothing I can do that you do not allow. You can shut me down as quick as a blink. Try it."

He lifted his right hand higher, and I felt the pressure of his fingers against my cheek, though he still stood ten feet away from me. It was real and present. I realized that this was the scene in the shower all over again, and the scene at the orgy in Rio as well. Armaeus had pushed, but I had allowed it—I'd welcomed him in. The thought made my head spin, and another surge of panic dropped a crackling barrier between us.

I staggered back, the loss of his touch jolting me, the swimming delirium of need, want, pleasure, and possibility cutting off so abruptly that it made me gasp.

"You're gone," I managed, feeling ridiculous as he continued standing right there.

He nodded. "I'm gone, and yet here. Again, there is nothing I can do to you that you do not allow, Miss Wilde. That's very rare among mortals, I can assure you."

"Why do you keep talking like that? You're human. You're mortal. You're standing right in front of me."

"I'm less interested in your assessment of me than in your assessment of yourself," he countered, and the dizzying dance started once again, the assault of sensation. "Would you like me to approach or to let you rest?"

I narrowed my eyes at him, but there was no way I had *any* intention of resting around this man. Not tonight. Maybe not ever. "You really have to ask? I'm not going to break."

He regarded me with a slow smile, his golden eyes intent on mine. "You will not break," he agreed. "You could break me, however."

"Yeah, right." A wave of delicious, bubbling possibility slithered through me, like champagne fizzing through my blood. I listed to the side, feeling almost like a Victorian starlet gearing up for a major swoon. Was I doing that to myself? Was Armaeus?

I didn't have time to piece it together before he was at my side, moving so swiftly it was as if he didn't even take a step. He was simply there. His arms wrapped around me, and I sagged against him, looking up into his beautiful face. His sculpted lips parted, and his golden eyes drilled into me with their intent stare. The air around us filled with the scent of jasmine and a new, almost heady perfume that hinted of sand, heat, and fire.

"Armaeus?" I whispered, and he jolted, physically stiffening as his hands tightened around me. It was the first time I'd ever said his name, I realized distantly, then his lips were on mine again.

This time, I was more prepared.

Pleasure shot through me, from the touch of his mouth, to the grip of his hands, to the long lean muscular lines of his body as he pressed against me. I pushed him back, the two of us toppling onto the couch, and attacked him like a woman possessed. I wanted everything about this man. I wanted him to fill me from the tips of my toes to the crown of my head, to feel his energy wrap around my bones, glide along my skin, and race through my blood. The need built within me, crashing and furious, so intense, it almost reached the point of physical pain.

"Miss Wilde," I thought I heard him say, but it was nothing compared to the driving need screaming in my mind. I pulled at his jacket and shirt, laying bare his chest, the expanse of coppery skin delighting my senses and making my heart pound in a furious staccato. I leaned in to taste him, the smooth, rippling muscles of his chest and abs causing everything south of my belly button to tighten with heat. My hands dropped to the waistband of his pants. I closed my fingers around his expensive leather belt, damned close to ripping it free, then Armaeus's cool hand covered mine, the strength of his touch flowing through me a shocking counterpoint to my own frenzied need.

"There is much you don't know about me. Much you should already have discerned, but I sense you have not. You should—"

"Oh, shut *up*," I groaned, pulling open the buckle of his belt, unfastening his trousers. His body sure as hell was reacting like an ordinary man's, and though I hadn't had a ton of experience in this department, I wasn't completely unschooled. I was also still dressed, I realized.

With that awareness, my brain caught up with my body, and I jerked my gaze up, my eyes going wide as I registered that I'd basically just attempted to have sex with my boss thirty minutes after kissing him thoroughly for the first time.

I should write a business book.

"Should I—should we—"

I didn't exactly understand what happened next, or why, whether it was because of the naked vulnerability on Armaeus's face, the fact that he was nearly naked, or the fact that I really wanted to become naked too, but suddenly, I was. My clothes disintegrated from my body, though that made no sense at all, and the Magician's clothes disappeared along with them. Then it was only the two of us, on the impossibly overstuffed couch in the impossibly expensive hotel room. He was breathing as heavily as a seventeen-year-old in the back seat of his dad's car, and mind-blowing need swept through me again, battering my senses.

I pulled myself higher on his body—want and need, panic and pleasure, fear and terror ripping through me as I braced myself on his shoulders, staring deep into his eyes. I lifted myself and gasped with utter, transcendent joy as his strong hands closed over my hips and he positioned me above him, his shaft pressing against me, the tip so close, I almost cried out in frustration and need and then—

Pain blasted through me. Mind-bending horror exploded through every bone, vein, muscle, and sinew.

I convulsed, practically levitating, my body and brain, my sinuses and synapses, my tendons and toes—all of them coming apart. I had the sense of a scream being cut off as if I'd been smothered by a Mack truck slamming into me.

And then there was silence, and I was dead.

28

"Miss Wilde."

The words poked at me from all sides, an angry buzz of bees that danced close enough to tease me before lurching away again. I struggled to respond, a clumsy bear swatting and pushing them away. I couldn't breathe, I couldn't see. I was buried so deep in a dark pit, lost beneath layers and layers of shadow, pain, and fear that I didn't think I could get out. I didn't know what I was, I didn't know who I was—

"*Miss Wilde.*" Okay, that was who I was, right.

This time, I didn't bat away the sound of my own name, but tried to curl my fingers around it, pulling it close to my chest, trying to internalize it. *Miss Wilde. Sara Wilde.* The name I'd made for myself, the name I'd embodied, to become the greatest, most successful artifact hunter on the arcane black market. I was strong, I was resourceful, and I would not die in this pit of darkness. I would *not* let this asshat destroy me.

A shot of anger rocketed through me, finally strong enough to overcome the pulverizing fear.

The Magician had harmed me, damaged me, him and his body that had seemed like a magical playground, open and inviting and everything I'd ever wanted in a man, but had never had the opportunity to take. He was a lie, a poisoned apple. He'd tried to have sex with me—

No, no. I shook my head, reorienting myself. I'd tried to have sex with *him*. I'd been the aggressor, the one whose need had seemed so strong and paramount. He'd merely allowed me close, never letting on that sex with him would lead to this deep dark place of loss, doubt, and formlessness. He would not do this to me. I refused to let that happen. I could break free of his thrall and regain myself. I could come back to life.

"Sometime today, if you would."

The unexpected pointedness of his derisive comment packed more punch than a dozen "Miss Wilde"s had before it. My eyes shot open, or at least they tried, the actions seeming to take a full minute as I gasped, oxygen slowly, laboriously filling my lungs.

Gradually, the details of the room filled in as I swung my head around, inch by painful inch. I was back in the hotel room, the expensive suite in New York City. I was curled up in a tight ball on the couch, but I was dressed in my own clothes once more. The Magician sat ten feet away on a wingback chair, his long lean form also dressed, though at least he hadn't bothered to put on his suit jacket again. He reclined at his leisure and studied me; his hooded eyes curious, watchful, unconcerned as I flailed toward full consciousness.

Anger built again. How had he gotten dressed so quickly, and how had I managed it when I was boneless with reaction? Why was I not still in control of all my limbs when he clearly was? I stared at him from beneath my brows, drawing in a painful breath as my lungs squeezed, desperate for the oxygen that didn't quite seem to reach them fast enough before I was forced to exhale again.

"Your reaction is completely unacceptable, Miss Wilde. And unnecessary, and overly dramatic," the Magician informed me. Definitely no problem with my hearing; I caught all that loud and clear. "I can only assume it is also unintentional, but you have the power over your own body's defense mechanisms, and you have the capability of fighting them. I do not pose the threat you seem predisposed to believe I do."

"You're a *dick*," I managed, the win of being able to string together the accusation muted by Armaeus's condescending eye roll.

"Surely, with the fees you command on the arcane black market, you have a more discerning analysis of the situation than that."

It was the reference to money that did it. Because he was right. He was my client, he was paying me. I'd broken the bounds of my own personal contract, and I never did that. I didn't mix business with pleasure. Hell, most of the time, the clients who hired me to find their magical McGuffins didn't appeal to me in that way. They were obsessed with their artifacts and the power they thought they could chisel out of them.

Armaeus was no different. He was hella hotter, sure, but he was just another megalomaniac with a fascination for shiny things. And I was one of those shiny things. He apparently was shiny to me too, but I should have known better. Shiny things were dangerous.

"Never again," I muttered, and this time, the words were clear and loud enough to carry across the room, the strength of them filling me as I straightened against the couch. Air flowed, the lights brightened. I was back.

"That would be a grave, grave disservice to us both, I should think," the Magician observed quietly, his voice equal parts amused, perplexed—and almost, I was sure, relieved. Had he been nervous about my blackout? Though he freaking well should have been, his apprehension spiked the fear in me once more. I got the feeling the Magician of the Arcana Council didn't go in much for apprehension, fear, doubt, or any of that. Which made what had just happened between us something he hadn't expected.

"You want to explain why I passed out the minute I tried to climb on top of you?" I asked, the ragged gravel in my voice seeming to pull him back from the edge of worry. He leaned forward, his expression losing some of the electric energy I hadn't at first noticed, but was obvious now that it was fading. His eyes sparked, his mouth twitched into a smile, and I instantly realized my mistake. My reactions were still too slow for me to raise a hand to forestall his words, and the lecture began.

"There was obviously a reaction between our innate abilities—your inner power, if you will, and my own. A recognition that such an intense connection between us could be transformative, and your absolute refusal to make that transformation."

"Yeah, well, it's the first date, I tend to avoid transforming until at least the fifth or sixth."

He flashed a devastating smile. "But don't you see? You have the capacity for transformation in a manner that is unlike anyone I have met in all my years. And I can assure you, that is quite some time."

He said this last bit with such assurance that irritation flared through me.

"Can I get some clarification on the 'I'm a great and powerful wizard' business?" I complained. "I mean, I get it. You're the Magician and a billionaire, you've got fancy clothes and fancy planes, and you like fancy magical toys, much like the entire top one percent of the arcane black market. You can zoom around like Tinker Bell and make coffee appear out of nowhere, but I mean—who are you? I mean, really."

There was a puff of smoke, and I blinked, but Armaeus now sat beside me on the couch, and he held a glass of amber liquid. "I thought you might need this," he suggested, offering me the glass.

I reached for it and realized my hands were shaking, but I wasn't about to waste good scotch. My fingers closed around the cut crystal tumbler, reassured by its weight. I touched the rim to my lips, felt the bite of the liquid. It was real. All this was real.

"So, what all *can* you do?" I asked evenly, staring at the Magician over the top of the glass. "Disappear and reappear, clearly. Read minds, I suppose."

Armaeus lifted a brow. "Except I can't fully read yours. Not without your permission. Which, as you may imagine, I find fascinating."

I took another bolstering drink, considering his words. They made me feel better. Knowing that he probably intended that, however, made me feel worse. I grimaced. "Can you travel a long way when you go poof, like shoot across the ocean or whatever?"

"I can." He nodded, trying and failing not to look pleased as I worked through his abilities. "My skills lie mostly in the power of discernment, the combining of disparate forces to make a new whole, generally through logic and the natural progression of most likely events."

"Yeah, okay. So you're super smart. That's not as cool as being able to poof and travel all over the world in a heartbeat."

He inclined his head. "As you say."

"What else?" I gestured at him with the glass of scotch. "Can you make this explode? Could you kill me with a thought? Can you set this building on fire?"

His lips twitched. "For everything, there is a spell or incantation, a path for magic to follow, to make the force of all things bend to a higher calling. With enough time and focus, nearly anything is possible."

"Time," I murmured, a new fear curling within me. He believed everything he was saying, believed it with such force that I did too. Was I that gullible, or did something inside me recognize the truth, the same something that could find an artifact with just a few hints from some well-chosen Tarot cards? But this was something else again. This stopped me a bit. "How old are you?"

He smiled and sipped a new drink I knew he hadn't been holding a second before, but the movement was so seamless that it didn't seem as if it had appeared in his hand at all. It simply was there, a part of him.

He studied me with dark and unsettling interest.

"I was born in the late 1200s, the son of an Egyptian priestess and the French Templar knight who had come to pillage her land in service to his king and his god. The campaign ended in disaster for the Templars, as many such campaigns did, and when the dust settled, the few survivors scattered."

"That means you're over eight hundred years old," I confirmed, taking another long pull of my drink to bolster me in the wake of so much math. "You're like a vampire who can walk in the sun."

Armaeus quirked a condescending brow, but kept going. "My mother, for reasons of her own, nursed my father back to life. He returned later to France with her, and wealth flowed to them. We lived in quiet comfort, our wealth slowly building, and my own psychic abilities growing as well. My mother, of course, was well aware of my burgeoning powers of intellect, manifestation, and manipulation, while my father was prouder of my strength and speed, not thinking to ask if it was beyond what was reasonable of a boy and eventually a young man my age." His chuckle was wry, almost bitter, and I felt an answering tug in my chest, an almost insane need to reach out and offer Armaeus comfort. I gripped my glass a little more tightly, fighting for objectivity...as if that were ever going to be possible again.

"I left them when I was twenty, moving to another town," Armaeus continued. "Their wealth had begun to attract attention that would have proven problematic to me."

At this point, I was staring, the scotch in my glass gone. Only it wasn't. The weight shifted, and I didn't need to glance down to know that the Magician had kindly refilled my drink as he swirled the amber liquor in his own glass.

"The call to join the Arcana Council came a few years later. I wasn't expecting it. I had resolved to make a life of study and quiet development of my powers, perhaps start a family."

This perked me up, and an unexpected and completely inappropriate twist of jealousy curled through my gut. I had known this man for all of a minute. I'd just blacked out trying to have sex with him. But I was going to be annoyed that he'd had a girlfriend in the freaking 1200s?

The Magician flicked a glance at me, clearly startled, and I burned with a new flame of humiliation that he might have caught any of that particular errant thought. I resolved to become a better person on the spot, and a brighter one. Dare to dream.

"So this Council was around all the way back then? They were based in France, I guess?" I asked, forcing myself to focus on a more important question than the Magician's love life.

"Recall, this was around 1300 AD. The Arcana Council had spent a few hundred years in the Far East, most recently in the city of Kaifeng. With the assault of the Mongol horde, the Council relocated to several temporary locations, but by this time, a permanent base was desired. And a new Magician as well, as it happened. We established the new base of the Council in Vienna. We did eventually return to France, setting up in Paris, but not until well after my parents and siblings had died and stories of my life had faded."

"You watched your family die?" I asked, aghast, the pendulum swinging back to me caring entirely too much. At this point, I was all in. The Magician could have told me he was from outer space and I would have bought it. "You're immortal?"

"Quite. One of the benefits of council membership. Perhaps one that may sway you in time to come."

I snorted. "Thanks, no. I've had enough crazy in my one life already. I don't need to borrow more."

To his credit, the Magician didn't pursue the question. Instead, his gaze remained on my face, and there was no denying the answering flush of heat across my cheeks.

"Would you not be intrigued to follow this thread to where it might lead?" He asked, his tone borderline offended. "You clearly have a reaction to me."

"I have a reaction to penicillin too, it doesn't mean that I try to seek it out. Not when I know it's not good for me." I gulped my drink, wanting to believe it was the heat of the liquor and not his gaze that was affecting me.

"Have you decided in our brief interaction that I am not good for you?" the Magician challenged.

Had he gotten closer to me somehow? He hadn't seemed to move, but I was already becoming quite aware that nothing was as it appeared when it came to him. "I don't think I want to stroke out again, thanks," I said, but my words sounded halfhearted even to my own ears.

"We've established that such a thing occurred at a specific point. No?"

I wasn't imagining it. The Magician *was* closer, leaning toward me perceptibly, his glass no longer in his hand while my fingers were still wrapped compulsively around my crystal tumbler. I held it between us as if it was some kind of ward.

"I don't understand how you make me feel horrible and yet wonderful at the same time," I said. "Maybe I'm just grossed out that you're eight hundred years old."

The Magician's smile was soft, amused, but there was no denying the urgency in his eyes either. He might be acting like he was the one in control, but I...I didn't think he was.

His laugh was quiet, almost grim. "I assure you, Miss Wilde, in this moment, I am not at all in control."

And once again, he leaned forward, brushing his lips against mine.

29

My fingers went lax, the tumbler living up to its name, only to be caught in a swift and dexterous movement by the Magician and poofed into nothing. At least I assumed it poofed. It flashed out of my hands and out of my thoughts as the Magician's arms went around me, and he pulled me close. Not roughly, not neatly, but with a rock-solid steadiness that surrounded me with heat and power. I groaned despite myself, sagging against him and tilting my head back, allowing him to deepen the kiss. His hand slid down my back, pressing me closer, and the tremor of fear reawakened in my belly. I stiffened, and the Magician eased back immediately, his golden eyes steady and sure as I blinked mine open, feeling a little dazed.

"What is that?" I gasped. "What is it I'm feeling?"

He stared down at me, his hands still holding me lightly, but away from him, both of us resuming our eighth-grade dance positions. We excelled at it.

"You're already adapting, but there's more work to do. What you're feeling could be a reaction to my power and the answering knowledge of your power deep within you. It could be fear," he continued before I could protest the unlikeliness of his first hypothesis. "Fear of the unknown, of the other. I certainly fall into both those categories for you at this time."

"I'm not afraid of you," I muttered, but the words rang false. Irritation snapped through me. I straightened, not needing to push the Magician away. He'd anticipated the move and was even now leaning back from me, regarding me with his best professorial gaze. I pulled my hands through my hair, retightening my ponytail.

"Right. So what else about you do I need to know?" I asked. "What am I missing about you and the jobs you're putting me on, whatever might be triggering all this? Exactly how powerful are you and this Arcana Council of yours?"

And that really was the crux of it, I knew. It wasn't only that the Magician had skills. He was part of a group of other high-level Connecteds, and that kind of organization was dangerous. I really, *really* needed to get Father Jerome's take on it.

"You will meet the Council in good order, as needs require. We don't make a habit of interacting with mortal magic more than we need to. Our charter is simpler than that. We seek to balance the magic that is in the world."

I frowned. "Balance? Like good and bad, right and wrong, dark and light? What kind of charter is that?"

"The kind of charter that will allow for the continuation of magic and not its destruction. There have been battles fought over magic many times throughout the millennia. It's a constant struggle between those who have it and those who do not, those who have a little and want more versus, well, everyone. Just as in every power struggle, there are those who would do nearly anything to augment or increase their power, even to, especially to, the detriment of others."

"Yeah, I got that part. There are some seriously bad actors out there. Are you telling me you're on board with taking them out?"

"No, I am not."

That rejection didn't surprise me, but it irritated me all the same.

"Why not? Have you seen what these assholes are doing to the vulnerable? They're taking out children, Armaeus. They're harvesting them for their blood and organs. That horror show been going on for centuries, and according to you, your little organization's been around for centuries and you've done nothing to fix it. What the hell is balancing worth if you can't fix the problems along the way?"

"You mean problems like these?"

The Magician waved a hand, and the walls of the luxurious sitting room shifted, the gilt frames remaining the same, but the paintings within them were replaced by screens. In each screen was a scene more horrifying than the last. Prison camps, village raids, abductions on street corners, attacks in homes. Children, the elderly, the young and strong, the old and infirm—attacked, robbed, killed, tortured. The scenes rushed too quickly for the eye to track, some of them present-day, others back in time, the vibrant, modern-day imagery making them look like period pieces in some Merchant Ivory production, but the action too visceral, too gory to be made for entertainment. It was an assault on the senses, and I pressed myself back into the couch as if I could escape it.

But there was no escape. Human beings were assholes.

"There is no stopping the tide of depravity, the voracious need for power and control, the depths to which the human condition can descend," Armaeus advised, but he was watching me and not the screens. "You are foolish for thinking you can make a difference in the way you are going about helping the vulnerable."

That struck a nerve, which I suspected was his intention.

"Yeah, well, at least I'm fucking doing *something*," I snapped.

With a short wave of his hand, Armaeus turned off the light show. "Your anger is misplaced, Miss Wilde. I am merely showing you that there are reasons why the Council does not engage itself at the level of individual interaction. We seek the balance of magic, nothing more. Magic must continue, because a world without magic is a far more dangerous place, I think you would agree."

"Honestly, that's kind of debatable," I said, staring moodily at the space that had just been filled with so much debauchery and carnage. "People can suck."

"But they are capable of so much more." With another elegant gesture, the screens returned, only this time, the scenes were far happier. Groups of people being cared for in makeshift beds spread across a field, standing, walking. More groups flickered across the panels, these people standing with arms raised, the energy of their joint prayer almost palpable. An old man leaning over cracked and parched earth, rivulets of green extending from his fingers as seedlings burst from the dirt. A knot of people staring at a computer, their fingers not on joysticks or keyboards, but stretched out, their eyes alight with wonder.

"In each new generation, magic finds a way to thrive, sometimes in the least likely places," he continued. "Again, we seek only to ensure its balance."

"Balance," I muttered. I didn't entirely like the sound of that, but I couldn't figure out why. It seemed to be...not nearly enough. Not when there were children suffering—kidnapped, abused, killed.

Armaeus lifted his glass to me. "Which returns us to David Galanis. In his current role with the Met and other museums of prominence, he has reached a level of particular influence. He now strikes fear in both institutional collectors and those with private holdings of great worth, but questionable provenance. His influence is greatest among the collectors of New York, but it is beginning to be felt across the country: Boston, Chicago, Los Angeles, Las Vegas."

"Las Vegas?" I frowned, unnerved by a shiver of dread the location served up. I hadn't been to Vegas since the bad old days, when I'd been a kid on the road and more or less on the run. "Why? Is there even a museum there?"

"Not exactly, but the city is possessed of a particular form of acquisitive magic. That makes it a safe repository for the highest-powered artifacts."

"Uh-huh," I said. Something poked at me, though, the sound of slot machines chattering and neon lights flashing far across the country. "Are you sure about that? You ever been to Vegas yourself?"

The Magician chuckled. "Las Vegas is a place most visit, but never stay for long. They can't, not if they feel the energy coursing beneath it, the hum and rumble of possibility. That strange urgency is what both draws the sensitive and repels the practical soul. It drives people to acts of foolishness and pride—yet opens the door to the extraordinary, a constantly spinning wheel."

"So you *have* been there," I confirmed.

He smiled then, almost wistfully. The expression tugged at me in a way I was wholly unprepared for. "A time or two."

"Well—either way. So what if Galanis is making a name

for himself among the collectors of the arcane black market. Why do you care?" I asked. Armaeus's gaze narrowed just enough for me to understand. "You're *jealous*. You're pissed off because he's getting his hands on these toys and you want them."

The Magician's elegant lips curled with disdain, which let me know that I was right on the money. "My personal interest in the acquisitions aside, there is a greater issue, given the level of power he is accumulating around him. Why does he need it? What are his plans? I've yet to find the answer to these questions, but we do know this: Galanis grows too strong."

"And you want me to hamstring this guy by outing his backer, because you can't. Officially."

He shrugged. "I would merely suggest there are many ways to accomplish one's goals."

"Yeah, by cheating. That's personally my favorite one too, so I'm good with it. And despite your little TED Talk just now, I do believe that I can make a difference by getting down on the ground with the people who are being hurt. So, let's get to it. We've got the relics, right?"

"We do," Armaeus said. He turned and pointed a long finger to an envelope I hadn't noticed before, tucked onto a side table. "And we have an official invitation, as well. To this evening's party at the Met."

"How'd you manage that? I only got here a few hours ago."

"Word travels very quickly when the message involves the kind of artifacts we have in tow."

"Fair enough," I said. "So we go hunting."

The Magician's smile only deepened as his gaze raked over my face. I was in complete conflict with myself. I didn't want to know what he was thinking, and I desperately wanted to know what he was thinking. I was wildly attracted to him, and I was deeply afraid of him. I needed to get away from the man—or whatever he was—and I wanted nothing more than for him to kiss me.

So, yeah. This client relationship was going well.

"Okay," I cleared my throat, pulling myself to my feet. "What is this party, exactly? A dinner? Cocktails? Square dance? What should I be ready for?"

Armaeus smiled with deep satisfaction, his eyes glittering as he met my gaze. "Anything."

30

The Met never disappointed, and the private party hosted in its august halls this dreary February night made the most of the venue, with LED torches lining the halls and throwing the exquisite artwork into unexpected shadow and light.

And it was true artwork too. Light and shadow revealed artifacts that whispered of age and wealth, from the tiniest jewel-encrusted objects to enormous sarcophagi and paintings. I knew there was a grand fashion event that took place in this venue every year, and it was easy to see why. The Met was over-the-top opulent. Exactly the kind of place that was one-percenter click bait.

Armaeus had spoken very little since I'd met him back in the sitting room of our suite, wearing the gown of super-special Connected silk. It was long, black, and ever-so-slightly heavy, with twin slits in the front that broke over my booted legs. I figured it would double as chain mail, but I particularly appreciated the pockets. This was one party where I wanted my cards handy—not to mention the two artifacts that would serve as bait for David Galanis.

My job here was simple. I was supposed to catch Galanis's eye as soon as possible after he arrived, arrange to show him the artifact—whichever one seemed like it would get me the most traction, based on our conversation. Once he expressed an interest in the object—and advised of his terms, since he wasn't one to pay for anything—I was supposed to delay the transaction as long as possible, which supposedly would anger whoever the real power was behind the deal. That guy would betray himself, Armaeus would swoop in, and I should dodge any flying body parts after that.

Now I turned and watched the Magician make his way back to me after having completed a tour of the long gallery lined with paintings, navigating around a few Bronze Age statues, making sure anyone who needed to see him, had. Given the ripple of interest in his wake, I was getting the impression that the man didn't circulate much, which made some sense. I'd never encountered him on the circuit, hadn't even heard of him, in fact, never mind all his mightier-than-Zeus powers.

I considered that, taking a long sip of my champagne as I studied his relaxed muscular form and the way his ridiculously expensive suit conformed to his body with enthusiasm. He turned both male and female heads wherever he passed. The man was undeniably hot.

Then again, attempting to have sex with him had almost killed me. Did that make him more attractive or less?

I caught the soft murmur of laughter in my mind. Then the Magician's smooth, rolling words vibrated against my skull.

"He's arrived, Miss Wilde."

I took my time, sipping another taste of champagne before shifting closer to the wall and studying the paintings beyond the discreet velvet rope. Transferring my glass to my left hand, I slipped my fingers into the deep pocket of my gown and riffled the cards. I'd studied everything I could find about Galanis, both on the regular web as well as using the arcane web resources Armaeus had access to.

Apparently, one of the members of the Arcana Council was a tech wizard who'd taken a deep dive into all things digital as they related to magic. I hadn't given much thought to the juxtaposition before, but it made sense. A lot of things made sense, once I wrapped my head around the idea of a clandestine hyperpowerful Council that was dedicated to the preservation of magic...if not necessarily the preservation of those who chose to wield it. An important distinction, and one I was still coming to terms with.

I glanced down at the cards I'd pulled, replaced them quickly, then took a stiffer drink.

Galanis, whose energy I could read far better now that he'd entered the room, was going to be a problem. The first card was the Magician, but in this case, I don't think it had anything to do with the man who was footing the bill for my work tonight. No, this was a not-so-subtle clue from the cards that this rando Connected had powers that approached the skill set of Armaeus Bertrand. Neat.

The second card was Judgment, powerful because it was a major arcana card, but also telling, as the scene it depicted most frequently was that of an angel raising the dead from their graves. Divesting graves of their artifacts was one thing that tied Galanis and me together. I could work with it.

And the third card sealed it. The Seven of Swords, which meant Galanis had a secret.

I could have pulled cards on this guy all day. Instead, I turned, my scan of the room stopping abruptly as Galanis met my eyes, almost as if he'd been waiting for me to search for him.

My psychic sense prickled. Non-card-related hunches weren't something I usually paid attention to, but ever since I'd started working with the Magician, I'd noticed them more. Merely a psychosomatic suggestion, a desire to be one of the cool kids? Or did I have a higher sensitivity than I realized? I'd been making my way in this world with the help of Tarot cards since I was a teenager, so it wasn't like I rejected the idea of being more deeply psychic. But I'd run into enough charlatans over the course of my life that I also had a healthy respect for the lies we told ourselves.

Galanis was no fake, though. Though he looked to be pushing sixty, he was lean, compactly built, and intense in his thousand-dollar suit and gleaming loafers. From the top of his snowy-white hair to his bright, beady eyes to his narrow, twitching mouth, I could feel the pressure of his touch as surely as I'd gotten to know the Magician's insistent press against my mind. I warded myself and didn't miss the sudden change of expression on the man's face. He'd noticed. Which once again put him in a very rare group of people.

I thought about my conversation with the Magician and his desire for me to delay and distract Galanis while keeping the guy's grubby mitts off my artifacts. I didn't think Galanis would be taken in by my feminine wiles. He was a small man, quick and hard, that lupine face practically quivering with intensity.

"They'll let just about anyone in here, won't they?"

The voice in my ear was all the more surprising because I wasn't expecting it. But I couldn't stop the smile as I turned to accept a new glass of champagne from none other than Nigel Friedman. The Brit was wearing a well-cut yet modest suit, nowhere near as expensive as the ones rocked by most of the gala attendees but he made up for it with the body beneath. Nigel was functionally athletic and surprisingly strong, as I'd had the occasion to observe up close and personal.

"You look so different with clothes," I commented, and he offered me a self-deprecating grin that wasn't fooling anyone. He was here on business, and probably the kind of business that was all about blocking mine.

"Are you here to buy or to sell, and on whose behalf?" Nigel asked, pitching his voice low enough that no one could pick up our conversation. I was well aware of Galanis's continued focus on us, though he had obligingly turned to engage an elderly set of partygoers. The duo were festooned in diamonds that looked real enough to my eye, but the two of them, especially the woman, appeared almost panicked.

"I heard about the party earlier, thought I would stop by," I deadpanned, then slanted him a glance. "I don't mean to cockblock you, Nigel, but I will if you get in my way."

"Maybe *you're* my job," he countered easily enough. But his energy was too loose for that, too relaxed. He looked around the room with the same surreptitious edge that I was employing. He was using me, but only as a shield until he was ready to make his move.

"Do I want to know?" A dumb question, because I always wanted to know.

He shrugged.

"If all goes according to plan, I will be recovering a small diamond-encrusted box from a secondary office deep within the museum. It's not on display, and very few people know it's here. It was a donation by my client that he has come to regret."

I lifted my brows. "He lost some of his mojo?"

"Quite," Nigel said. He quirked one corner of his mouth into a pained smile. "As it turns out, some artifacts *are* worth the price these people pay for them. My client is quite keen to retrieve the object in such a way that the museum will be forced to make restitution to cover their lapse, if you will, since it's only on temporary loan. He's an avaricious soul."

"Okay, but how are you going to get back to this private office? There've got to be security guards and cameras all over the place."

"My words to my client exactly. I haven't quite worked that part out, but I was hoping there would be the opportunity for a distraction. Now that I know you're here, I suspect my fondest wishes will be realized."

"I can be discreet," I countered, and he snorted.

"You can, but chaos follows you around. Don't look for me this time, okay?"

He made as if to turn away, but I snaked out a hand and laid it lightly on his sleeve. "Are there others here? Operatives? I don't know the field as well as I should. I generally don't work with as many people around."

"There are not," Nigel confirmed, giving the room another quick scan. "There are plenty of potential clients, though. And they all seem rather nervous. Did you notice that?"

"I did." I frowned, feeling Nigel leave me as I turned to study the room again. There was more chaotic energy now that I was focusing on it. If anything, Galanis wasn't the most notable in his energy signature. I couldn't quite see what I wanted, but I felt myself straining as if this were a muscle I'd just discovered and needed to train. I watched as a young woman approached Galanis and nodded at him, and then I was back to sipping my champagne as Galanis turned abruptly and made his way toward the front of the room. The Magician was nowhere to be seen.

Less than thirty seconds later, Galanis trotted up the steps of a makeshift stage I hadn't seen in the crush of people. He turned and smiled. "My friends and associates, I'm honored by your presence here tonight. Your generous donations are allowing the Met to protect some of the most valuable artifacts and works of art in the world, ensuring their safety and celebration for generations to come. I will see to it that you all are personally acknowledged for your contribution to the future, and rest assured, I'm committed to your safety and the safety of your collections."

He went on for a bit more like that, until people obligingly applauded. His speech over, he headed down the steps and directly for me. I casually patted the two miniature relics I carried with me, completely unsure how to play this, but ready to roll.

My fingers brushed over the relic of the One True Cross as David Galanis approached.

Here we go.

31

"Ms. Sara Wilde," Galanis began. His mouth creased into a smile that didn't reach his charcoal-black eyes. Up close, he was smaller than I expected, barely taller than me at five foot eight, and his body wasn't muscled beneath his expensive suit, just narrow. But his face remained every bit as arresting, his expression shrewd, and brows lifted. Everything about him seemed to twitch. "Your reputation precedes you. And your request to join us this evening was unexpected. My sources still placed you in Rio."

"They don't make sources like they used to, I guess." I shrugged. "I don't know you, right? I feel like I know you."

His smile merely deepened, the avaricious gleam in his eye sharpening.

"I'm hurt, Ms. Wilde. You can't still be upset about the Merovingian tiara," he tutted, and it was all I could do not to react.

"That was you?" *Well, crap.* My opinion of Galanis grudgingly elevated a bit.

I'd been hired to steal the Merovingian tiara from a

private collection two years earlier, only to have it stripped from me in the dead of night by what had felt at the time like thirty-five hooded assailants, but in retrospect had probably been three. My client had never responded to my failure report, and of course I'd never been paid, even though I had succeeded in lifting the daggone thing from its hidey-hole. Such was the life of a thief, but the original owner had never leveled a claim against the loss of the piece and no other requests for me to find it had been forthcoming either. "Funny, I didn't see any press releases about its inclusion in a museum or repatriation to its rightful owners."

Another smug smile. "A great deal of my work is for the public good, it's true." Galanis gestured around the gallery. "But there are some artifacts too precious to be displayed, lest they are seen by the wrong people and cause more chaos than pleasure."

I narrowed my eyes. "The wrong people?"

"The uninitiated, the unprepared," Galanis said, once again surprising me. I had expected an elitism of money, not education, but we were talking about artifacts designed to augment psychic ability. I'd only maintained possession of the Merovingian tiara for a short time and had never once put it on my head, which, of course, was where it was intended to go. But I had felt its resonance, the energy that sparked and slid along its golden wires and carefully positioned stones. I'd assumed I was psychically attuned to the thing because I was hunting it, but what if it had that effect on everyone, even low-level Connecteds who didn't understand what it was? I could almost see the guy's point.

"Where is it now?" I asked, genuinely curious.

"An interesting thing," he said. "Its owners, though grateful that I had recovered the item, didn't want it returned to them nor displayed publicly for the reasons I've already given. As a result, it's safely tucked away where it can do no harm."

"Well, that's a relief," I said drily, not believing his story for a second. Collectors didn't donate their precious treasures to safety deposit boxes not controlled by them. I also noted that Galanis had stopped short of saying that the tiara also could do no good. It didn't take a genius to discern that he'd stashed the magical piece away in his own private collection.

I took a harder glance at him, struggling to see what couldn't be seen. The Magician had been the first client I'd encountered with legitimate high-end magical abilities, but I sensed a similar energy coming from this man—no, coming *through* him, I decided. As if from a source outside his body. Could that be possible? I didn't dare lift my mental barriers to ask the Magician directly, because I sensed the pressure assaulting me from my supposed mark. In this moment, I felt ever so slightly out of my depth. I wasn't a fan.

"And now, I understand, you have something for me," Galanis said, offering me a delighted smile. "I assure you, I'm eager to see it. Walk with me?"

We turned and strolled down the length of the party room, two security guards nodding at Galanis as we stepped out of the chamber and into a large, well-lit hall.

I nearly jolted out of my skin to see the Magician at the far end of the corridor, admiring a large painting. What was he doing? I glanced away, then back, and he was gone.

"For all its international acclaim, this room exemplifies what I love about this museum," Galanis said, drawing my attention as we headed toward the same painting. "A history of the city in the oil, capturing its life, its energy. Carefully curated, you see, over the years, to convey a very specific ambience."

"I can see that," I said, though I couldn't see any such thing. I longed to pull a few cards to give me some clue as to what the importance of this gallery was. It definitely jangled my nerves. But whether that was because of the energy waves coming at me from the thickly caked paint bracketed by heavy gold frames, or because I was beginning to suspect that Galanis was every bit as psychically souped-up as the Magician feared, I couldn't say.

We continued down the hall, Galanis serving as an impromptu tour guide, pointing out the various locations immortalized by the paintings. We passed a few other appreciative donors, Galanis stepping close to share a private conversation with each of them. He might not be the host of this soiree, but he certainly was one of its star attractions.

His brief reprieves didn't leave me enough time to swipe a card, unfortunately, so I focused on the paintings, streetscapes, and port panoramas brimming with life. In one of the paintings, a card game with men hunched over their hands drew my eye, only a few cards visible clutched in their grimy hands.

I blinked. The cards visible were the Ten, Nine, and Eight of Spades.

In the world of Tarot, the Ten, Nine, and Eight of Swords all sucked. They also didn't offer a hell of a lot of context all lined up together like that. Was that another card peeking out from the corner of one of the men's hands? I'd shifted forward to peer at it when Galanis's voice startled me.

"We can speak in private just through there," he said, pointing back to a door that had been opened in the paneling of the wall next to the painting Armaeus had been admiring. A cheery light shone from behind the door. "We won't be missed."

Panic leapt within me. I felt deeply that I needed to avoid being alone with Galanis at all costs, but why? I thought of the three cards from the painting. Once again, the Ten of Swords nearly always meant betrayal or an ending of some kind, the Eight was all about restriction, and the Nine was the nightmare card, but it wasn't like this man was going to tie me up and stuff me down a dumbwaiter. Why did he feel like such a threat?

"What's this painting?" I asked casually as we approached the door, mainly to stall for time. I gestured to the painting Armaeus had been studying—a party scene, with men and women in...colonial wear. I froze, remembering the young painter from the party at the Morris-Jumel House. Surely, that couldn't have been the guy who'd painted this, right?

Right?

I stared into the perfectly rendered, painted face of Armaeus Bertrand, and the beautifully clad *moi* twirling beside him in profile, as Galanis glanced up beside me. Out of the corner of my eye, I could see recognition light Galanis's features, and I winced as he jolted. He stepped forward, staring at the painting with undeniable urgency, then swung around toward me, his face flushed.

"What do you have for me?" he demanded. "I must see it now. At once."

As I tucked my hand into my pocket, I glanced up at the painting that caused the problem. It looked like any of the two dozen oil scenes that lined the gallery, some grand party filled with men and women in opulent European-looking outfits and powdered wigs. Still, my fingers slid off the relic of the cross and grazed over the reliquary I had procured in

Savannah. Maybe I should keep the conversation a little lighter than offering up a relic of the risen lord.

"It's a small family piece," I said, slipping easily into the well-worn patter that I'd perfected over the years of working with operatives on the arcane black market. As with most collectibles, they weren't simply buying the piece, they were buying the stories. "I'm not sure if you're familiar with the Ambrose family?"

I was pretty sure he did know the Ambroses, but I wasn't sure how well. Ophelia could have been dangling lures in a lot of dark corners of the arcane black market, so she could have dropped Galanis's name at her club without having an official relationship with the guy.

Galanis's brows shot up, but his interest seemed purely of the tea-spilling variety. "Of course. Such a tragedy, William Manchester dying abruptly, leaving such an estate and all its complexities behind for his poor, frail wife to manage all on her own."

His voice was thick with sarcasm, and I offered him a conspiratorial smile. "Then you know that the rumors about the family on the mother's side are true. She's considering beginning production of Ambrosia again, with a result that's every bit as potent as it was during its heyday over the last century."

I pulled the six-inch reliquary out of my voluminous pocket and presented it to him. He bobbed up on his toes with excitement. He angled us expertly toward his pocket office and gestured me inside. I looked around, desperate to see if the Magician was witnessing any of this, but he was nowhere in evidence and I felt trapped. Eight of Swords all the way.

Still, we were in an adjunct office in the middle of the Met, and my date for the night was an eight-hundred-year-old Magician who seemed rather possessive of my abilities to help him get what he wanted. How much danger could I be in?

A thin trickle of sweat trailed between my shoulder blades. I suspected that was the wrong question to ask.

Breathing out a tight, controlled breath, I allowed Galanis to usher me into the small room. The place didn't look like it was even close to a primary location for him. A nondescript desk, walls refreshingly bare after the cacophony of artifacts and artwork throughout the rest of the building, two comfortable chairs in front of the desk, and an executive seat behind it.

"Please make yourself comfortable," Galanis said, gesturing me toward one of the two chairs as he took the other. He held out his left hand for the reliquary as he slipped free a magnifying glass with his right. I held on to it for a second longer.

"You know who I represent?"

"I do not. I know *what* you represent, though. The same kind of power that I do—power to change the world, power to rule the world. I assure you, I'll make any exchange well worth your client's while—either now or in the future, whenever he or she most has need of my assistance or inter-cession. But show me."

He wiggled his fingers, and I dropped the reliquary into his hand. Armaeus had told me to stall, but for how long? He was an immortal Magician, for freak's sake. Surely he didn't need a lot of lead time to karate chop this guy?

"Mrs. Ambrose wouldn't have given this up easily," Galanis confided with a professorial primness as he examined the reliquary, peering at the slender vial of blood inside. "How did you come by it? How might I know for sure that it's real?"

I smirked, but this question, at least, put me back into my comfort zone. "Seriously, you're going to question the provenance of this piece? Because I've got plenty of other buyers. If you know anything about my reputation, you know that's the case."

Irritation flashed across Galanis's face, and a darker emotion that I'd also seen too often. This guy wasn't just an asshole, he was powerful. He was used to getting what he wanted, but more than that, he was used to people being afraid of him. I obviously hadn't gotten the memo, and that ticked him off.

He tilted the reliquary, and there was no mistaking the shift of the blood inside its interior vial. His brows tented, and he glanced at me, excitement lighting his gaze. "Fresh blood," he observed. "The seals on these devices weren't so perfect that blood would remain liquid indefinitely. Especially since the blood in question was intended to be sampled, not merely admired. Whose blood is it? Not the old woman, I don't think. Not if she could help it."

I grimaced. He was right, but more to the point, he was talking. "Why wouldn't she use her own? She's a powerful Connected."

I spoke with the authority of one who would know, and Galanis took me at my word.

"She's not that strong." He snorted. "And if for some reason she's been hiding her gifts, she wouldn't want to make herself a target. No. The donor is someone she believes she can protect and also manipulate. Ah! The daughter? No, even better, the granddaughter."

"You seem to know an awful lot about the family for never having worked with them," I noted with a slow drawl.

"It's all connected, can't you see?" Galanis punched a button on the console on his desk, and the lights of the room dimmed while projectors beamed images on the wall. This presentation had been queued up, and not only for me, I was pretty sure. Who else was Galanis sharing his crazy with?

But the images on the screens captured my interest. A forest of genealogical trees burst up across the wall, stemming from locations all over the world, but focused primarily in Europe. Galanis, no doubt tracking my expression since he knew the contents of the presentation, chuckled.

"Oh, we're quite aware that there are other families whose bloodlines we haven't captured. The rest will get added in time, but to start, there's a network building. A network ready-made to take the power of the gods into the next millennium, where only the strongest Connecteds will survive."

I pushed through my annoyance at any sort of Connected meritocracy—where one set of people decided what level of skill should be rewarded, and what shouldn't —and focused on the real crazy of his statement. "The power of the gods?" I asked carefully. "You mean Connecteds with godlike ability?"

He sighed with deep satisfaction. "I mean the return of godlike powers among humans. Not those we were born with, though that can be impressive. Not that which has been augmented, though we would do well to prepare ourselves as best we can."

Okeydokey, smokey. Everything that hadn't already been clenched inside me seemed to twist up, and I watched Galanis tilt the reliquary, his eyes fixed on the viscous fluid within. This guy had not only drunk the Kool-Aid of the full possibilities of Connected development, he was looking to top off his glass. For the first time, it occurred to me that he might drink Maria's blood right there in front of me. I shuddered in revulsion as he continued. "But there are powers the ancients knew of that we forced away in our fear and disbelief," he continued. "Relegating them to the heavens from whence they came. But they are close, very close. And they are eager to return to this earth."

Did you know about this? I thought fiercely to Armaeus, never mind that Galanis could be tuned into my radio frequency too, but the Magician didn't respond. I grimaced internally.

Of course he knew about it. Of course he understood the level of crazy I was walking into, and of course he hadn't warned me about it. Why had I thought otherwise?

Punching down my own internal monologue, I offered Galanis an easy smile. "Look, Mr. Galanis, I'm not really here to dispute your belief. You've seen the reliquary. What can you offer for it?"

But Galanis only laughed. "You're asking entirely the wrong question." He laughed. Then, in a swift, dexterous move, he unclasped the reliquary's tiny door and pulled the small vial free.

I started to lunge for him, only to hear Armaeus's bark of refusal in my mind. *"Allow it."*

"So now I will show you," Galanis said, apparently missing the fact that I gripped the sides of my office chair, which was all that was keeping me from launching for his head. "You and all who would deny me the Connection I crave."

As I stared in queasy dismay, he uncorked the slender three-inch long vial and took a delicate sip of blood.

"Ahhhh," he murmured, clearly savoring the vintage. He looked at me with genuine delight. "I hadn't expected the assist for this evening, but I appreciate your timing all the same. And now, I believe your second gift to me will become even more useful. A piece of the One True Cross, borne by the hand of a woman. It could not be more perfect."

I shifted in my seat as he capped the blood vial and stowed it in his suit jacket, leaving the ornate reliquary on his desk. "Oh yeah?" I bluffed, as if I knew what the hell he was talking about. "Perfect for what?"

"For this." He smiled. He reached almost lazily to the side of his desk and tugged a drawer open. I braced for him to pull a gun free, but instead, he picked up a remote, smiled down at it almost lovingly, and punched a button.

The lights flickered; the room went dark.

Then the walls exploded.

32

"**M**r. *Galanis*," I shouted, reacting without thinking. I flung myself over the odious man as debris shot out in all directions. The two of us hit the floor, but Galanis wrenched away from me, leaping up with delight as I blearily stared around the room.

The back edge of the office now opened out into a large, cavernous space, a museum storeroom, filled about a third full of overladen tables and shelves. Actually, based on the debris in the space, a few other walls had been blown as well, making the room far larger than it had originally been. Emergency lights swept on, klaxon bells rang out overhead. I could hear screaming and running from the world outside, but we were in no danger that I could see, other than from the swirling smoke at the back of the room.

"What is this?" I gasped.

"This is an attack on the Met," Galanis advised with an offhanded smile. "The main reception area has been assaulted by a series of small explosions carefully placed by anonymous bad actors, not enough to damage anything truly irreplaceable. It will come out later that, as per typical museum protocol, the most famous relics were replaced by facsimiles for safety purposes. Insurance companies, you know. I assure you, I already had the explosions in this room planned, not anticipating the added bonus of your offering. I'd merely sought to expand one of the interior storage spaces to serve as a holding area. But one must make the most of one's opportunities, yes? And now you can serve as my sword and my shield."

"Your what?" I asked guilelessly, as I sent another irritated mental message to Armaeus. I didn't know if the explosions had interrupted our connection, but the Magician didn't respond. He really needed to work on his teamwork skills.

My mind flitted elsewhere, quick as a rabbit slipping under the garden gate. Nigel would so be taking advantage of Galanis's fireworks, as he raced through the Met to swipe his client's artifact. Even if I didn't directly cause the distraction, the guy totally owed me.

"You have a relic of the One True Cross, which means you can brandish it as protection for us both, should we need it," Galanis said. "One god against another, no? It should be interesting to see who is stronger."

"Stronger," I echoed. If I hadn't thought the man was crazy before, he was making an admirable case for it now. But there was no questioning his sincerity, as messed up as it sounded. "You're working...for a god."

"With, Ms. Wilde. We are working *with* the gods. Your efforts in collecting the Ambrose reliquary and the relic of Christ are laudable. If I didn't have a more pressing use for you, I could see our relationship evolving to one of mutual benefit. Alas, artifact hunters are a dime a dozen."

I narrowed my eyes at him. "I appreciate the pep talk, but you should be careful. You don't know what the blood in that vial will do to you—and you sure don't have enough mojo to do much of anything on your own."

"And you are *wrong*," Galanis retorted, his eyes sparking with fury. There was nothing that pissed off truly magical people more than being accused of being ordinary. And I was more than willing to let the guy's unhinged nature get him into trouble. "I've prepared for this day for the past twenty years, since the first relic stolen from Sumer was reclassified and returned to its homeland. I received my first vision from Enlil that night, and it changed my life."

"You had a dream that the gods of Sumer checked in to thank you for repatriating their statues?" I confirmed, hoping derision didn't make it into my tone. The Magician better have some sort of recording device trained on all this crazy, or I was going to be pissed.

"Far greater than that," Galanis assured me. His gaze fixed on the far end of the room, but I didn't follow it. He was clearly expecting somebody to show up, and when he was disappointed, I needed to be ready. "The gods came to me and told me how I could bring them back to walk among their subjects once again. Our world was a finer place when the gods had dominion over mortals. There was no chaos or destruction. There was no disease. There was only peace and prosperity."

"Yeah, if you were a *god*, maybe," I pointed out. "If you were human, there was also no freedom."

"And what have we done with our freedom?" He smirked at me. "Kingdoms rise and fall. Humanity continues to destroy itself and all that's beautiful in this world. Who's to say that we're better stewards of this planet than the gods?"

"Well, me, for one," I pointed out.

JENN STARK

Galanis raised his hands. They glowed, and I looked at him sharply, noting the fire prickling along his fingers.

"How are you doing that?" I demanded, backing away from the sparks.

He ignored the question and instead raised his voice. "Listen not to her disbelief. She knows not what she says. She speaks only from fear and the shame of her weakness."

Irritation flashed through me, but before I could tell the asshat off, the sound of falling material jerked my attention to the far end of the room. It sounded exactly like a curtain dropping off its pole and thumping to the ground, but what I saw was no theater production.

Stepping out of the shadows was a male-ish-looking figure, easily nine feet tall, covered in shimmering garments and a helmet with multiple horns, standing in the center of the room, its arms spread as if for the world's biggest group hug. This...was, um, Enlil? The god itself?

I stared, trying not to gape. It was one thing to accept that Armaeus was hella stronger than any Connected I'd ever met, any Connected I ever hoped to meet. It was another to see the object of David Galanis's fixation in the flesh. As in real flesh, with eyeballs and arms and even a vaguely human expression on its face, emanating godhood like it was its job. The power that flowed from the being was irrefutable—alien and boundless, with a curious neutrality to it that somehow set it apart from every living being on Earth. This was a creature that would rule because it could do nothing else, that would plunder and destroy without thinking, pursuing some random whim only it could track. Standing in front of me, fierce and undeniably real, was our past, I realized in a heartbeat.

I sure as hell didn't want it to be our future.

Beside me, Galanis dropped to his knees, babbling

something incoherent as he raised his arms as well, an infant ready to be taken up in his father's embrace. I was more concerned about the creatures that burst out of the shadows to cavort around Enlil. I wasn't completely up on my ancient psycho mythology, but these looked like golems to me. Demons of the underworld who didn't eat, didn't sleep, didn't drink, and delighted in nothing more than torturing whatever poor souls were given over to them. It was an impressive display. They even stank of spoiled meat and mildew.

"On your knees, lest the gallûs eat you alive," Galanis hissed, even as the central figure spoke.

The god who was maybe Enlil spoke, or at least a flood of unintelligible words fell from its lips, making Galanis sway. I wasn't up on my ancient whatever language the god was speaking, but I glanced around. Who was this show for? The Magician had permanently broken my skepticism button, so I'd given up hoping what I was seeing was merely CGI. This was real. My skin felt cold, an aching chill sliding along it, and there was a pressure in front of me and then behind, batting me back and forth.

"Miss Wilde, I can't reach you. Not right away. You will have to fight Enlil yourself. The relic should help protect you."

What? I shot back mentally. The Magician sounded bored, but I wasn't buying it. I didn't know what he was doing, but the impression he was trying to give me that he was merely caught up in a book and couldn't be bothered to help me didn't wash.

What's going on? I pressed.

"Enlil remains entangled in the veil. But it has breached it this far by mortal will—a mortal must return it back to its side," Armaeus said.

Irritation ripped through me, followed by white-hot fear. *And you're just figuring this out now?*

I rounded on Galanis, shoving my hand into the pocket of my gown to grip the relic of the One True Cross. I wasn't all that big on prayer, but now seemed like a really good time to start. "Did you summon this asshole?" I demanded of the man. "If so, you need to send it back."

But Galanis was in full-on fanboy swoon. "Enlil is the savior of our people, and I will be his right hand, preserving knowledge and beauty from the horde and placing the power in those with the right to lead."

There were so many things wrong with that statement that it took my breath away, but Galanis's announcement appeared to draw the attention of Enlil. The god turned its face toward us, and now it was my turn to stagger back.

Summoned to save the people or not, Enlil was *pissed*. A loud crack of thunder boomed overhead, making Galanis gasp and convulse in almost sensual transport. He struggled to his feet, his arms still out, his fingers splayed, and the tenor of his words changed. He shifted into the same ancient tongue or one awfully similar to what Enlil had spouted, and his voice rang with authority, even pride.

The guy wasn't reading the room. Enlil's face darkened as Galanis spoke, and the gale around it grew agitated, jumping and hissing, roiling around.

"You may want to cut that out," I advised Galanis.

He turned and backhanded me so hard, I went sprawling. That was out of nowhere, and *completely* uncalled for.

"You will know your place among the scrabbling servants," Galanis roared at me. "You will speak only when spoken to."

I rolled back to my feet, my hands loose, my weight on the balls of my feet. I glowered at Galanis, unreasonably hopeful that his descent into insanity was at least partially triggered by the flapping gallûs around him. That still didn't give him a pass. I started to lunge at him and realized something else. We weren't alone in the storage room anymore. Three dozen men had come in behind us. I recognized several as the Met's security guards, only instead of their regulation Met uniforms, they now wore shimmery gold robes and horned hats similar to the one Enlil was rocking, though with fewer horns, naturally.

I backed away from Galanis, staring from the security guards to the gallûs, then from Galanis to Enlil. I was feeling distinctly outnumbered. "Are we going to have a dance-off?"

"We are ready to serve, Enlil!" Galanis asserted, turning to his god. "I have strengthened my blood and bone to stand as your right hand, I can teach you all you need to know of every society, from the ancients to the present."

I sent the crazy dude a sidelong glance. He wasn't just talking about his super sip of Maria Ambrose's blood. In his role in antiquities these past twenty years, Galanis had doubtless amassed an extraordinary knowledge of ancient civilizations dating from whenever Enlil had last terrorized the planet to present day. One of his hardier security guards, apparently unfazed by the roiling demon mosh pit surrounding the ancient god, stepped forward with a gorgeous heavy yoke of gold and jewels, spikes radiating from it. It took only a second for Galanis to don the necklace, while another guard set a golden helmet on his head. I noted immediately that his hat had almost as many horns as Enlil's.

Enlil picked up on that little detail too. It flicked its hand with the slightest gesture, and I felt the wave of pressure sweep through the room, could almost hear the change of direction in the howling wind outside. Galanis staggered back, but before he could defend his sartorial choices, the gallûs leapt for him, fangs and claws bared.

Totally saw that coming.

I didn't even like the guy, but despite his need to play Dress-Up Ken, I wasn't going to let Galanis get sliced and diced by a bunch of demon wannabes.

Christ on a crutch, what was *with* this job? Since when were demons—real or aspiring—an actual thing for me to have to deal with on a heist?

Stuffing down my own building hysteria, I turned to the nearest security guard, who finally seemed to be registering the real threat in the room, and whipped off the closest weapon I could get my hands on, which was regrettably his shiny helmet. I turned to his neighbor, who already had his hat in hand and was shoving it at me.

The other guards were already breaking ranks and running. I couldn't blame them. I wasn't sure what recruitment pitch Galanis had offered them, but it probably hadn't included gallûs.

The demons' screams filled my ears, their voices a nattering combination of breathy yelps and clicking pointed teeth that I didn't think I was ever going to be able to unhear. Belatedly, and reluctantly, Galanis defended himself as well, the rings on his fingers glittering every time he lashed out at a gallû. They fell back with yips and cries, surprising me.

Something in those rings had helped Galanis knock me on my ass as well, I realized. That made me feel better, but only slightly, as the battle raged on. The gallûs seemed to have one trick, and that was to surround you and start dragging you off.

Unfortunately, when they couldn't get purchase on me

or Galanis, they made for the next easiest target, the fleeing security guards.

"Miss Wilde," the Magician began.

"A little help here," I yelled back, not bothering with my inside voice.

But the mere force of his address had me looking up and over the battle in the center of the room. Enlil had turned, facing a wall that now shimmered with the force of his attention. It suddenly occurred to me that Galanis wasn't a complete idiot. Enlil had been entangled in some kind of veil, Armaeus had said, but I had a different suspicion. Galanis had reinforced these walls inside the Met. He'd sought to ensure he could contain Enlil at least until they'd worked out the terms of his employment. And now Enlil was looking to get out. I crashed my way through the outer ring of gallûs and headed for the god at top speed.

I didn't know what I was doing. I didn't really care. I flung one of my sharp pointy hats at the guy's back. Through no intention of my own, it physically enlarged as it hurtled through the air.

By the time it careened off the shoulders of the ancient god, it was packing quite a punch. Enlil staggered forward, then whipped around, his flowing robes creating a mini tornado that sent the gallûs behind me into a new level of screaming hysteria.

But Enlil's eyes were only for me. Lasers shot straight out of them.

Aiming for my head.

33

I didn't have any choice. I dropped flat to the ground, rolling away as the eyeball beams etched a deep gouge in the tile floor behind me.

I scrambled to the left, into the rows of artifacts. Gleaming statues, gorgeously jeweled necklaces and belts, and tiny clay pots gave way to larger gold and silver chalices that expanded still further to golden discs studded with jewels—all of it hidden away, the personal playground of David Galanis, safely under lock and key within the museum so he wasn't technically stealing them...just borrowing their power.

Maybe he would return these pieces to their rightful owners, maybe he would use them in his own dark designs to rule the world with Enlil, but one thing was sure. Galanis believed these artifacts had power. He believed that magic was embedded in them right along with the precious stones and inlayed gold and silver. Given his particular line of business, I was willing to go with his recommendation.

Another surge of lasers shot over my head, crashing into

the wall and leaving a scorched scar. I narrowed my eyes at it, impressed once again by Galanis's preparation. He might be a megalomaniac sorcerer, but he wasn't an idiot. He'd built serious reinforcements into these walls. Reinforcements that might be strong enough to cage a god? That remained to be seen.

I grabbed the closest, heaviest objects I could pick up and clutched them to my chest with one arm, while hooking the other around a pile of small statues, each of them no longer than my forearm. Then I dove back to the floor, scrabbling out of sight as Enlil turned, its body unnaturally stiff. Was it getting used to the atmosphere after a couple of millennia in the ether, or wherever it was gods went to hang out after people stopped believing in them?

Whatever the problem, it was making adjustments fast. I dumped the pile of treasures and picked up a disc at random, hurling it like a frisbee toward the ancient Akkadian god.

It connected with his shoulder, and Enlil staggered to the side. Direct hit!

Enlil mostly seemed confused as to where the attack was coming from, so I didn't give it time to react. Hauling up another disc and then a third, I ripped them across the open space, then grabbed two of the smaller statues, hurling them like bowling pins straight for the god's head. It didn't duck—maybe it didn't know how?—and instead took the statues straight to the face.

My immediate amusement was quickly cut short as Enlil roared with bone-jarring rage and the wall behind me caught fire. There were screams, one of the most hysterical coming from Galanis, but I grabbed a chevron-adorned collar and ripped it across the room, gaining some ground as I did so. That weapon wasn't such a good choice, as Enlil reached up with an almost languid gesture and caught the necklace in one hand, a fiery glow radiating from its fist as it did so. A bolt of that fire shot directly back at me, and once again, I hit the floor, scrambling to get away.

As I rolled, my hip ground against the heavy chunk of wood in my pocket. I didn't hesitate. I'd already come to appreciate that the power of things mattered less than the belief of people in the power of things, and the fact that this relic was ascribed to a prophet turned savior who'd showed up three thousand years after Enlil first did didn't matter. He would have heard of Jesus at some point along the line.

"I banish you with the power of the One True Cross!" I howled, forcing myself not to focus too much on how ridiculous I sounded, but only on my utter conviction that this asshat needed to *go*. "Begone!"

I plowed into Enlil and shoved it back toward the blackened wall of the storeroom. A rent appeared in the darkness, exactly as if a curtain had been ripped and flung aside. I glimpsed the sight of a lantern deep in the shadows as Enlil's hands closed around my throat and clutched hard. I struggled against it like a cat up against the bathtub, knowing if it was going back to whatever hellhole it crawled out of, I was going too.

"You may stand aside, Miss Wilde," the Magician ordered in my mind, his voice calm and unhurried despite the chaos raining around us.

I would have snapped back something cutting to him, but it was a little hard to retort with Enlil's hands crushing my esophagus. The god loosened its hold on me ever so slightly, then, shifted to take in this newer threat. I turned with it—I didn't have much choice—and my eyes nearly bugged out of my head.

The Magician had been transformed.

No longer merely tall, dark, and exceedingly attractive, he looked dead-on the Magician of the Tarot, with long red robes, his hands stretched up, a corona of fire above his head in which the Möbius strip of infinity hung suspended. Other artifacts spun around him as well—a short sword, a cup, a wand, and a large gold disc. The symbols of his power.

Enlil dropped me unceremoniously, which was when I realized it'd been holding me about three feet above the floor. My knees buckled, but I managed to stay more or less upright as I lurched away. For a half second, I scanned the back of the room, but the gallûs and security guards remained in a roiling deadlock, and Galanis was nowhere to be found. Maybe he'd stepped out to score a Starbucks.

Enlil roared something at the Magician that sounded vaguely Egyptian, and the magician answered in the same language while he took a step toward the ancient god.

"Your place is not on this earth. It has not been for a very long time," the Magician said, helpfully translating his words into English as they rang through my mind. "It's time for you to return from whence you came."

Once again, I caught some movement in the darkness behind Enlil. Was there someone waiting on the other side, a sort of cosmic ferryman to take the errant god back to Hell? A light that looked like a lantern swung deep in the shadows, and I felt the most curious pull. Who was back there? And why did they seem familiar?

"No!" From the back of the room, Galanis burst out of the scrum of men and gallûs and rushed forward, way too far away to grab. He had a book in his hands that he flung not at the god, but at the Magician. The trick was an old one, but it proved extraordinarily effective as the Magician's focus veered away from the god and focused on the book. Meanwhile, Galanis flung himself toward Enlil, not going down to his knees as I would have expected, but spreading his arms wide once more.

"We can take this world, rule it. They are ready for your dominion. They can no longer stand in the way of your might—"

"Watch out," I gasped.

The gallûs swept by me, not even hesitating as they plucked up David Galanis and hurled him toward the shadows at the back of the room. His screams were instantly muffled. I raced forward. The guy was an asshat, but he didn't deserve to die like that. I reached him a second later, the gallûs parting to either side of me as heat swept through my body. I assumed the Magician was adding fuel to my fire, but I would take it. I reached Galanis, shaken by the stark insanity in his eyes. This guy was going to need *a* lot of therapy, but I unraveled him from the gallûs' clutches, staggering as he collapsed against me.

The gallûs howled in triumph, and I looked up to see the Magician now struggling with the ancient god. The ancient god who was now pulling him toward the same rip in the universe.

"*Armaeus,*" I yelled.

The Magician stepped aside just enough to allow me in to take the lead on shoving at Enlil beside him. Between the two of us, we were finally able to get Enlil through the hole, the Magician reaching out to pull me back when I nearly went tumbling in after the god.

The shadow wall vanished, the gallûs along with it. Galanis was in a dead faint on the floor. The remaining guards, very much worse for wear, were sprawled in muttering, delirious heaps. I took a step, then stumbled.

The Magician was right there to catch me.

"If you will allow me, Miss Wilde...?"

Before I could respond, he wrapped his arms around me, and the world disintegrated into smoke.

34

I thought I was fainting. I kind of wanted to faint, but I remained obnoxiously conscious as I felt my body come apart, my molecules descending into puffs of nothingness as the Magician's body turned into a rush of smoke. The world around us suddenly blanked, and I realized how noisy it had been, the chaos of the storeroom, the screams and groans of the men, the riot of color and the smell of sulfur, the far-off wails of klaxon bells and police sirens.

Everything vanished in a heartbeat. Then we were shooting through walls and windows and out into the street beyond, far above the chaos of a crowd assembled on the rainy streets of New York City. A fine mist drifted down, the rain turning harder as we whisked away. I couldn't breathe, but I didn't have to, suspended in time as we flashed through the city in barely a blink.

Then suddenly, we were back in the hotel suite, the fireplace roaring cheerfully, the couches and chairs shimmering with muted splendor beneath the soft light. We materialized, still wrapped in each other's arms, and I gazed up at my partner in crimes. The Magician met my eyes, his now a swirling dark gold with hints of black smoke in them even as the world around us came sharply into focus.

"Armaeus," I whispered. His grip around me tightened ever so slightly, the subtle movement the only indication of the fierce control he was imposing on himself.

But I was not to be deterred. "My rates are *totally* going up again."

I pulled away from him as he stood back, and despite myself, my heart caught as he barked a sharp laugh, his face transformed with such immediate and genuine amusement, joy even, that I had to break my gaze away to keep from staring at him.

He shook his head and gestured to the seating area. "I assume you have questions?"

I snorted, mostly to cover my own embarrassment than anything. I needed to take back some control here. Armaeus had already nearly gotten me killed on several occasions. I was willing to allow him to pay me handsomely for that, but I couldn't risk more. I couldn't trust the tremor that I felt every time our gazes connected, every time we touched. He was dangerous and unpredictable, and around him, so was I.

"Answers would be good, yeah. Starting with what's going to happen to Galanis? Because he went around the bend so far that I don't think he's coming back."

I didn't miss the satisfied smirk on Armaeus's face, and I pounced on it. "You *knew* that was going to happen. You knew that this series of events was going to end in him being taken out of the action, didn't you?"

He didn't bother denying it and went further to incline

his head in sort of a noble acknowledgment of his nefarious plans. "Galanis was a problem. The worst-case scenario would be that he continued to be a problem. That was followed by the possibility that he could be banished along with Enlil."

"Banished to where?" I frowned, but when Armaeus didn't respond, I recalled the not-at-all-there look in Galanis's eyes. He might not have been banished or whatever, but he definitely hadn't had a good day. "Is he going to be all right?"

The Magician turned to me, drinks in hand as he strolled back from the sidebar. "Would you like him to be?"

I scowled as I took the drink, choosing a wingback chair to settle into. A couch seemed like a very, very bad idea around this man, demigod...whatever he was.

"What kind of question is that? Of course I do. I mean, he has a life. He has a family or he could. If he'd broken a law or killed people in the pursuit of his artifacts, then he should be punished and forced to stop doing those things, but if he's just a guy trying to scrabble out some power in this world, well, there's no inherent crime in that. We're all just trying to figure things out."

"And if, in the course of his work, he allowed children to be sacrificed?"

"Then screw him," I said succinctly. I took a long satisfying drink of the amber liquid Armaeus had given me. "What is this?"

"Glenmorangie. Not the most exclusive brand of scotch, but it has a particular taste I thought you would enjoy."

"You thought correctly," I acknowledged, then met his gaze. "*Did* Galanis sacrifice kids to get all the toys he collected?"

"As it turns out, no. David had a wealth of opportunity

through other channels to secure his treasures. The artifacts he worked with were all several hundred or even thousand years old. Trafficking of the stolen merchandise is a dangerous gambit, of course, but in his case, it was generally not true Connecteds who he worked with, but merely looters. And, of course, the occasional morally challenged artifact hunter."

I lifted my drink in the Magician's general direction, accepting the designation with a smirk. "I don't need to worry about that group. We get what we get. It's the price of doing business."

"And you are engaging in this business to protect those who cannot protect themselves."

I shrugged. "I'm here to make money, Armaeus, no more and no less. What I do with my money is my choice after that. Right now, I've made that choice. What I do tomorrow, who knows? I could start a shoe collection."

His wry smile told me that he didn't believe me, but I didn't care. I didn't have to explain myself to anyone, at this point. I'd gone through my share of crap since those long-ago days in Memphis, reading second-hand tarot cards in my mom's dumpy kitchen with its peeling linoleum floors and faded wallpaper. Now I was drinking fancy scotch in a fancy hotel room with a fancy man who'd just helped me shove a god back across the veil. No big deal.

I took another long pull on my drink as Armaeus chuckled. "Oh, I assure you, Miss Wilde, you are a very big deal."

Irritation ripped through me on the heels of panic. "You know what? If I'm such a big deal, you need to stop reading my mind even when I'm not focusing on you not reading my mind. You don't belong there."

As I spoke, I mentally imagined my barriers dropping into place, blocking out his touch, and I blinked as I realized that it was effective. I could feel the pressure of his attention, the push of his mind, but he was once more on the outside looking in. And he could freaking well stay that way.

"You should be aware that you remain the only person I have ever met who can withstand my touch on their mind. It should not be possible. Who is your father?"

The question jolted me, particularly since I'd literally just been thinking about my very alone, very single mom.

"You don't have any shame, do you?"

"Very little," he acknowledged. "But the question is a deliberate one. I have obviously done my research on you, Miss Wilde. I know of your modest upbringing in Memphis, of your mother and the tragic accident that separated you. I am not trying to pry any more than I need to."

"Who says you need to pry at all?" I didn't like this. I didn't like any of this. "I'm here to do a job for you. I've done that job. And I expect to be paid a lot of money for it. End of story."

The Magician nodded. "The money is already in your account, and your fees, as always, are yours to set."

"Well, they just doubled. Again." I put the drink down and stood, crossing quickly to my bedroom where my jacket and clothes lay. I pulled the phone out of the jumble. Wheeling back toward the suite's living room, I tapped a few icons, ready for a fight. Then swayed a little on my feet.

"Double, in arrears," the Magician confirmed, raising his own glass to me.

"How do you do that?" I asked, though honestly, manipulating money and accounts was a kind of magic that even non-Connecteds had perfected. But it was of such visceral importance to me, the key to my heart, and Armaeus Bertrand was twisting it. As I watched, the numbers doubled again.

"Money is an exchange of energy, Miss Wilde, and I value your energy a great deal. Whether you know how to use it fully or not."

My mouth had gone dry, but I managed to form the words anyway. "But how is this actually possible?"

To my surprise, Armaeus took my question seriously. He put his glass on the coffee table, neatly positioned on its coaster, and stood, not closing the distance between us, even though I stiffened and gripped my glass as if it somehow could protect me. Now, that would be some pretty impressive scotch.

"My abilities come from long practice, as any good magician would tell you," Armaeus began. He lifted his hands, and a web of energy erupted between his palms as he held them facing each other, about two feet apart. I stared at the arcing energy, mesmerized. "You should know that the base of my power lies in the core of my being, the root chakra, to use different parlance, also known as the sexual core."

That snapped me out of my haze, and I blinked at him. "Did you actually say that out loud? Did that just happen?"

His smile was soft, knowing, and unmistakably sensual. "I'm quite serious. If it were possible for me to touch your mind, to run my fingers along the current of your energy systems without a sexual charge, I would. However, it is not in my nature to do so. I would argue that it is also in your nature to respond on that deeply intimate level."

"You're kidding me, right? You're using sex magic to fuel your..." I flapped a hand at him, embarrassment warring with legitimate fear, especially because I absolutely understood what he was talking about. The Magician was ringing enough chimes in me to give the "Carol of the Bells" a run for its money. I was responding to him on levels I didn't even know I possessed, and all systems were yelling *go*. "Um, powers? That's a thing?"

Armaeus chuckled, not at all put off by my awkward protest. "Not necessarily sexual, though you have those depths, but emotional," he corrected. "A deep core of empathy drives you beyond all human possibility. Would you not agree, Miss Wilde?"

"I wouldn't." I rejected the idea without hesitation. "I'm kind of a bitch."

He chuckled softly. "But are you, though?"

The question swirled through the open air, curling around my head, riffling through my hair. I opened my mouth, closed it again, and somehow, without even moving, Armaeus was in front of me again. He gently plucked the glass of scotch from my fingers before I dropped it.

Then he lifted his hands to my face and cupped my jaw, his long cool fingers giving me incredible relief as my skin flushed hot in his hands.

"You can feel the energy flowing from me to you, yes?" he asked.

Only I was lost in the golden smoke of his eyes, which in the Magician's case were not windows to the soul, but to a vast playground of possibility that extended far beyond my capacity to see. I couldn't understand what I was looking at —spheres and angles with arcing lines of energy connecting them, electrical coronas of fire that leapt and beckoned, and deep ravines of shadow that threatened to swallow me whole.

There was a darkness far beyond the edge of the last glimmering spheres, and I yearned to explore that darkness, to dive down into it. I wanted to know everything about the Magician, except I also wanted to run. The fear struck me with the same intensity as the pleasure, and I stiffened, instinctively pulling back from Armaeus's hands.

He let his fingers drop from my face, but didn't move them any farther, and I couldn't edge back another inch. I was held, transfixed by my own indecision. Not in his arms, never that...but not willing to step away from them either.

"Miss Wilde, you should know I have never encountered this particular level of ability before. And I have looked."

"I bet you say that to all the girls," I tried to smile, my connection to sanity swinging by the thread of the only joke I could muster.

"You don't have to protect yourself from me," he murmured.

Though I held on to that proclamation with both hands and a foot, I understood the real truth in a flash.

He was right. Very right. But he was also dead wrong. Because I didn't have to protect myself *from* him...but from the person I could become *through* him? That was a different question altogether.

"Noted," I said drolly, and it was as if my feet had gained purchase on the floor again, strength flowing back through my legs, solidifying my bones and bringing my body back fully to the present.

The Magician might be the Great and Powerful Oz, and he had some mad skills, but he was *not* the boss of me. I now knew more than anything in the world that I could not let him become the boss of me either. I would need to maintain some level of separation, because as ridiculous as it sounded, *he* needed to be protected from *me*. Everybody did. I didn't understand how or why, exactly, but I knew it all the same.

Unfortunately, in the midst of this soul-shaking realization, my mental barriers clearly slipped a notch. The Magician's brows shot up, and his eyes gleamed with an almost feral intensity.

In that moment, I could believe that Armaeus *was* driven by sexual power, because the naked yearning that leapt in his gaze was unmistakable. He wanted me more in that moment than any who had come before, and we were standing a foot away from each other, not even touching. The guy was *good*.

"You believe that you can hurt me," he said, his words nearly a gasp. "You know it to be true. It is written in your bones."

I squinted at him. "Seriously, did you take an online class to learn those lines? Because you should ask for a refund."

If anything, my retort seemed to drive him to a higher level. "Miss Wilde, I will never push you beyond your limits, but you need to understand that I *will* push you to those limits. That my entire purpose in this world is to poke and prod and shove you into whatever incarnation you are supposed to embody."

Alarm bells jangled, sirens blared, but everything was jumbling together in my mind as Armaeus's energy swirled around me, a living, breathing rush of possibility. "And how do you propose to do that?" I asked, or I thought I asked. Reality shifted like a kaleidoscope, and without warning, all I wanted... All I really, seriously wanted...

Time fractured. The energy between us was unmistakable. Dangerous. Sensual. Demanding.

Deadly.

"Kiss me, Miss Wilde," Armaeus murmured, his voice a predatory purr. "That's all. Nothing more."

"I don't want to have sex with you," I blurted. I sounded almost believable, and there was no denying the unnerving anxiety swirling in my belly at the thought. I actually *did* want to have sex with the man, bone-melting, brain-frying sex. It was just that I was pretty sure that all that bone melting and brain frying were going to leave a permanent mark.

"Then don't have sex with me." His smile curved in pure, carnal invitation. "But what *do* you want to do?"

35

I closed the distance between us in less than a breath. Lifting up on my toes, I reached for Armaeus, my fingers tangling in his hair as I pulled his face to mine. Our lips touched and the world spun out around me, an electrical fire of opportunities taken and chances missed, racing through my blood, gilding along my bones. The Magician was light, hope, and magic, and he was pouring every ounce of himself into that kiss, his hands loose at his sides, no part of him touching me other than that which I directed.

It wasn't enough.

Despite the growing hysteria that swirled through me, I snaked one arm around him, flattening my palm against his back as I pressed his chest to mine, our bodies lining up. The world tilted and my sight dimmed, a scream building deep in my throat. I wanted him, I needed him, and he would kill me or I would kill him. He would be the reason for my death, the reason for everything to die, unless I was that reason instead, unless together we—

"Miss Wilde."

I snapped back into reality. The Magician stood in front of me, his hands gripped around my wrists, holding me as if I were some kind of wild creature that he might need to wrestle to the floor, and not for a good reason.

"What?" I demanded, shame and anger ripping through me. I had no idea what had just happened between us. Once again, I'd blanked out just when we were getting to the good part. "What the hell is wrong with me—with you? What is happening here?"

I wrenched my hands away from him, but he didn't let me go, not at first. His grip was a vise, unyielding, a rock to hold me in the maelstrom of need, fear, doubt. It also set off a frenzied burst of emotion that I'd felt on more than one occasion, usually when I was tumbling down some deep dark hole in an artifact hunt gone terribly wrong. I blacked out in those moments too, but only briefly, and then I'd figured out how to save myself.

I could do that here too.

"There is nothing wrong with you, Miss Wilde. There is only you," Armaeus said. "You are a woman unique on this earth, in the way that all mortals are, yet your abilities surpass the great majority of those mortals. It is your choice whether you want to tap those abilities, and it is my duty to challenge you to become what you most need to be. I can do no less."

With that, he let me go and then took a full step back, giving me the slightest nod of deference. His meaning was clear. This was a man who would absolutely test me, but only as far as I let him. This was a dangerous man. Demigod. Whatever the hell he was.

"So now what?" I grumbled, more to stave off the returning surge of desire that goaded me to body tackle the guy to the floor. I was antsy, on edge. I needed to get away. I needed a new job.

It finally occurred to me that I hadn't quite finished the old one.

"Oh, right." I reached into the deep pocket of my gown and pulled out the relic of the One True Cross, the knotty piece of old wood blackened with handling over the centuries. "I guess you can take this now. I think it helped, back there at the Met, but I didn't feel like giving it up to Galanis. He had plenty of his own problems on board."

Armaeus took it, allowing his fingers to brush mine as he did, but paying no attention as my hair stood on end and my heart froze in my chest, every cell in my body separating for a microsecond before fusing back together again. He took the chunk as if he was used to dismantling people on a regular basis and studied it as I took in a labored, shallow breath.

"You did that on purpose, you asshat," I muttered.

"Of course."

But his smirk was more for the artifact, it seemed, than for me. He held it up to the light his expression amused and even a little surprised. "Do you know if you put together all the pieces of the One True Cross that currently reside in reliquaries and crypts, and in churches, in private collections throughout the world, you would have enough wood to build a city?"

"Sorry?"

He waved the chunk of wood at me. "This, Miss Wilde, is a fake, I regret to say. A piece of olive wood that, once carbon dated, will be revealed to have come from sometime in the late nine hundreds, I think. Lovingly handled, polished to a high sheen, and undoubtedly either sold or given to a gullible believer in exchange for something of far greater value to the charlatan who created it."

I scowled at him. "What are you talking about? I used that thing against Enlil. It broke his concentration. Heck, I think it injured him. How could it be fake?"

"As you pointed out, the value of most religious artifacts is not based on the magical properties they inherently possess, but in the belief that humans accord them. You believed that there was power in this piece, David Galanis believed the same, and that belief carried to Enlil, a god who is no stranger to the strength of human belief. Most mortals are far more powerful than they give themselves credit for, and those who truly believe have found a way to utilize that force."

"You mean I knocked him over with the power of positive thinking?"

The Magician turned and put the relic on the table. He didn't toss it down indiscriminately, though, and strangely, I liked him better for it. The fact that this was just a meaningless chunk of wood didn't take away from the grace that had been bestowed upon it for centuries on end. But if it wasn't truly the One True Cross...

I narrowed my eyes at him. "Then why didn't you pick it up yourself? Back there during Washington's time. If it wasn't real, you could easily have done so."

"I believe I've told you about the organization that I work for," he countered, my attention ping-ponging between the relic—which maybe wasn't just a useless hunk of wood after all—and the Magician, who was once again beginning to piss me off. This was much more comfortable territory for me, though, so I rolled with it.

"Are you telling me this was some kind of screwed-up

test, that you legit hauled my butt to eighteenth-century New York to *test* me? You don't have an app for that?"

I didn't believe it for a second, but the Magician pushed on. "I would like very much for you to come back with me. To work more closely with the Council. There is a great deal I believe I can learn from you, and, to be frank, far more you could learn from my colleagues at this point in your development than you think."

"Wait, are you offering me a corporate job?" I made a face. "I'm really more of a freelancer."

"I am offering you more money than you could possibly imagine in exchange for your full-time presence at our base of operations. I think you will find it quite stimulating."

"Only in the way that I find cattle prods stimulating." I held up both hands as he turned to me. "Armaeus. You want me to find artifacts for you, I'm your girl. A simple exchange of money for services and the occasional drink, I'm in. I'm not going to be exclusive to you and your precious organization, though. I reserve the right to work for whomever I want, wherever I want."

A flicker of annoyance flashed across the Magician's face. "I assure you, I have more than enough work to keep you busy."

I smiled, feeling more like myself than I had in a long time. I knew I'd made the right choice. "Yeah, well. I find ways to keep myself busy all on my own."

Underneath the veneer of my banter, though, the uncertainty deep within me had stirred again. I didn't know what the Magician's end game was, I didn't know what this work was he wanted me to do for the Council that required my physical presence. I didn't want to be tied down, and I especially didn't want to be tied down to him. I mean, not really, anyway.

I shook off the errant thought. I needed space. Clarity. I needed to stop tugging on the dragon's leash.

"You know, maybe it would be a better idea for both of us if we took a breather for a minute," I suggested. "I've got other jobs I gotta follow up on, other treasures to find."

The Magician merely studied me. He hadn't changed position. There were only a few feet between us, yet that space had become a chasm that neither of us was willing to cross. Partly out of pride, and partly out of fear—at least on my part—but I didn't care. I teetered on the edge of the chasm right now.

At length, he nodded. "I too have other jobs for you, in whatever way you wish to work them. I can wait, Miss Wilde. But you should be aware, I won't give up on you."

I didn't know what he meant specifically by that last comment, but tears suddenly sparked behind my eyes, and I blinked rapidly, pushing them away. What the hell was wrong with me?

"I'll be in touch, then." I nodded. "When I'm ready."

He inclined his head. "I have arranged for a car in your name. It will be waiting outside the front door when you reach it. Oh, and go ahead and take the relic. While it is not precisely what it purports to be, it *is* imbued with power. If there is someone who would like to buy it, you are welcome to sell it."

"Right." I swallowed, but before I could change my mind, I scooped up the chunk of wood, turned on my heel, and made for my bedroom. I didn't know whether to laugh or choke back a strange little sob when I saw my slightly battered backpack on the bed, full of God only knew what the Magician might think I'd need beyond rolls of money. Beside it was stacked a pair of jeans, a hoodie, tank top, and a sweet pair of boots.

By the time I made it back out to the living area of the suite, I was surprised to see Armaeus still there, a drink in hand, his golden eyes trained on me as I emerged from my suite and made my way across the living area.

"I will never pass up an opportunity to see you, Miss Wilde," he murmured. "Even if only to say goodbye."

Our eyes met. For one long moment, energy crackled between us. Then I was through the door and gone.

36

After a long conversation with Father Jerome on the ethics of pawning off a potentially fake chunk of religious memorabilia, I'd lined up a client meet in Philly to offload the relic. That ended up not working out, mainly because it was less a meetup than an ambush. Apparently, word had gotten out of the supposed treasure I was carrying, and three separate goons had come to see if they could take it from me.

I grinned, settling back in the driver seat of another parting gift from the Magician as I lightly grazed my hand over my swollen jaw. I'd needed the fight. I hadn't realized how much.

In the end, I'd sold the chunk of wood to a fourth party, an agent of one of my more regular clients, who'd sent only one man with plenty of money and no brass knuckles. I hung around Philly for another day to make sure I wasn't being trailed and to work out the details of wiring this latest windfall to Father Jerome, who seemed at peace with the arrangement now that he knew that the fake shard was in the hands of a black market syndicate. Those asshats deserved what they got.

It was a sunny day on the Pennsylvania turnpike, a stretch of highway I didn't usually travel, certainly not in a deceptively understated sleek sedan that seemed to get a thousand miles to the gallon. Say what you would about the man, the Magician had mad auto skills.

The extra-large coffee with triple cream had finally seeped its way through my system, and I pulled off at a rest area that was remarkably well maintained. There were a few cars parked when I pulled in, along with two separate groups walking dogs. By the time I headed back to my car, only one guy and his dog were cavorting around a picnic table near my vehicle.

The guy wore an orange knit cap with a sugar skull on it, a white long-sleeved shirt beneath an army-green T-shirt, frayed jeans, and canvas sneakers. His pack looked not all that unlike mine as it sat propped on the table next to a water bottle. A tall, well-worn walking stick leaned against the table beside them, though the guy couldn't have been more than twenty-five years old, far too young to need the support of a stick, unless he was using it to fight off bears.

Were there bears in Pennsylvania? Things I probably should've asked earlier.

I smiled at the exuberance of both the guy and his dog, then hopped back in surprise as the pup spun around toward me, suddenly bounding in my direction, its forward momentum impeded only by the maniacal waving of its entire hindquarters. Not just its tail, but its entire butt shook so hard that the dog looked like it might spontaneously combust as she ran up to me.

"She's friendly! I promise!" the guy shouted, and I

laughed as the small white ball of fluff hurtled up at me with a joyful yip.

"I can see that." I awkwardly grabbed the pup and held her as gingerly as possible until her feet slowed down enough that I could set her down again. It wasn't that I didn't like dogs, I just didn't have a lot of experience with them. The pooch didn't seem to mind my awkwardness, but spun around in circles at my feet, wriggling with joy.

I glanced again at the parking lot and realized that, other than mine, all the cars were gone save for a new SUV pulling in.

"Where's your ride?" I asked the guy, and as I expected, he shrugged.

"Don't know yet," he said cheerfully. "Snowball and I are kind of just making our way back home. I'm Simon, by the way. You're the first person to talk to me beyond saying hi to Snowball, so things are already looking up."

Something in the unaffected innocence of his delivery struck a chord deep within me.

Look, I got it, okay? Young guy, walking stick, white, fluffy dog. The incarnation of the Tarot Fool in the flesh. If I'd been looking for signs this morning, I couldn't come up with much more of a signier sign.

As it happened, I wasn't looking for signs, but I couldn't help remembering another girl several years before, younger than this guy by a lot, out there on the road, making her way. That girl hadn't been looking to go home. She'd been running away from the only home she'd ever known. But the similarities were still there. She'd met a kind woman who had been good enough to take her along for the ride.

Maybe it was time for me to return the favor.

"I'm Sara," I said. "And I'm heading to Chicago, more or less. Does that help you at all?"

"Anything heading west helps me." He grinned, his blue eyes wide and guileless beneath his mop of curly black hair. "Let me grab my pack."

A few minutes later, we were barreling down the turnpike, Simon immersed in the electronic dashboard of the Magician's car. I hadn't taken the time to figure it out. I wasn't much for music or podcasts or any of that, happy enough for the open road and silence, but between Simon's delighted mutters as screen after screen appeared on the dash and the spinning delirium of Snowball in the back seat, prancing on her own special blanket, it didn't occur to me to ask for more details until we were a good fifty miles down the road. "What brought you out here, anyway? And where's home?"

Simon laughed, and Snowball yipped behind me. Then he peered ahead as something electronic dinged on his wrist. He crouched forward like a lookout. "Take your foot off the gas, but don't hit the brakes. We've got company over this next rise."

"Seriously?" I asked but did as he suggested, and only then noticed that I'd been driving a cool ninety miles an hour. I wasn't sure what the speed limit was in this neck of Pennsylvania, but it probably wasn't ninety.

Sure enough, a cop complete with a speed gun hung out the window of his car, tracking us. By then, I'd slowed down to what had to be a respectable speed, but he still glared at me balefully as I cruised by.

I squinted over at Simon. "You have a portable police scanner tracker thing?"

"I've got a thing for tech." He grinned. "And I've been

traveling for a little while now, but it's time for me to head home. How about you? This is a pretty sweet ride."

"Payment for a job," I said, and couldn't deny the spurt of validation when Simon's brows lifted. The idea of getting a car as payment probably would be pretty sweet for a gearhead his age. He was maybe only a year younger than I was.

"It's been a few years since I hitchhiked," I continued. "You run into a lot of trouble?"

"Not usually. I let Snowball pick out my drivers, and she hasn't failed me yet."

Snowball greeted this validation with a sigh of contentment, circling around in the back seat until she settled in a fluffy heap.

"What put you out on the road, back when you got started?" Simon asked.

I smiled a little at the question. I didn't think about the bad old days that often, but the question was an open and honest one, and I felt myself drawn to answer.

"I got into some trouble. I was seventeen. I dipped my hand into occult stuff, reading Tarot cards, that kind of thing. I was pretty good at it and caught the attention of the wrong kind of people. They took out my house and everything I ever loved. After that, it didn't make much sense to do more than run."

He nodded, watching me. "And you've been running ever since?"

I slanted him a glance, but his large blue eyes remained guileless, his mop of dark hair under his knit cap poking out in all directions.

"I don't know," I said as honestly as I could. "Maybe. Or maybe life is just one big adventure and I haven't quite found my way through it yet."

He laughed. "A friend of mine always says that to me,

that I haven't yet embarked on my greatest adventure. I don't know about that." He laughed and shrugged, waving to the world outside. "I think I'm doing pretty good. But now it's time to head home for a while, because there's some shit starting to go down and I want to be there for it."

"And home is...?"

"Las Vegas," he said.

Though half of me had been expecting that location without realizing it, the other half of me gripped the wheel, my foot pressing more heavily on the pedal.

"Have you ever been?" Simon continued. "It's really awesome. The bright lights of the Strip, the chatter of the slot machines, all the people, like an endless stream of souls coming and going into the morning and all through the night."

"You live on the Strip?" I blew out a long breath. "Like permanently?"

He snorted. "As permanently as it gets, I suppose."

"And what do you do there?" I asked. The question felt heavy in the air between us.

"I guess when you boil it down, I help people," Simon said. "I help there be a little more magic in the world, and I make sure that magic stays balanced. There's a whole lot of people who don't understand their own magic. They're just waiting for the adventure to find them."

"Right." I stared out at the rolling landscape of Pennsylvania in the early spring. The leaves were coming out. It had rained recently, and the sun was shining. The damp highway seemed to shiver with promise, and the bright sun glowed high overhead, lording over an endless sky.

"So now I suppose you want me to go with you to Vegas...and to meet the Arcana Council. Is that what this is about?" I glanced into the rearview mirror, but wasn't surprised to see that Snowball had disappeared. In her place was a shiny white deck of cards.

"I mean, what could it hurt?" Simon asked, drawing my attention, all arms and legs and goofy smile. In the brief moment that our eyes met across the front seat, I didn't see a twenty-five year old guy, barely younger than me. His eyes were older. Wearier. Not as old as the Magician's, of course, but the Fool of the Arcana Council had already seen some things in his young life. And if I hooked myself up with that same Council, I'd probably see some things too. Maybe go places I couldn't come back from. Maybe learn things I couldn't unlearn.

Armaeus had sent Simon to do his work for him, not giving up on his quest to get me to work more closely with the Council. I wasn't really surprised. Part of me wanted it to happen, knew it had to happen. Without question, I'd get a lot of money out of the arrangement, and I had lots of people who needed that money.

I couldn't deny the anxiety that skimmed along my nerves, though. If I drove all the way to Vegas and walked through the Magician's door, I might not find my back out again. Was I ready for that?

I didn't think so. But that didn't mean I wasn't going to do it.

"I don't like any of this," I muttered. Or maybe...I liked it too much.

"Well, maybe just think about it, then." Beside me, Simon flashed an easy smile and leaned back against the seat. "I mean, when it comes to taking an adventure, the choice is always yours. What do you want to do?"

THANK you for reading WILDE MAGIC! Sara and the Magician meet again in Paris—and then Sara jets off to Rome to hunt for the Devil of the Tarot in **GETTING WILDE...**

THE ADVENTURE CONTINUES...

Using her well-worn Tarot deck, magical-artifacts hunter Sara Wilde can find anything—for a price. And the price had better be right, since she needs to finance her own personal mission to rescue several young psychics recently sold on the paranormal black market.

Enter Sara's most mysterious client, the wickedly sexy Magician, with a job that could yield the ultimate payday. All she'll have to do is get behind Vatican walls... and steal the Devil himself.

But play with the Devil and you're bound to get burned.

From the twisting catacombs of Rome to the neon streets of Vegas, Sara confronts ancient enemies, powerful demigods, a roiling magical underworld about to explode... and immortal passions that might require the ultimate sacrifice. But oh, what a way to go.

No matter how the cards play out, things are about to get *Wilde.*

Buy **GETTING WILDE** NOW—OR turn the page for a sneak peek!

～

GET CONNECTED! Keep up with all things Sara Wilde (new books! inside information! Tarot!) by signing up for my mailing list at www.jennstark.com. Other places you can find me online include my website, Twitter, and Facebook. (I'm most often at Facebook though!)

I appreciate your help in spreading the word about my books, including telling a friend. Reviews help readers find books! Please leave a review on your favorite book site.

Turn the page for an excerpt from **GETTING WILDE**...

GETTING WILDE - EXCERPT

The Devil was in the details. Again.

I leaned against the sticky countertop at Le Stube and glared down at the faded Tarot cards, the best Henri could scrounge up on short notice. The Devil trump looked particularly foul in this deck: all leering grin, fat belly, and clawed feet. Worse, it was the third time in as many days he'd shown up in my reading.

This time, he'd brought along some friends. I'd turned up the Tower, Death, *and* the Magician card in quick succession. Heavy hitters of the Tarot who had no business being in my business, at least not tonight.

Tonight's transaction, while unpleasant, wasn't supposed to be complicated. It *wouldn't* be complicated, I'd decided. I'd had enough of complicated for one evening.

Le Stube's front door opened. I sensed Henri peering past me with his sorrowful bartender eyes—just as I caught a whiff of the guy coming in. I sat up a little, blinking rapidly. Dude was *pungent*. Even by Parisian standards.

I tapped the Prince of Pents card lying in the middle of all the Major Arcana cards. It was covered by the Five of

Wands. Since pentacles equaled money, I was pretty sure this newcomer was my contact: some low-level knuckle dragger muling cash for his king, the buyer who'd commissioned this deal, here to relieve me of the artifact I had snugged up against my right kidney. Unfortunately, I was also pretty sure said contact was spoiling for a fight. Which might become an issue, since neither prince nor king was going to get his trinket tonight, if the payoff wasn't right.

Not my problem, though. I wasn't the one who'd lied.

"Un autre?" Henri sighed. Like most bartenders in the City of Light, Henri was a master of the resigned sigh.

I swept the cards into a stack, pocketing them as I nodded to him. It wasn't the prettiest deck, but it was trying, at least. I owed it a one-way ticket out of Paris. Henri plucked my glass from the counter, making a big production of concocting something way too involved to be my drink.

He set the mess down in front of me and scowled, gloomy concern evident in every line of his thin, hunched body. Which was more than I could say for the guy shuffling up to the bar, who stank of sour cheese and bad karma, and maybe...peanut butter? Didn't want to think too much about that.

I barely avoided a wince as he sat down. "You 'ave it?"

"You didn't tell me about the competition," I said, picking up my glass. "The price has gone up."

"You *do* 'ave it." My contact leaned toward me, his gun nudging into my side. Henri was applying his bar towel diligently to nonexistent dust at the far end of the bar. As if nothing that happened here would bother him, as long as I kept it tidy.

I could do tidy. The cards and their crazy were not the boss of me.

"If you have the money, we have a deal," I said, Miss

Congeniality all the way. "Just at double our original price. What's more, I suspect you do have the money, honey, because you knew what I was walking into. Unlike me, for the record. Which, frankly, wasn't very neighborly of you."

His face didn't change expression. "You agreed to the terms."

I shook my head. With the mule this close, we could talk freely without being overheard. If only I could manage it without breathing. "No. I agreed to lift a minor, plate-sized relic off a clueless museum intern. You missed the bit where said flunky was also being targeted by the *Swiss Guard*, who, by the way, apparently don't wear pajamas when they're not at the Vatican. You also missed the part where the Swiss Guard had become ninjas. All that's a little out of my pay grade." I took a sip of my drink, wincing at the tang as I set the glass down again. *Horseradish.* Nice. If I had to use it on this guy, it was going to sting like a bitch.

"But you *'ave* it." Clearly the guy thought he could get what he wanted simply by boring me to death. I considered my options. He was powerfully built, with a thick jaw and a boxer's nose—but his curled upper lip shone with sweat, his beady eyes looked just a teensy bit feral, and his cheeks were flushed. Something wasn't right here. He was too nervous, too intent.

"The transaction was compromised." I spread my hands in a "what can you do?" gesture. "I wasn't given full information. With full information, I never would have taken the job. But, I can be reasonable. Which means your new price is merely double. So go talk to your boss, get the extra cash, and then we'll have something to discuss."

"No." Again with the gun. Harder this time. Sharper. "You must give it to me *now*." The man practically vibrated with concentration, and my Spidey sense went taut. This definitely was too much reaction for the relic in question. We weren't talking the Ark of the Covenant here, no matter how much I was going to charge the guy.

I reclaimed my glass of horseradish whiskey and took in Henri. He remained at the far end of the bar, well out of the way of any untoward blood spatter. Very efficient, our Henri.

"Take it easy, my friend," I said, as casual as all hell. "We're just having a conversation." It wouldn't be long now, I thought, watching his nostrils flare. The golden seal of Ceres suddenly weighed a hundred pounds in its slender pouch against my body.

It was a pretty thing, really: a flat gold disk the size of a dessert plate, imprinted on one side with an image of the Roman goddess of fertility and grain. On the flip side, a half-dozen thick, raised, symmetrical ridges lined its surface at odd angles.

Not the most spectacular artifact I'd ever been asked to locate, but not the most mundane either. And with the help of the cards, I'd tracked it down easily enough.

Then again, I probably should have asked a few more questions before I headed out this evening. A third-century BC seal featuring a corn-festooned pagan goddess shouldn't have been entrusted to your average intern for a late-night museum transfer. And the guy had been really *young* too. Too young, too clueless.

Which might have caused me to stop and reconsider what I was doing, if I hadn't been so distracted by the ninja shadows of death who'd swarmed the Metro platform the moment I'd made the grab. I'd immediately thought the Swiss Guard had come to swipe the relic out from under me, but why? What had I seen to tip my mind that way?

And why would the Swiss Guard give a crap about such a minor artifact?

"Give it to me," my contact hissed, officially signaling the arrival of the next stage of our negotiation process: brute force. Then he lunged at me.

I moved just as fast. With a sharp, cutting jerk, I splashed the horseradish whiskey into the guy's eyes, then shattered the glass against the bar as his hands went to his face, his scream a guttural bellow. Henri was right beside me, ripping the man's gun away as I shoved my contact flat against the bar, the cut edge of the glass tight against his collarbone, pressing into his thick, sweaty neck.

"And now the price is triple." I glared at his clenched-shut eyes as tears rolled down his cheeks. "You want to pay, you know where to find me. You don't want to pay, I got plenty others who will."

"You wouldn't," he sputtered. He tried to open his eyes, but that wouldn't be happening anytime soon. "You were 'ired to—"

"You bet your crusty baguette I would. Tell your boss that if he's got the money, then he'll get the package. Otherwise, no deal." I stepped back as Henri and Le Stube's bouncer moved in. Henri whipped a spotless white towel off his shoulder to help my contact get cleaned up, while his muscle stood ready to hold the guy tight until I got out of there.

No wonder I liked this place so much.

Stepping into the warm, muggy night, I strode toward the Luxembourg Gardens without too much hurry, the popular tourist destination still illuminated despite the fact that it was nearing midnight. I angled my way through a dozen or so manicured plots, waiting for a tail to materialize. None did that I could see, so I changed course. I still had that creepy crawly feeling of being followed, but there was nothing for it.

I had more work to do.

Continue the adventure with **GETTING WILDE** now!

A NOTE FROM JENN

With the launch of Sara's adventures with the Arcana Council in this book, it seems fitting to start where all adventures of the Tarot begin, the Fool.

The Fool

What do you want to do today? Where do you want to go? The Fool is here to tell you that your adventures are only limited by your imagination, and you would do well to take the leap and see what happens, vs. stay quietly at home, longing to explore the world but afraid to get started. The Fool not only says that everything will be okay, but that this adventure is yours to take—that you've got what it takes to see it through to its ultimate end, and be all the richer for it. She say the Fool is naive, a dreamer, and, well, foolish to believe that everything will be okay when he steps off that cliff. But the Fool knows that you first must leap if you want the net to appear.

What adventures will you be taking next?

BOOKS BY JENN STARK

Immortal Vegas

~complete~

Wilde Magic

Getting Wilde

Wilde Card

Born To Be Wilde

Wicked And Wilde

Aces Wilde

Forever Wilde

Wilde Child

Call of the Wilde

Running Wilde

Wilde Fire

Wilde Justice Series

~complete~

The Red King

The Lost Queen

The Hallowed Knight

The Shadow Court

The Wayward Star

The Night Witch

The Untamed Moon

The Shattered Tower

The Demon Enforcers Series

Demon Unbound

Demon Forsaken

Demon Bewitched

Demon Ensnared

Demon Betrayed (2022)

Demon Beloved (2023)

ACKNOWLEDGMENTS

Writing this new series starter has truly been a labor of love, with both the Magician and Sara finally willing to share a little about their past. I hope you have enjoyed getting to see the early days of their adventures! As always, my sincere thanks to all my readers, who wanted to learn more about the primary couple of Immortal Vegas and Wilde Justice. I am delighted to also thank Elizabeth Bemis for her beautiful work on my site and her ongoing support; Gabriela of B Rose Designz for her truly stunning re-imagining of my series covers; and my editorial team of Linda Ingmanson and Toni Lee (as always, any mistakes in the manuscript are most definitely my own). Judi Soderberg provided a brilliant copy edit, and Edeena Cross (as always!) caught errors in tone and style. I especially thank Kristine Krantz, who is an amazing dev editor and also an amazing friend. I would also like to express my appreciation for Sabra Harp, who has the never-ending task of trying to keep me sane. And, of course, sincere thanks go to Geoffrey—who was with me to the end, and all over to start again. It's been a *Wilde* ride.

ABOUT JENN STARK

Jenn Stark is an award-winning author of paranormal romance and urban fantasy. She lives and writes in Ohio. . . and she definitely loves to write. In addition to her Immortal Vegas and Wilde Justice urban fantasy series and her Demon Enforcers paranormal romance series, she is also author Jennifer McGowan, whose Maids of Honor series of Young Adult Elizabethan spy romances are published by Simon & Schuster, and author Jennifer Chance, whose Rule Breakers series of New Adult contemporary romances are published by Random House/Love-Swept and whose modern royals series, Gowns & Crowns, is available wherever ebooks are sold.

You can find her online, follow her on Twitter, and visit her on Facebook!